Merry Christmas 2...
Pass this on to Pete & Jenny,
Lone, Carol & Alan

T5-CCV-355

Yvia Voi:
Land of Grace

Roy L. Hill

AmErica House
Baltimore

First printing

ISBN: 1-58851-372-6
PUBLISHED BY AMERICA HOUSE BOOK PUBLISHERS
www.publishamerica.com
Baltimore

Printed in the United States of America

Dedication

I dedicate "Yvia Voi: Land of Grace" to my mother, Carol, for her technical support and to my loving wife Loli for her emotional support.

CHAPTER 1

Bara, Commander of the small Terasian space fighter Larow, was transfixed toward the stars in meditation. What better object to focus on than Revus Senra, a red giant centered in the middle of his three-dimensional viewing screen. Meditation was common practice among his people, the Terasians, to combat stress and as an aid to sleep. Yet Bara took meditation to a deeper level by freezing his thoughts. This activity allowed his mind to harvest strange psychic perceptions.

After three days of living in a trance and collecting information, an electrode wired to Bara's forehead discharged. Fragmented thoughts were perceived and he began to feel the warm air around him. A part of him longed to remain in a blissful state of meditation. Although many would have been seduced, Bara forced his being into a state of mindfulness.

Bara was sitting alone in his spaceship's pilot room. Control panels rimmed the oval, ten-by-seven foot enclosure and were lit by brilliant and red geometric shapes standing out against the black vastness of space. He once found refuge in that vastness meeting the need for quiet, stillness and introspection. Yet tranquility was a faint memory now. Life had become consumed by intrusive, horrible memories spanning from his youth to the present.

"What is this?" Bara had asked his father.

"A memory chip."

"I realize that. But the war-"

"Has bankrupted the family. Yes, I know that son. I have liquidated my assets to pay for the neuroimplant."

Bara opened his mouth but said nothing. His father never acted without sufficient reason, confronting him would only invite humiliation.

"The data from this chip holds a few select memories of personal success and lessons learned. At least you will inherit some of the richness of my brief life. That is the highest gift that a father can give a son."

Bara dismissed the words 'thank you' as feelings of loss overwhelmed him. "You said lived," he challenged. His father never made verbal slips.

"As an old man, I will have little value in the years to come. Civilians such as myself will not be protected sufficiently against the Vesder attacks."

"Your age doesn't make your life any less meaningful, father. Terasian forces will quickly dispatch the Vesders, if it even comes to that. Personally, I believe that the diplomats will be successful."

Qerba shook his head. "The Vesders are not interested in negotiation. You have so much to learn, my boy."

Bara conceded that his father was right, he had been young and ignorant some eighty years ago. Yet his ignorance had been short lived. Bara had learned quickly when war came the following year.

"Bara," Commander Luv barked. Bara turned around to meet the large red-haired man. His white wrinkled face looked like chiseled stone. "I have a message from Terasia."

"Yes sir."

"Your father was killed in latest Vesder attack. I could offer my condolences, but I won't. We all have lost family. I expect that your grief will not compromise your duties. That is all." Commander Luv turned and left. Alone in his quarters, Bara wept.

Bara forced his eyes away from the viewing screen. "I have never compromised my duties Commander Luv," he whispered. "Like you, I have become a product of death and destruction."

Bara wondered if he was being too hard on himself. He had little choice but to live the life of a soldier; it was every Terasian's destiny of his generation. An unknown species, the Vesders had attacked Terasia en force. More than fifty years of fighting had transformed Bara into the very thing he loathed: an efficient, callous, killing machine. To survive, he detached every human emotion except anger. Yet whether it was by choice or destiny, Bara understood that he sacrificed a part of his humanity in defense of his people. In retrospect, the price seemed too high considering that the humans lost the war.

Bara stared into the view screen and clenched his fists in anger as he vividly relived the last day of the Human-Vesder War in his mind. Only hours long, the final battle had occupied every dream and most of his waking hours.

Roloto Station orbited the giant gas planet Nalu like a dead, barren rock. Although the station lights burned steadily against the swirling, dark-blue, mass of gas below, Roloto Station was ominously quiet. For the third time in the last ten minutes, Bara tried to gain clearance. There was no response. Not even static came through.

"Computer, assess damage."

"No structural damage," an unconcerned voice returned.

"Any vessels in the area?"

"Negative."

Bara stared at the outpost with narrowed eyes. "Computer, establish contact with Terasia."

"Transmission time, five minutes."

Bara waited patiently as five, ten, and then fifteen minutes passed, no response. "Computer, what is the status of the Roloto scanning shields?"

"Shields are down."

"Computer, scan station."

"Scanning."

"What is the status of the crew?"

"Scanners report no life forms on Roloto Station."

"Are the bio-conditions normal?"

"All bio-conditions read normally."

"Can you access the Roloto Station computer?"

"Checking . . . Access confirmed."

"Display a visual of the Roloto command center."

Decaying bodies filled the view screen and Bara's stomach constricted like a vice. The implications of his discovery were catastrophic. The Vesders had somehow infiltrated the station with deadly chemicals. If they could infiltrate the defensive systems at Roloto Station, the entire human population would be at risk. Trembling, Bara tried to contact his home planet one more time. Nothing. The absence of response could only mean one thing.

Arriving at Terasia near light speed, Bara's worst suspicions were confirmed. Billions of decaying bodies littered his home world. All outposts had been destroyed. The hopes, dreams, and future of his people had been obliterated. Bara was alone.

Noticing blood trickle from where his fingernails pierced his hands, Bara shelved the intrusive memories and opened his fists. He then took a deep breath and fought off the present urge to join his people in death. The task was not easy; it was hard to derive meaning in an empty universe. Yet dealing with his own internal universe, the mind, was even more challenging. Bara desperately needed a distraction. Exiting the pilot room, he entered a small narrow corridor and veered into a small room to his left.

A dim whitish hue appeared as Bara sat at a small desk constructed out of deep-blue wood. He placed his hand over a glowing red ball and began to communicate with the ship's computer.

All the necessary mathematical computations were calculated in nanoseconds. The data hovered over his desk in dark-blue holographic symbols. Taking a deep silent breath, Bara scanned thousands of characters. Computations regarding speed and heading were read, understood and silently approved. After several minutes, the last subheading, CHARACTERISTICS OF THE BUROOS TE PLANETARY SYSTEM, suddenly materialized. Below this heading appeared the word, UNKNOWN.

The data offered no surprises. At a distance of approximately 148.72 light years, no one had attempted travel to Buroos Te. According to the data, Buroos Te was just another middle-sized binary star. Yet Bara believed otherwise.

During meditation, Bara had sensed immense power being generated from the Buroos Te coordinates. The power was too organized, subtle, and complex to be natural. Something, or someone, was calling out and luring him to the alien star system. Bara sensed that critical questions were waiting to be answered. Yet what were these questions? Although a part of him didn't care, another voice, perhaps stemming from a remnant spark of life deep within his soul, urged him to explore. Bara decided to accept the challenge and live or die doing something meaningful rather than die slowly floating aimlessly in space.

* * *

Bara watched stars creep forward in his view screen. His ship was slowly gaining momentum and would eventually reach a sustained speed of .896 times the speed of light. Although this speed skimmed along the steadfast barriers of physical law, it would still take 165.9 years to reach the Buroos Te system.

Bara gazed at the shrinking Terasian sun and greeted it with a nod. Silently, he exited the pilot room, walked down the corridor, and entered a small, empty, egg-shaped enclosure known as the hyper-freeze chamber. Slightly larger than himself, the room was uniformly white. Any sense of depth perception would have been lost if not for a myriad of small dark

YVIA VOI: LAND OF GRACE

holes burrowed in smooth, glossy walls. In a flicker of a moment, the universe he had known, loved, and fought for would be gone forever. Yet there was no sense flying aimlessly in a galactic graveyard. Bara closed his eyes and commanded, "Computer, engage hyper-freeze." A red-tinted translucent substance instantaneously filled and solidified the chamber. Bara became a frozen statue for the next 165.9 years as his ship penetrated into uncharted space.

* * *

Bara awakened and felt a warm tingling sensation course through his body. Had he been sleeping for a second, a thousand years, or one hundred and sixty-five years? Lifting his eyelids felt like lifting hundred-pound weights. The "egg room" was immaculately clean and offered no hint to the passage of time. Only Bara's body seemed to have been affected by inactivity in that his muscles felt stiff like wood and his head throbbed with pain.

Bara exited the hyper freeze chamber and began the difficult process of stretching. His muscles quickly regained some of their flexibility and a singular, pink pill tamed his migraine. Satisfied, he entered the pilot room and relaxed in a comfortable black chair. Sunshine flooded the small oval room and bathed his waking senses. On the left side of the screen, Bara gazed upon a bright, yellowish-white disk surrounded by long, sharp, needles of white light. To the right side was a smaller disk radiating a crown of soft blue light. The computer confirmed his suspicions. He had reached the Buroos Te star system. "Computer, set and engage course to planet number four. Set arrival time for two hours and forty-five minutes."

"Course set and engaged."

Although the ship's fusion reactors should have remained unaffected by a hundred and sixty-five years of inactivity, Bara watched the ship's instrumentation carefully as the main front thrusters roared softly. To his relief, the ship performed perfectly. Buroos Te #4 grew slowly from a white dot into a stunning blue globe peppered with light brown geometric shapes and white clouds. A part of Bara became engrossed in the purity and magnificence of the elements as he looked over rows of copper colored mountains, deep blue lakes and reddish-brown canyons. The view was so vivid that he felt the urge to reach out and touch the surface. These natural elements seemed to coexist in harmony, blending with a unitary brilliance against the backdrop of space. At that moment Bara realized that the Terasian genocide was light years behind him. Instead of looking at a planet in destructive ruin, he was beholding a virgin world that seemed simple and pure. After some reflection, Bara renamed Buroos Te #4 to Yvia Voi, meaning "Land of Grace."

Bara noted two satellites orbiting the planet. The larger moon was large enough to maintain its own atmosphere, but was too cold and poisonous to support life. Covered by thin, white clouds, the black and gray surface was dotted with craters, mountain ranges and inactive volcanoes. In contrast, the smaller of the two moons lacked an extensive atmosphere and was covered by a number of active volcanoes and red lava fields.

Looking at the planet, Bara wondered whether there was intelligent life below. The ship's alarm quickly diverted this question, however. A host of holographic graphs, mathematical configurations, and a three-dimensional globe of Yvia Voi popped up on the screen before him. The computer was registering a strong, diffuse, energy surge. Bara bounded out of his chair and rechecked the data. Yes, there it was! He was looking at energy patterns identical to those he had perceived earlier, actually a 165.9 years earlier, during meditation. Someone or something was activating the energy field. By the intensity of the readings, Bara knew that the technology was advanced. Then, suddenly, the pattern intensified, narrowed and took aim.

"Defenses up!" Bara barked. The computer raised the ship's shields instantly. "Full thrusters, quadrant 6 by 83, engage." The ship's engines roared for a second and then stopped. All the lights in the pilot room went black as the ship's oxygen flow ceased. His ship was dead.

An invisible force grabbed Bara's ship and turned it directly toward the planet's surface. Yvia Voi was instantaneously transformed from the land of grace into the land of death. The continent below rushed toward him and grew in size exponentially. Red-gold mountains looked like winding caterpillars, lakes deepened in color, and individual puffy clouds could be seen hovering over a shadowed landscape. These images faded as the ship became engulfed in flames as it entered the stratosphere. Bara knew that heat and gravity would combine into an explosive, deadly mixture. Only years of training allowed him to suppress his fear and review options. He found none. Taking one final deep breath, Bara blacked out.

CHAPTER 2

A strong cold breeze brushed against Bara's face and stirred him into consciousness. Groggy, he concentrated on what sounded like a stereo of grass rustling around his head. The warm sunlight penetrated deep into his skin as a ballet of bright spots danced beneath his eyelids. Bara opened them. A rush of blinding light made him squint and turn his head away. He tried again more slowly. Shades of green flooded his vision.

Bara found himself lying on top of a gentle rise covered with thick, stubby, green grass. Ignoring the pulsing persuasiveness of aching muscles, he sat upright. He was amazed to find himself sitting on an alpine meadow looking down into a deep valley laced with white and green vegetation. Above the valley were layered, pinkish, granite peaks crowned with snow. The view fondly reminded him of the rugged mountains from his boyhood on Terasia, except now there were two suns rather than one. Bara quickly redirected his thoughts to the question of why he was standing here, on the surface on a strange world, without his ship.

Bara had cheated death again. A part of him found little pleasure in that fact. Another part of him, however, was deeply concerned about his current situation. Some powerful force had tracked him in space and knocked his ship out of the sky. Yet it had saved his life and then abandoned him on a mountaintop. The responsible agents must have had some purpose in causing such an odd series of events. Yet what that purpose might be, he didn't have a clue. After all, why would the local inhabitants want his ship? Their technology was evidently superior to his. And why would they rescue him and let him wander around their planet unaided or without introduction? Although the forces responsible for his present situation abducted his ship, Bara had not been left completely defenseless. His lase-gun and multiuse-analyzer were still strapped to his belt and in functional order. What had perplexed Bara most was that his ship's instrumentation had not detected any spacecraft, artificial satellites, planetary communications, or advanced civilizations on the planet. Where were the advanced inhabitants of this world? How would he find them or his ship? Perhaps assuming that the Yvia Voi had the same societal signatures of his own people was arrogant. Still, nothing made any sense and this left Bara feeling helpless and lost.

YVIA VOI: LAND OF GRACE

An undifferentiated snapping sound distracted Bara. He reacted instinctively by drawing his lase-gun and pointed it toward a rustling bush. He examined the bush and relaxed. Bundles of thick green stalks branched into tangled, orange streamers. Within the center of the plant fed a small, flat, oval, blubbery creature. Oblivious to Bara's startle maneuver, the creature continued chewing at one of the green stalks. It's small oval body was packed full of fat, stubby legs. Bara thought he had counted twenty of them, but was not sure. The creature also had a curved tail that looked like it could be used as a highly efficient digging instrument. He realized that this tail, along with the creature's flat proportions and blubbery consistency would serve it well in its alpine environment. Anyway, the alien was obviously some minutely intelligent herbivore. Bara lowered his lase-gun and moved his attention to a more important issue, namely his survival.

A cold wind ascending from the mountain valleys stung Bara's exposed face. He noticed that the planet's primary sun was setting over distant western peaks. Long shadows filled tree-studded valleys like silent creeping arms as the snow-capped peaks were turning a soft shade of purple. It was time to move to a less exposed area.

Bara worked his way down to a nearby alpine lake and peered into the shallow, pure waters. The lake mirrored a tall broad, man, with black hair and ivory-white skin. Pronounced cheek bones and a wide chin made his face look like an amateur sculptor had chiseled it. Two large, purple eyes glimmered in the rippling water of dwindling light. Although the orbs hid emotion, they whispered many secrets. Bara's face, in fact, seemed to speak of many such contrasts, hard but soft, rigid and flexible, dark yet light, obvious but still unknowable. Bara was oblivious to these contrasts, however. He was more focused on the fact that everyone and everything in his world were gone. Who he was didn't seem to matter anymore. Bara gently stroked the thick stubble growing on his face, taking note that he must have been unconscious for at least a day. Confirming that the water was safe to drink with his analyzer, he drank deeply from the lake and then started down off the mountaintop at a brisk pace.

The landscape changed as Bara descended. Tundra grasses eventually gave way to a sparsely studded forest of gnarled trees that reminded him of wizened old men. The trees straightened as he descended into the warmer recesses of the valley. Branches grew in flat, straight, symmetrical rows from the tree's leathery, yellowish bark. The branches flattened at the tips and were transformed into long, thick, ribbed leaves. Beneath each leaf grew small bulbous pods. Bara took a spectral analysis of the seedlings, determined their in edibility, and continued his downward trek.

The long-leafed trees thickened and multiplied as Bara entered the darker recesses of the valley. Within the growing darkness the forest floor became a dense thicket of blue vines, hooked thorns and grayish mist. Although thorns pricked Bara and slowed his descent considerably, he steadily made his way toward the bottom of the valley. Night ruled the heavens by the time he encountered a fast, raucous, mountain stream. After drinking from the cold clear waters, he propped himself on a large solid boulder at the edge of the embankment. The cool mountain air and cold spray of river water actually awakened feelings of contentment. Could there someday be life after tragedy? Bara sighed. The heavy blanket of despair would smother him very quickly, of that he was certain. But for now it was enough to look at the stars, and ponder the beauty of eternity.

Both the large yellow sun and the smaller blue sun had set and the two moons were close together this night. The silvery large giant cast an eerie glow over the granite boulders and the flowing water. The smaller red moon's glow only tinged the edge of the surrounding plant life. Bara recognized many constellations in the sky, although some of the closer stars seemed out of place. Then Bara saw his own star, the Terasian sun, shining brightly in the night sky. After a moment of silence, the feeling of despair returned. It was time to get moving.

Bara wasn't sure just where he was going, but following the stream seemed logical. All night he followed the winding, flowing path. Occasionally he heard noises and strange shapes bound into the dark forest, yet nothing threatened him. At one point he considered using his lase-gun to kill an animal for dinner but saw little point in wasting the effort. He had enough energy stored in his artificial bio-cells to last him a month. Anyway, Bara decided that if he didn't find anything interesting within that time he might as well lay down and let his body die of malnutrition. He didn't see any sense in prolonging the agony that accompanied lonely wanderings. He was tired fighting for the pointless life.

The larger of the two suns peeked over the eastern horizon as Bara worked his way between and beyond the towering, winding fingers of mountain terrain. The landscape began to flatten as the river widened and slowed. Broader trees that supported a singular, rounded, red and green

13

leaf that looked like a page from an open book replaced the tall, yellow-truncate trees. Eventually the trees ended and Bara walked into a large, open field. At the end of the field, to Bara's wonderment, stood two rock buildings tinged yellow by the early morning sun! Bara could barely make out candlelight flickering in the open window of the smaller house as he hid in the shadows. The house looked very ordinary. In fact, the house looked much too ordinary to be built on such an alien world.

After a moment of careful observation, the owner of the house walked by the window. Bara gasped. Nothing could have prepared him for the sight he had just witnessed. He had made a discovery on an alien world that was not alien. The resident of the small house was a man, a human, not so different from Bara himself.

Bara whipped out his multi-use analyzer and took a careful reading from the humanoid. Although the man's biological signature patterns were similar to any Terasian, they weren't exactly the same either. Only eight to ten thousand years of divergent adaptation could explain these genetic differences. Terasians had not invented the plow, much less space flight, that far back into history. Bara frowned. He had hoped that this person might be a refugee from the Vesder War, a survivor like himself. But if the man wasn't Terasian, who or what was he? Parallel evolution accounted for biological similarity between worlds, not near duplication.

Bara stared at the simple rock house, dumfounded. He again scanned the man's biological signatures to rule out any false readings. The bio-signs were reliable. Bara scratched the stubble on his chin. He couldn't remember a time when scientific data had appeared so contradictory. Bara told himself to be patient and collect more data. It was only through patience that he could solve these plaguing questions.

Bara watched closely as a tall, muscular man emerged from the small rock cabin. He was deeply tanned and dressed in some type of rust-colored leather cloak and trousers. Thick, red hair tumbled from his scalp and bright, green eyes glinted brightly in the morning's first light. Judging by the ruddiness of his face, it appeared that this was a man dedicated to the earth.

The man lumbered into the open field, stretched his arms, and deeply sucked in the chilling morning air with a raucous yawn. "By the Divu, it smells like a glorious morning. By the Divu!" he exclaimed. The man turned toward the larger rock building that served as a barn. "Come on old Bernka, it's time to haul your lazy butt out to work."

"Gegawah! Gegawah!" some creature bellowed as the man headed into the barn.

Bara was able to translate the spoken words instantly. The man spoke some odd dialect of Terasian, easily understandable with a little effort. This fact alone strongly supported the notion that this man, although genetically different, had interacted with Terasians on a frequent enough basis to speak the language with fluency. Bara felt a swell of hope that he had not experienced for a long time. Might his species have another chance? Would there be another chance for him?

The stranger reemerged from the barn tugging on a thick rope of twine. A massive four-legged beast reluctantly followed. Thick black blubber covered the creature's stocky body from head to tail. Three large glowing orange eyes dominated a hefty triangular head that bobbed up and down with every step. Although the creature appeared harmless, a group of three long spikes growing out on its tail that gave Bara pause.

"You'd be a stubborn Dithler today," the stranger commented. "How about if I feed you to the Varuk, eh?"

"Gegewah, Gegewah!"

Bara boldly stepped forward out into the field. The man saw him immediately and stood back warily with a knife in hand.

"Good morning sir," Bara shouted in Terasian, mimicking the man's difficult accent with moderate success.

"Who are you? Why you dressed so strange? You speak funny."

"My name is Bara. I am a stranger to your land. Strangers sometimes dress strange and do funny things. We can't help it. But this stranger has just crossed the mountains and is very tired. And, I might add with some embarrassment, quite lost."

The man eyed Bara for a moment. "Crossed the mountains, huh? See any Varuk?"

Bara shook his head. "I took great pains to stay out of everyone's way."

"My name is Duqat," the man said, easing a little but keeping his knife in hand. "Come on inside. You must be hungry."

"Thank you."

Duqat tied his beast to a tree branch and escorted Bara into his modest dwelling. Although a large area of the one-room house was filled with shadow, morning light beamed through an east facing window and illuminated a sparkling table made out of polished mountain granite. Crude wooden bowls and a black metallic pot sat haphazardly on a chiseled table. Duqat sat on one of two bare wooden chairs and offered the remaining chair to Bara. Bara obediently sat and then took an inventory of all items in the house. He noted a shelf, a fireplace, a mattress made of straw, and a few other odds and ends. Although nothing interested him that in itself was interesting. He saw no evidence of any manufactured items that hinted of civilization. His people, the technologically civilized Terasians, would certainly not live like Duqat. So the central question remained where were the Terasians?

"I have a little soup left over from breakfast," Duqat said, "I apologize that it has grown a bit thick."

"Don't worry yourself. I think just about anything would taste good to me right now." The soup was starchy, cold and bland. Bara finished it quickly and thanked his host.

"I don't make it a habit of finding out other people's business, stranger. But no offense, but you look different from other folks. I'm not sure I have seen anyone look like you, purple eyes and dark hair and all. Yet, somehow you look familiar. Are you sure you don't mean anyone any harm?"

"I mean you no harm. My purple eyes are no more dangerous than your blue eyes."

Duqat laughed. "Rightly so, I suppose. No offense."

"No offense taken. My features are very rare, even among my own people."

"I see."

"Are there any cities nearby, Mr. Duqat?"

"Nope. There's a fortress nearby and several towns beyond. I'm afraid we're living on the frontier."

Bara breathed deeply and casually asked the question that weighed heavily on his mind. "Duqat, have you ever heard of the Terasians?"

"No, can't say that I have," Duqat answered with indifference. "Should I know them?"

Bara shook his head. Although he was not surprised by the man's answer, he felt the darkness of his despair deepen.

"What's the matter?"

Bara looked away and watched the sunbeams stream down into the Spartan room from the Eastern window. Finally he spoke, "Death has tainted my soul, Mr. Duqat."

"Are you dying Mr. Bara?"

"I have died a million small deaths, yet somehow I continue to breathe."

"You speak oddly, stranger. I don't like the feel of you. I thinks you be a magical creature, like that witch woman in Gloroveena, Lonovina. What do you want?"

"Nothing. I am just babbling. I will leave you in peace. Thank you for the meal."

Duqat grunted. "If you continue to follow the river you will reach Capoca Fortress. Maybe you will find what you are looking for there. Oh, and remember to keep an eye out for the Varuk."

"What are the Varuk like in these parts?"

"Extremely vicious. They run in packs now."

"I see. I will be very careful," Bara said, confident that his lase-gun could resolve any Varuk threat to his favor. Bara left the premises, soon finding a winding trail that followed the contour of the river. His stride was quick but his thoughts were slow. Very few mysteries escaped Bara's power of reason, yet nothing he had observed so far seemed to make sense. He had witnessed an alien power of enormous sophistication. Yet the physical presence of this power, as well as his ship, remained hidden. Rather than making contact with an advanced alien life form, he had discovered humanoids! With some thought, Bara decided that dreaming was the most logical way to explain these inconsistencies. Bara found this explanation unlikely, however, as he was aware of all sensations associated with dreaming and other states of consciousness. Perhaps his present reality was just a farce, a stream of realistic images inserted by some alien malevolence running behavioral experiments. Was his every reaction being monitored and measured? Although this hypothesis seemed the most likely, it was also the most repulsive. Yet how could he be sure? How could he measure the unmeasurable?

Bara eventually gave up on what seemed like a futile endeavor. The mysteries of the planet would not reveal themselves on this day. The trail eventually opened up into several clearings. Dozens of rock dwellings were scattered between fields of dark earth segmented by large, convoluted, green lumps of harvested vegetable. Ruddy men, dressed simply like

Duqat, were throwing their produce into wooden carts for market in preparation for the coming winter. Some of the farmers noticed Bara and hastily pointed at him to the others. No one approached.

In the distance a stone wall wrapped around a rocky bluff. Small, simple, and uninviting, Bara guessed that the structure was none other than Capoca Fortress. He stopped and took stock of his surroundings as instinct told him that something was amiss. Bara reached for his lase-gun and continued on cautiously.

Bara traveled another mile before he heard the rhythmic pattern of pounding earth. He placed his lase-gun under a catch in his sleeve. The pounding became more intense as he waited silently behind a large, granite boulder. Three men suddenly appeared riding on the back of large beasts. Four muscular legs propelled the beasts and a thin layer of greenish blubber covered them. The animals stood nearly six feet high and were more than nine feet long from front to back. A large nose dominated the face of each animal and the head was covered with horns. Nine reddish eyes glared at Bara menacingly.

The three riders stared at Bara. Each man was broad, muscular, alert, and rode his beast confidently. The men were clothed with loose black trousers and flowing red shirts. The shirts were weighted down heavily by thick steel chain links and thick broadswords hung at their sides. The soldiers surrounded Bara reigned in their beasts. The leader was a muscular man with a large rounded face, a trim black beard, and two large black eyes. Bara bowed confidently. The man looked unimpressed.

"Who are you?" the leader asked gruffly.

"My name is Bara."

"You are not from here."

"No, I am a stranger. I mean no harm."

"That will be for my Commander to decide. Right now, you will come to the fortress. A Varuk attack is imminent."

CHAPTER 3

The leading soldier with the trim black beard kicked Bara in the backside and pointed him toward a dirt path forking to Capoca Fortress. The architecture of the fortress was uninspired; the four surrounding walls defied the colorful countryside and the vibrant river below. Only a stained wooden door penetrated the five man high walls. The three soldiers followed behind Bara in silence with their swords pricking at his back. Bara silently turned up the path and focused on the fresh morning air flowing cleanly through nose and throat.

As the armed complement approached, faces peered over the battlements and glared down at the stranger. Bara challenged their unrelenting gaze but, to his surprise, found neither malice nor curiosity but rather fear. Of him? That would be ludicrous. Then it occurred to him that his own presence was incidental. The looming faces reminded Bara of other men about to die in battle; men with tormented souls contemplating their own private, impending doom. The party responsible for their fear would clearly be that creature the old farmer talked about, the Varuk.

With a command from the bearded man, the white doors of Capoca Fortress opened. Two entrance guards allowed the company to enter a small courtyard enclosed by the four perimeter walls and several simple stone buildings. The brunt of the bearded soldier's sword pointed Bara in the direction of the closest, most recently built, structure.

The day's brilliant sunshine was snuffed out as Bara entered through the low doorway into a small room. A simple white wooden desk, a map, a few bulky chairs furnished the area, a small shelf lined with books, and some scattered documents. A middle-aged pot-bellied stood across the room with his right foot propped on his desk. He was busy picking at his fingernails and examining his hand with great care. Wearing black trousers, a flowing bright red shirt and a breastplate of armor, Bara guessed him to be the Commander of the small fortress.

The Commander seemed oblivious to his audience and continued to examine his hand. Eventually, the man brushed his fingers through sparse grey hair, cleared his throat, and shifted his gaze toward Bara. Bara returned his gaze without wavering. The man's gray eyes and face were expressionless.

"Report, Herak."

The broad, trim-bearded soldier behind Bara stiffened. "Commander Dukuk, we observed this man on the eastern trail. He was apprehended moments ago and was immediately brought here. He is a stranger . . . "

"I can see that Herak! What's his name?"

"Bara, sir. I believe he might be a spy."

"A spy? From where?"

"I . . . I don't know sir, but he was traveling the eastern road alone and unannounced."

"Well, I dare say, Herak, that Bara the spy will be sorely disappointed after snooping around this pisshole. Unless, of course, he is not a spy . . . Are you a spy, Bara?"

"No, sir," Bara answered with relaxed confidence.

"If you are not from here, Bara, where are you from?"

"Mohasa, sir."

"Mohasa, huh. Land of heart. I never heard of it."

Bara sighed, as if bored to explain. "It is an island, of a sort, to the east, far beyond the mountains and the great waters."

The Commander eyed Bara suspiciously. He eventually glanced back down at his hand, picked at his fingernail, and spoke. "Well, if you say so, Bara. In fact, you can be a spy for all I care. We have no secrets here. I only have one question. Can you handle a sword?"

"I have years of formal training and experience as a soldier."

The Commander nodded and removed his boot off the desk and placed it on the dusty, rock floor. "We are going to be attacked by the Varuk tonight. We estimate that they will number more than fifty. Unfortunately, we are just twenty. You may choose to assist in our mission, or, you may travel south and join the villagers." The Commander then stared intently at Bara and spoke in hushed voice. "Safer that you go, boy. We aren't expecting reinforcements by tonight. You don't have much of a Gevoi's fight'n chance on walking out of here alive if you stay."

"I have no concern of death. Besides, the Varuk are just as likely to ambush me this time of night. I will stay and fight."

"No concern for death! Commander, this is a worthless man," Herek inserted. "He will probably hurt somebody, or at the very least be in the way."

"I am not picking men for the academy, Herek. If this man can handle a sword, then he will be useful. You will escort Bara to Moluq's squad and give him the necessary equipment. And Bara, you are to follow orders without question. Understand?"

Bara nodded in agreement.

"Follow me," Herak commanded in a deep, low voice.

Herak escorted Bara across the compound past a hive of soldiers swarming in preparation for the coming battle and into an elongated stone building used for the storage of armaments. The trim bearded soldier wiped sweat off his eyelids and grudgingly handed Bara a broadsword. Bara took the sword and examined the cool, steel blade gingerly.

"Standard Coana sword," Herak said acidly. "Don't cut yourself."

Bara ignored the remark and lifted the sword gently in his hands. Although the sword was heavy and awkward, Bara knew that he could handle the weapon with confidence. Ancient weaponry had always fascinated him. Although Bara had time to master many activities throughout the last two centuries, his skill in fencing had been particularly renowned. The beauty of simplicity had been the catalyst of his interest. He had always marveled at how one could transform such an unsophisticated weapon into a graceful wand of moving art. Indeed, as Bara familiarized himself the weapon, the blade began flow eloquently in an orchestra of circles, arcs, and lines. Finally the blade blended into a blur of motion. Abruptly the sword stopped just short of Herek's boot.

"This will do fine," Bara said.

Herek's immediate response was silence, although his pale face betrayed amazement.

"And I promise not to cut myself," Bara added momentarily.

"Hmm, perhaps you will be of use to us after all," Herek answered regaining his composure. "Here is your archery equipment and shield," he continued while handing Bara supplies. "I don't have any more chain, so we are done here. Come and I will introduce you to Moluq."

The twenty odd soldiers began spacing themselves in small even groups around the battlement perimeter. Moluq was found pacing his section of the battlement, seemingly absorbed in thought. With Bara walking three paces behind, Herak silently strode behind the unsuspecting man. "Second rank Moluq!" his voice boomed.

Moluq jumped and whirled his lithe body around with jerk reaction speed. His face was contorted as he gawked at Herak. Moluq mastered himself quickly and stood rigidly at attention. "Yes sir!" he snapped.

"This is Bara, Moluq. He will be under your authority for the duration of the Varuk attack."

"Yes sir."

Herak turned and headed off toward the Commander's quarters.

"I think the man has chronic bowel problems," Moluq whispered and winked.

Bara decided to offer a faint smile. Moluq returned the smile with a grin, a wide grin that complemented two small blue eyes, straw flowing hair, and a large bulbous nose. These features, in combination with his crumpled and torn shirt, seemed to defy any seriousness about the man.

"How do you do?" Moluq asked lifting his hand skyward. Bara mimicked the movement and clasped Moluq's hand.

"Not from around here, I bet?"

"No," Bara answered. "I'm from a place called Mohasa."

"Land of heart. I have never heard of it."

"Well, you would probably be the first around here if you had."

"So, you have come all this way to join our fun at Capoca Fortress, then?"

Bara cracked a smile, this time genuine. "Let's say that fate brought me here."

"Well mister, fate don't like you much."

"No, you're right about that."

"We're going to have a wild party tonight," Muloq said gazing over the northern battlements. "Wait until you see who's on the guest list."

Bara joined Moluq and gazed out onto the velvet green expanse. Gentle curving hills repeated themselves until they became lost in the evening haze. Large three-stemmed trees dotted each grassy rise, their leaves glowing silvery-green from the evening sunlight. Granite boulders also crested a number of these hills and glowed in a shade of watermelon.

"A beautiful place." Bara commented.

"Yes . . . Yes, it is." Moluq said quietly. "We should try to get the most out of this sunset. It may be our last."

Bara shrugged his shoulders. He knew that he would probably survive the present ordeal unscathed. Whether Moluq and the other soldiers perished or not was a whole different matter.

Bara had already decided not to use his lase-gun to kill the Varuk, unless necessary. Undo attention was the last thing he wanted. Besides,

Bara decided that he was tired of being the hero everyone depended on for their survival. He had taken on that responsibility before and failed. He wanted to solve the mystery of his ship and explore this mysterious planet without interference so that he could later do, well, whatever came next. He certainly didn't want to become involved in these people's lives. There was no sense in making attachments in a universe filled with suffering and death. Still, if this were entirely true, why was he aiding these people at all? Habit, Bara told himself. Yet he knew that this answer wasn't quite true, either.

"You are a hard man to read, stranger. The look on your face, well, never mind."

"Yes, it looks . . . "

"Tortured."

"I wouldn't know, Moluq."

"Say Bara, do you think we have a chance?"

"I don't know. Why don't you tell me about the Varuk?"

"Why? Don't you . . . "

"The Varuk don't exist on Mohasa."

Moluq gazed at Bara with astonishment. "No Varuk! Your land is truly blessed, sir. I wish we could rid the world of such evil." Moluq spat, paused momentarily, and then continued. "Well, let's see. The Varuk is an animal. Although more intelligent than most, it is an aggressive, meat-eating, blood sucking, filthy animal! They used to live by themselves. Generally, they lived in caves or rock shelters. If a man stumbled upon their lair, they'd tear him up. Otherwise, they generally stayed clear of civilization. About three moons ago, a group of Varuk started attacking solitary farmhouses. Despite our efforts in organizing defense against the raids, they have continued to grow larger and bolder every day. Now, by the Divu, they have the audacity to attack a military fortress. Retaliation will come swift, and I assure you. Our deaths will be avenged!"

Moluq's description was disturbing. Something didn't sit quite right for Bara. "You say that the Varuk once lived individually?"

Moluq looked at Bara quizzically. "As far as I know," he answered. "At least, it has been that way since the time of my father's father.

"Do the Varuk have language or tools?"

"No, none to speak of. They chip away at rocks, utter a few grunts, and throw sticks. Basically, they're pretty stupid. Why, what are you driving at?"

"What you suggest is impossible. How can a solitary animal evolve into a pack animal overnight? And how would a nonverbal animal organize, plan and orchestrate a massive attack against anything, much less a small military fortress during a new moon?"

"Well, ah, I don't know." Moluq thought for a moment and then glanced at Bara perplexed. "What do you think, sir?"

"I think someone with imagination and intelligence strategically planned this attack; say somebody with influence over the Varuk."

"By the Divu!" Moluq boomed. Nearby soldiers glared and loudly whispered, "Quiet!"

Moluq lowered his voice. "Why? Is that possible? But, ah, who would be capable of doing such a thing?"

Bara shrugged. "I don't know."

"Disturbing thought, indeed."

Moluq looked out across a landscape shrouded in shadow and began to shiver. "They will be coming very soon," he whispered, "before the blue sun rises. Tell me something, Bara. What are you doing here? Did Commander Dukuk threaten you or somehow force you into this?"

"No," Bara answered, "he did not. I believe that maybe I can help you stop them."

"Perhaps," Moluq replied flatly and sighed. "However, it is the new moon, and Varuk have eyes built for night. You haven't seen them. They also have sharp talons, speed, strength, and travel in great numbers."

"Yes, but we have a defensible position, weapons, and intelligence," Bara replied.

Moluq shifted his gaze and stared out silently into the enveloping darkness. Bara noticed that his eyes were glossy, his cheeks were weighted, and his ears drooped. He had seen the look before, and recognized it as an expression of hopelessness. A self-fulfilling prophesy, that, he thought sadly. Those who feel beaten are beaten.

Moluq finally spoke after several minutes of silence. "I never had children," he muttered. "I wish I had children. Oh, I, ah, mean, I have no legacy, you see. If I die here, no one will really care, will they? I mean, what's the point?"

Bara felt a welt of anger sting from deep within. He really didn't want to hear this from a man who might be getting his face ripped to pieces. Moluq's emotional baggage was not his responsibility. Yet some other emotion, nameless and suppressed over time, surfaced and gave him pause. "Do you have fond memories, Moluq?" Bara asked gently.

"Yes, of my mom, brother, a few friends, I suppose."

"Nobody can steal those experiences, Moluq. The people you have cared for, helped, and worked beside, have all been touched in meaningful ways. The past cannot be erased with the passing of time. That, I suppose, is the point."

"Do you think?"

Bara nodded and wondered if he really believed it himself.

"Yes, perhaps you are right," Moluq replied. "And, of course, one should not discount the possibility of an afterlife. The villagers believe that the righteous will live peacefully on a spiritual mountain, eating Yuga fruit, and digging out lost spirits from the Nuba Nuba. That doesn't sound very appealing to me."

"No, I suppose not. I know nothing of that. Yet I do know one thing. If this campaign were as hopeless as you suggest, I wouldn't be here. All is not lost, yet."

"Ah, you speak rightly, my friend. We must have courage, yes? Without it, we are doomed. Truly, I will fight with hope and dignity." Moluq feigned a smile, looked out to the west, and silently watched the sun disappear over the mountains.

Capoca Fortress became as quiet as a tomb. Stars began to twinkle in the coming night sky. Bara detected an evening breeze as leaves began to rustle from the hillside trees below. Some soldiers closed their eyes and silently moved their lips in prayer. Most simply stared over the battlements, stiff and still. Herak and Commander Dukuk walked the battlements and whispered words of confidence to the frightened soldiers. Bara, for his part, kept his anxiety at bay. It was easy for him. Unlike the neophyte soldiers that surrounded him, he had more than seventy years of practice.

As the night strengthened its short reign with the passing of time, the Milky Way Galaxy bowed majestically across a moonless sky filled with millions of twinkling stars. Bara shifted his artificial vision to the infrared spectrum and hunted for the enemy. He didn't have to wait long before shimmering red bodies began scaling a nearby hillside.

"Moluq, Go fetch Herek," Bara whispered. "I'll man your post."

"What are you talking about?" he whispered back.

"Just do it."

Reluctantly Moluq hurried toward the man and whispered in his ear. Herak turned, frowned, and approached Bara.

"This had better be important, stranger," he whispered acidly.

"I believe it is sir," Bara replied in low voice. "Look directly ten degrees west from north, then down another twenty."

"Yes, and . . . "

"Look carefully and you should see Varuk coming over that large rock outcropping?"

"Huh, . . . wait! Goka! I saw something move. Goka, you got good eyes," he said looking at Bara in astonishment. "Keep me informed if you see further movements."

"Very well."

Herak darted off and informed the rest of the men. Soldiers scurried and repositioned themselves near the northwest battlement. They notched bows, piled rocks, and placed magnesium flares into small catapults. Dukuk lumbered alongside the battlements and placed his hand on Bara's shoulder. The Commander's body reeked with the odor of clothes drenched in sweat. His long weathered face announced concern and suspicion. "Do you see them?" he asked gruffly.

"Yes. A couple hundred are coming up from the northeast. The closest are, I would say . . . approximately sixty feet . . . there," Bara replied and pointed.

"Ahhhk, I can't fathom how you can see through that blackness," he retorted skeptically.

"Some of my people can see very well in the dark, Commander. Here, let me demonstrate." Bara notched an arrow and aimed at the closest glob of shimmering red heat. The arrow flew smoothly and was answered by an "Eeahhkk!" and a faint, muffled thud. A choir of deafening battle shrieks followed.

"Flares!" the Commander, yelled over the mayhem. Four magnesium flares sailed through the air illuminating the immediate ground below. The Varuk, momentarily frightened by the brilliant spectacle, were easy stationary targets for a rain of arrows released by the Fortress men. This advantage did not last long, however, as the Varuk regained confidence almost as fast as the flares were spent.

"You're, you're, a wizard," Moluq stammered.

"No lad, I was just built to see in the dark." Bara notched another arrow and let it fly toward the mass of shimmering heat. "Ten Varuk climbing the northwest corner!" Bara yelled. Several soldiers raced toward a pile of rocks. Pumped by adrenaline, they lunged massive boulders down upon the ascending horde.

Bara noted that Moluk was accurate in his assessment of the Varuk; it was an animal built for violence. Long muscular arms and stout legs supported a massive frame covered by a thick, black, blubbery hide. Their body was defended by sharp talons and layered, back spines. Their faces were nearly featureless except for three red glowing eyes. A large gaseous maw served as a mouth that opened at the neck and belched out corrosive drool. Bara knew that the animals would be difficult to kill.

Again, the magnesium flares flickered into nothingness and Bara let another arrow fly. Then he launched another, and another, and still another. Eventually, the Varuk began to climb the battlements directly under Bara and Moluq.

"You hand and I slam!" Bara barked. Moluq nodded and preceded to hand Bara large boulders. Propelled by artificial strength, Bara smashed the heavy boulders down on the oncoming Varuk with deadly precision. Many animals squealed as he hit them, but others kept scaling without fear. Other parts of the fortress were not so efficiently defended. The Varuk began to breach sections of the battlements and hand to hand combat followed. As the soldiers fought for their lives, fewer men were available to throw rocks down on the encroaching mass. The Varuk breached the walls in greater numbers, and soon the battlements were flooded with the raging animals.

A Varuk rushed toward Bara and leaped. Bara swung both arms with an inhuman force and deflected the three hundred pound animal over the battlements. The second Varuk immediately followed and swiped at Bara with razor sharp talons. It's three triangular eyes were blazing red and drool flung out in every direction. The animal was extremely fast, but Bara was even faster as he heaved the heavy broadsword upward into the creature's stomach. It shrieked as it fell over the wall. Another Varuk attacked Bara from behind. Bara did a backward air dive and clobbered the animal in the head. The animal stunned, Bara ran his sword well into its chest. The Varuk fell with a thud.

Moluq was engaged with a smaller Varuk, yet the beast was overpowering the lithe young man and had already sliced into his smooth skin. Bara hurled a stone at the animal. The projectile hit the animal in the face, stunning it long enough for Moluq to end the challenger with one blow.

Bara quickly jumped to his feet to meet the next challenger, but there was none. Both the Varuk and human ranks had thinned considerably. Moluq supported himself against the wall, bloodied and panting. Herak and Commander Dukuk were defending against six Varuk on the northwest corner and were quickly losing ground.

"Moluq! Man the walls and cover my back," Bara barked. Moluq nodded and grabbed for a rock. Bara notched an arrow and aimed for a Varuk closing in on the Commander. The arrow sliced through the air and gouged itself into the beast's neck. Red blood and green mucous spurted out. The creature stumbled, screeched, and fell. Another arrow fell the next Varuk in a similar manner. The reduction in the enemy allowed Herak to cut down a nearby Varuk. Running into the mayhem, Bara and the Commander finished the sixth and last beast with relative ease.

Suddenly the battlefield was bathed in soft blue light. All living eyes turned to East. Buroos Te-2, the solar system's blue dwarf sun, was burning brightly on the horizon. Sensing a turn in events, the remaining Varuk bolted over the battlements and retreated into the brightening night. The few remaining soldiers cheered.

"We did it!" Moluq screamed. Tears wallowed up in his eyes. "By the Divu, we did it!"

Bara placed a hand on Moluq's shoulder. "You did well," he replied.

"You deserve the credit, I would be dead without you," Moluq said with conviction.

"We all did what we had to do, Moluq. The important thing is that you fought with hope an honor."

"Yes!" he replied excited, "Yes I did, didn't I?"

Bara nodded in agreement and scanned the premises. The battlements were littered with corpses. Blood glistened in the soft blue starlight. Only seven men were still standing. "We had better start attending to the wounded," Bara stated flatly.

All of the luster in Moluq's face quickly vanished. "Yes . . . yes, I suppose you're right," he muttered.

The seven remaining men, tired and grim-faced, toiled during the remaining night to save the wounded and bury the dead. Bara endured much of the labor as he was less fatigued than the others were. He served the company efficiently and silently, yet had personally wondered what had possessed him to volunteer for such a difficult undertaking that was none of his concern.

CHAPTER 4

Bara accompanied the survivors of Capoca Fortress toward the nation's capital, Gloroveena where they expected the company to give reports to various generals and politicians. Rain had sporadically pummeled the men and their uncooperative mounts for three days and the provisions had become soaked and cold. Silence and curses were their only defense against the lashing drops. On the fourth day the landscaped brightened, warmed, and gained definition. The men rode along a heavily traveled, dirt road sheltered by deeply creviced, dark-brown cliffs. Shrouded by clouds from the passing storm, the jagged spires looked ominously alive behind the moving mist.

"I think the rain has finally stopped for good!" Moluq said looking at the sky. "We should reach Gloroveena later this afternoon."

"I hope the weather holds," Bara mused, glancing at the bright sun overhead. "After traveling four days in the rain and mud, Capoca Fortress seems a world away right now."

"Gloroveena! It's been years since I saw her last. Did I tell you about the blue royal spires?"

"Yes, I think twice now."

"Ah, but they truly are beautiful, sir. Imagine dozens of them, as high as these rock cliffs, all plated with vivid blue glass. I can almost see them sparkling from here," Moluq added stretching his neck up to gain a little height. "Indeed, our glorious bravery will be honored under the glittering glass. Medals and promotions for all of us. I hope to make fourth level soldier and live in the capital."

"Stationed under the royal spires, I bet!" a voice boomed from behind. Moluq turned and discovered, to his dismay that the booming voice belonged to Sub-Commander Herek. Of course the Sub-Commander was grinning.

"Possibly," Moluq granted. "Spires or not, Bara will join our glorious fighting force and be placed under my command. Together we'll defend his majesty's glorious spires with life and limb."

"I do not serve anyone's glory," Bara replied, "especially if it involves losing body parts."

Herak shook his head and grunted, "After my report, Moluq, you'll be lucky to promote to latrine duty."

"Ha, they won't pay any attention to your ravings," Moluq returned and shifted his gaze to the road. "Yes, I'll settle down in Golorveena, make a good living, find a wife, and raise lots of children to carry on my legacy. What about you, what do you want Bara?"

"I would settle for some hot food and a bath."

"I'll go along with that," Herak agreed, bringing his beast up alongside Bara. "You are a more patient man then I, listening to all that man's rubbish. Perhaps I should order him to walk far behind us, preferably in the mud."

Moluq scowled and turned silent. Quickly becoming bored, Herek shook his head in disgust and sped his mount forward toward Commander Dukuk. For his part, Bara welcomed the silence that allowed himself to enjoy basking in the warm sunlight beneath towering, steep-cliff canyons. Although he had learned about local customs by observing passing travelers and listening to his company's idle conversation, he had not learned anything regarding the incredible source of power that stole his ship. Bara believed that there was a strong force operating on the planet; perhaps some sixth sense perceived it's tantalizing call. In the rock and air, this force seemed to permeate everywhere, yet it was nowhere. Bara even perceived a power in the fat, leathery, purple succulents that flourished in the fertile, volcanic soil. The plants interested Bara in their own right. Layers of twisting, overlapping, thin arms and nodules created a tangled mass of vegetation that reminded him of wind-blown hair. The most amazing thing about the mass was its size. The plants followed the contours of the canyons and seemed to have no beginning or end. "Moluq," he said breaking the silence, "do you know anything about the thick vegetation down there at the bottom of the ravine?"

"Ah yes. That is a good question you asked. That THING is named the Asid."

"Thing?"

"Oh yes! You're not looking at a colony of plants, Bara. That monstrosity is the largest growing thing ever known to man. Millions of vines intertwine and grow together as one organism. In fact, the thing stretches throughout the Asid mountain range."

"Fascinating," Bara replied, truly amazed.

"Oh yes. Legend has it that first woman was berthed in the Asid womb."

"Womb?"

"You see, the Divu, our god, created it hollow like a pipe. The city of Gloroveena drinks from the main river. Lonovina may have also been berthed by its headwaters, although the river is much too pure to beget such a sordid individual, in my opinion.

"An old farmer referred to her. The name Lonovina means nothing to me."

"Yes, well, we must be careful what we say about her," Moluq whispered. "The woman has ears."

"Is she some sort of deity?"

"I'm not sure what she is," Moluq whispered again, this time more eagerly, "but she is as real as ground beneath our feet. I have heard stories, Bara that would make skin crawl. Some are likely to be fabricated, but many come from reputable sources. One thing for sure, the woman has supernatural powers."

Bara gazed at Moluq with an expression of surprise. Could this be the break he was looking for? Supernatural powers might either be equated with myth or technology. Bara was hoping for the latter.

"Do you know this from personal experience?" Bara asked.

"Well, I never met the woman," Moluq continued. "We don't exactly maintain the same circle of friends. Still, I do know this, Lonovina has single handedly created the most profitable manufacturing and trading empire in the Caonan Empire."

"Just because a woman is good in business doesn't make her sorceress. She probably has just found an edge over the competition."

"Indeed. No one can match her quality of products for the price. Her factories, they say, are run by objects of magic."

"Probably machinery," Bara stated flatly.

"What?"

"Never mind. Please continue, Moluq."

"Obviously that kind of wealth equates with power, political power. Even the emperor grudgingly pays her heed, or so they say."

"People fear her," Bara surmised.

"Absolutely! As they should, too. Some say that Lonovina can make a woman barren just by looking at her in a certain way. Like this," Moluq offered by crossing his eyes and sticking out a gigantic purple tongue. Bara couldn't stop himself from smiling.

"No really, it's true!" Moluq said wounded. "Many respectable people even say so."

"I'm not mocking you, Moluq. It's just your expression."

"Yes, very funny. Well, as I was saying, Lonovina has many political enemies, including the church. A heretic they call her for all the uproar she creates. Some say the church has been responsible for several assassination attempts."

"A resourceful woman to survive such a formidable foe."

"She probably survives by using magic. Scary stuff if you ask me."

"Who supports her?"

"Mostly the traders back her. Some say various military hot shots support her too. Only the Divu knows why."

"Probably because the rumors about her are nonsense. Lonovina intrigues me. Someday I hope to meet her."

"Meet her? Are you crazy?! Personally, I would rather engage another Varuk."

"You may have to deal with both. Anyway, I think I see your city coming over that ridge."

"Yes," Moluq said grinning. "Splendid!"

Although Gloroveena was provincial by Terasian standards, Bara recognized the splendor of the city given the inhabitants limited population and technological sophistication. Even from a distance, the metropolis was clearly a cultural, political, and religious center. Sporadic, tall, ornately decorated spires cut into the sky, graceful columns softened rough granite walls, and pointed, dark green roofs added texture to the complex patterns of the city. A vast valley lined by jagged brown and purple colored cliffs cradled the city itself. The gigantic plant Asid stopped just short of the city limits. A mighty white river poured from an opening in the plant, snaked through the city, and flowed into an ocean of brilliant blue water. Dozens of sea-faring ships dotted the ocean's horizon, no doubt bringing in commerce from other coastal ports and making merchant traders, like Lonovina, very rich.

Commander Dukuk had ordered the small company to rest briefly on the grassy ridge so that he could discuss private matters with Sub-Commander Herek. The delay was clearly difficult for the anxious, young Moluq who twitched in anticipation of home. His Rovan mount, already tired from the day's journey, began to wrinkle its blubbery hide and shake its sharp horns in protest. Reading the animal's behavior accurately, Moluq eased off his mount and leaned against a nearby twenty foot tall bluish-green plant. The plant was shaped like an animal's ear and quite unlike anything Bara had ever seen before. He guessed that the ear portion of the plant trapped moisture from the ocean breezes.

"So, Bara, can you find all the landmarks I described?" Moluq asked trying to relax and fill time.

"The Emperor's palace is right there in the center of the city," Bara said flatly pointing to dozen blue glass spires twinkling in the late afternoon sunlight. "The large gold-leafed domed building standing to the palace's right must be the Xinct building, or the house of politicians. That large black alabaster building, shaped like a star with a silver bubble over its center, must be the Central Church."

"Very good, and our destination?"

"Would be the fortress to the right," Bara answered pointing to a hill crowned by a complex of fortified rock walls, battlements, large plain rock buildings, courtyards, and towers."

"The Pillar of Caonan Justice."

"Will be swift and harsh," Herek barked over Moluq's shoulder, "if you don't line up in formation."

"Sorry, I didn't hear you, sir. I was busy talking," Moluq explained.

"As usual," Herek returned and then grunted.

Moluq hurriedly fell into formation with the rest of the men. With Dukuk and Herek in the lead, the company proceeded down the hillside, weaving their way through a maze of travelers, soldiers, dignitaries, wagons, mounts, and strange beasts of every sort. Opulent estates dotting the hillsides was quickly replaced by larger communal dwellings as the land flattened. Markets and other businesses began to appear and the buildings began to compete for space. The road, once little more that a dirt pathway, was now paved with polished rock and lined with painted white stucco buildings five stories tall. The crowds became thicker as the company made their way deeper into the center of the city. Used to solitary living, Bara became uneasy with the continued pressing of bodies, the acrid smell of sweat, and the loud voices of haggling consumers.

Thankfully, the crowds finally thinned as the company reached a large treeless square that allowed entrance to the towering battlements of Gloroveena Fortress.

The heart of Gloroveena Fortress remained hidden behind a massive, dark grey, rock wall towering more than a hundred feet over their heads. The company stopped, unmounted, and waited for admittance into the fortress's massive gate of interlocking iron rods. The head entry guard was an enormous man that looked as permanent as the stones surrounding him. Two expressionless eyes set deeply in a meaty face carved up by years of weather peered vacantly at Dukuk.

"Papers," he muttered mechanically.

Dukuk obediently handed over the relevant credentials and a sealed order of business. The man briefly scanned through the papers and locked eyes with Commander. His gaze abruptly shifted toward Bara and the other remaining soldiers. "All of you, come with me," he muttered.

Dukuk glanced over his shoulder nervously and obediently followed the sentry. The company followed Dukuk as if he were their mother. The guard opened an inconspicuous door and entered the gate tower. The seven men were directed into a small office with a sign saying, GATE SUPERINTENDENT. A tall, brown-skinned man looked up.

"Yes," he muttered, not looking at anyone in particular.

"These are the soldiers from Capoca Fortress, sir. I brought them directly to you, as ordered."

"Thank you. You are dismissed." Without expression, the thick man bowed slightly and quickly disappeared.

"So, these are the brave men who gallantly defended our glorious frontier against the raving vicious Varuk mobs," the Gate Superintendent announced. "Well-done Commander Dukuk."

"Thank you sir," the commander replied beaming.

"And who is this, Dukuk?" the superintendent asked pointing toward Bara. "You have brought a stranger in our midst.

"Ah, this is Bara sir. He was most valuable during the Varuk attack. I humbly request that he be boarded with our company."

"Very well," the superintendent replied with indifference. "Just so that he knows the consequences of entering secure areas."

"Understood, sir."

"I was expecting you earlier this morning, Dukuk. No matter. Commander Dukuk and Herak, you will brief the generals at five bowoa tomorrow morning."

"Yes sir," both answered in unison.

"Oh, and one other thing. Lonovina will want to meet all of you at eight bowoa tomorrow evening."

Several men coughed. "Lonovina, sir?" the commander asked.

"You heard me, Dukuk. Don't ask me what that woman wants. She has pull with your superiors, so you all better be there."

Bara turned toward Moluq and saw that his face had turned a light shade of purple. For his part, Bara was looking forward to meeting the woman in the hope of discovering the mystery of her magic.

Dukuk, Bara, Herak, Moluq, and the rest of the company arrived at Lonovina's residence at a quarter to eight. Although the building's white stuccoed walls and dark green roof shingles blended in with the rest of the city, the house was eccentric. Dark glass windows, covered by black iron rail, reflected sparkling sunlight to the observer. Dark blue blots and lines crisscrossed over the white stucco forming complex, abstract patterned designs. Bara visualized concrete shapes embedded within the abstraction, shapes that were lost and then replaced by others. Bara realized that the painted designs allowed the viewer to project their own unique images on the picture, like one might do looking at clouds. Bara guessed that Moluq was seeing monsters, judging from the look of him. The other soldiers also seemed uneasy. Gone was the continued bantering between the young men that annoyed Bara. Everyone was silent now.

Two tough guards manned the entrance gate. They were both outfitted with black uniforms and gold-sheathed daggers. The larger of the two soldiers was thickly muscled fellow with ebony skin and black curly hair. Most noticeably, he had an extensive pink scar that snaked across his face. With the sound of footsteps, the man turned and glowered at the oncoming soldiers.

"I have a bad feeling about this," Moluq whispered to Bara.

"Shhh, not now." Bara commanded.

Commander Dukuk warily walked up to the dark-skinned man, bowed slightly, and announced, "We are from Capoca Fortress."

The guard lifted his arm and opened his hand. Dukuk hesitantly placed his fingers over the guard's fingers and both squeezed.

"Greetings, Commander Dukuk," said the guard warmly. "Lonovina has been looking forward to your company's arrival. Everyone, please follow me."

The men followed the guard through a yard overgrown with thick bushes and stubby trees.

They could see various human figures melding with the shadows as they approached a large metal door. The guard unlocked the door with a heavy metal key and led the company into a spacious foyer. Soft sunlight streamed through large ceiling windows illuminating curving pillars of pink marble that shadowed the white floor with erratic designs. A large door, leading into the main part of the house, was locked. The guard ignored this entranceway and led the company into a receiving room off to their left.

The receiving room was spacious and generously lit by large elongated side and ceiling windows. Banners representing various trading interests hung neatly over light blue walls. At the center of the room stood a large, simple, rectangular table complete with chairs. The guard instructed the men to sit, then bowed and exited the room. Silence pervaded in the room until a woman briskly walked in unannounced.

The men stood as the woman joined with them at the head of the table. Bara stared at her with intense curiosity. She wore a simple black dress that fell slightly above her knees. Although she was tall and muscular for a woman, she had delicate facial features like many people in Gloroveena. Yet unlike other humans Bara had seen on Yvia Voi, the woman had long, thick, curly black hair, large, almond-shaped purple eyes, and slightly translucent skin. Bara's likeness to the woman was not lost on the rest of the company. Heads turned in silent double takes.

The woman also stared at Bara in utter amazement. It was a look that vanished as quickly as it had appeared, however, as she shifted her gaze toward Dukuk.

"Commander Dukuk, I presume."

Dukuk stiffened. "Yes, Ma'am, ah I mean sir, or, ah-"

"Ma'am is fine, Commander."

"Yes, Ma'am."

"I am Lonovina. I'm glad that we have had a chance to talk," she said raising her hand. Dukuk timidly grabbed it and squeezed.

"The pleasure is mine," he returned, relaxing slightly.

"Thank you all for coming," Lonovina announced while making eye contact with each member of her captive audience. "The Varuk attack, although relatively small, has monumental significance. We have reason to believe that the Varuk will strike again in even bolder numbers. Not only are my trading interests at risk, but innocent lives will be lost if we do not act promptly. Thus, any information you chose to share with me today will be highly valued and appreciated. I would like to begin by asking Commander Dukuk to describe the events before, during, and immediately after the attack. But before you start, Commander, I would ask you to be as precise as possible. Do not to leave anything out. Understood?"

"Yes Ma'am."

"The rest can add anything you like, anytime."

As instructed, Commander Dukuk carefully recalled the events leading up to the attack. Lonovina nodded occasionally but otherwise listened attentively without interruption. She did shift posture, however, when Dukuk described Bara's sudden appearance at Capoca Fortress. He followed up by carefully describing the initial meeting with Bara and emphasized the stranger's willingness to fight against the Varuk.

Time passed slowly as Dukuk dwelled on defensive strategy and company bravery. More than one soldier blushed as Dukuk lavishly praised the men for specific acts of heroism both during and after the attack. The stranger was not exempt. Dukuk expounded on Bara's uncanny eyesight, skill, and strength. "To be honest, Ma'am," he said. "I don't think we would have succeeded without him. The military really needs a man like him and should actively recruit his services. I have already mentioned it to the generals."

Lonovina shot a quick glance at Bara, but said nothing.

"I guess that's all I have to say," Dukuk said, feeling awkward in the silence. "Does anyone else have anything to add?"

The men shook their heads.

"Frankly," Lonovina stated, "I find it alarming that the Varuk could attack with such organization."

"Yes, those are my thoughts exactly," Moluq blurted out, and then reddened with embarrassment.

"And your name would be?"

"M-m-mooluq Ma'am. I-I was just saying, th-th-th-th-that my friend Bara here believes the Varuk were helped, somehow. Right Bara?".

Lonovina turned toward Bara, her gaze soft and liquid. Bara couldn't help but feel some sexual interest. He quickly squashed this feeling, however, and concentrated on the functionality of the woman. Could she help him find his ship? No doubt she knew something of technology, at least more than the rest of Caonan society. What secrets was she harboring?

"Bara?" she probed gently.

Bara bowed slightly. "My rationale is as follows. The Varuk, according to Moluq here, is a solitary animal. Group organization and cooperation have never been in their repertoire. Animals don't change complex social patterns of behavior overnight."

"Yes," Moluq added with new confidence, "impossible for them to get all chummy."

"Another thing," Bara added, "the Varuk lack linguistic ability. How did they organize and plan an attack during a moonless period? They must have had outside influence."

"Interesting idea. Lacking language, as you say, how could anyone communicate and direct the animal."

"Language is not necessary. One can radically alter the disposition of animals through genetic engineering, which simply means tampering with their biological blueprints."

"Genetic what?"

"It would take too long to explain. Sufficed it to say, it would involve selective breeding."

Lonovina was momentarily speechless and beset with questions. Where did this man come from? Was he for real? She had never met anyone like him before. He knew either too little or too much. "Interesting hypotheses," she eventually said. "I have heard about selective breeding. Except, the Varuk changed suddenly, not over generations."

"Not necessarily. A grouping could have been corralled and bred in secret."

"You have given me something to think about, Bara, as you have Dukuk. Perhaps we can talk about selective breeding and this genetic engineering some other time. Unfortunately, I now have another engagement. I thank you all for your time."

Following Dukuk's lead, Bara and the other men bowed with respect.

"Guard," she commanded. The large dark-skinned man appeared suddenly, as if from nowhere. Lonovina reached over and whispered something in his ear. The guard nodded nonchalantly.

"The guard will escort you all out now," she said smiling. "May the Divu be with you." Lonovina then turned and walked out.

CHAPTER 5

Bara wound through a web of black cobbled streets toward Lonovina's estate. Although it was late morning, the autumn air felt cool and moist as he walked beneath thick, swooping trees. Relieved to exit the noisy, cramped quarters of Gloroveena Fortress, Bara embraced the delicate hiss of rustling leaves. Momentary serenity was quickly lost, however, when his companion Moluq coughed and spat on the street.

"Nervous?" Bara asked.

"Naw."

"But what if Lonovina looks at you cross-eyed and makes you impotent?"

"All right, all right, you've made your point," Moluq returned gruffly. "I may have exaggerated about her earlier. Still, I still don't think she's normal. She's probably related to you, by the look of her. No surprise in that, I suppose."

"I'll take that as a compliment."

Moluq bit his lip and checked a snicker.

"What?"

"I think she likes you. Didn't you see the way she first looked at you? Or are you all that blind?"

"Lonovina's expression suggested astonishment, not infatuation. Her surprise was reasonable considering the circumstances."

"She asked you to lunch, didn't she?"

"Intellectual curiosity motivates her, as it does me."

"Then why was I invited, huh?"

Bara frowned and walked faster.

"I agree that curiosity motivates the woman, but our invitation was definitely social. And I," he said grinning from ear to ear, "will be your chaperon."

Bara halted. "You will be my what?" he asked in a tight, well controlled voice.

"Your chaperon, thick skull. And, as your chaperon, I must meet certain obligations."

"Such as?"

"Like making sure you two, ah, you know, march steadily into the blissful arms of love."

43

Bara shook his head. "That's about the stupidest thing I ever heard, Moluq."

"Yeah, well, I kind of specialize in stupid."

"Yes you do."

"But sometimes I'm right."

Lonovina's estate came into view as the men rounded the street corner. The same two guards stood rigidly at the front gate. The ebony skin man bowed and guided Bara and Moluq into the compound. Entering the foyer, Bara noticed that the main door into the house, previously locked, now stood open. The guard motioned the men into the house and retreated to his post.

Moluq and Bara walked through a long spacious hallway that emptied into a large courtyard filled with dazzling colors, eccentric shapes and rich textures. At the center of the courtyard was an extensive garden filled with a variety of exotic floras partitioned by a gurgling stream and marble pathways. Surrounding the garden were eight perimeter walls made from slender slabs of white, petrified wood and black onyx. At the corner of each intersecting wall was a patio.

"Good morning," a voice sounded from above. Lonovina entered from an octagonal shaped door, strode across a balcony made of silver, and descended down a circling staircase. "Thank you both for coming," she resumed approached the two men. "My personal chef has prepared lunch. I hope that you're hungry."

"I sure am," Moluq replied heartily.

"Yes. Thank you," Bara added.

Lonovina was dressed in a black dress, similar to one she wore the day before, but shorter and less modest. She also wore high black leather boots that drew Bara's attention, not for their enticing texture or color, but for the wicked-looking dagger bounded in its material. The dagger and boots were of little consequence, however, in comparison to a single glittering, red jewel hanging from her neck. An expert in minerals, Bara knew that the jewel had been manufactured. He felt vindicated. The jewel proved that he had not been hallucinating about his ship being knocked out of space; advanced technology was indeed active on the planet and was shaping the very fabric of its history. Nevertheless, the technology was illusive, quiet, and well hidden from the native human population. But why? Who were these illusive architects of the jewel? What role did humans play in their convoluted cosmic plans? More pointedly, what role was he meant to characterize? A symbiosis of purpose existed and Bara was certain that he was on the verge of a breakthrough. Previously he had no leads in answering these questions. But alas, the presence of the jewel changed that. Lonovina would be a starting point in his search for answers.

"My jewel fascinates you," Lonovina stated.

Before Bara could answer, a loud shriek reverberated throughout the courtyard making Bara's companion, Moluq, jumped when a large four-legged beast came bounding toward them through the courtyard. Unlike all the other animals Bara had seen on Yvia Voi, this creature was covered with thick white hair, not tough blubber. It stood waist high and was about six feet in length. The beast had a long thin tail, a generous pink nose, two bright emerald green eyes and two nasty incisor teeth protruding from its upper lip. Bara watched the bounding creature with fascination. Here was yet another mystery to be solved. Moluq, on the other hand, retreated in horror.

"Its O. K.," Lonovina reassured them. "He won't harm you."

The animal trotted straight toward Lonovina and gently butted its head against her left side. Lonovina placed her hand on the massive head and scratched a pointed ear.

Bara stared at the creature as if communicating some private message. The animal warily came forward and sniffed Bara's outstretched hand.

"Ah, Bara, be careful," Moluk stammered, now standing far in the background.

"Amazing," Lonovina announced. "I've never seen Tilar take to anyone like that before!"

"I think he senses familiarity."

"I don't know. The animal does seem to have a sixth sense. Anyway, I have generally found him to be a good judge of character."

Bara glanced up at Lonovina and offered a faint smile, but hurriedly looked away when she smiled back with more intensity than expected.

Moluq gingerly reached out an arm toward Tilar. The beast growled menacingly and Moluq recoiled.

"Best leave him alone," Lonovina warned.

"I should think so," Moluq replied.

"Perhaps we should go eat."

45

Bara and Moluq followed Lonovina to a patio at the far corner of the courtyard. A variety of odd looking plants, meats, and creamy dishes were eloquently centered on a white metallic table. Lonovina seated herself on one of three cushioned chairs and the men followed her lead. No longer the center of attention, Tilar plopped himself beside Lonovina and closed its eyes.

"Quite a beast, there," Moluq said cutting into the silence.

"He's a Dulavat," Lonovina explained glancing down at the snoozing animal. "They live in the North, far away from people. I found this boy lying around the frozen tundra bleeding to death. I patched him up and brought him home. He has been a loyal friend ever since."

"Have you really traveled all the way up into the tundra fields?" Moluq asked in astonishment.

"Several times."

"Incredible!"

Lonovina shrugged.

"I heard that the Northern lands are home to voracious man-eating bogs that swallow their victims in the most horrible manner. How did you survive?"

"Don't believe everything you hear, Moluq. Travelers exploring the Northern Lands are ill prepared for the cold and generally die of exposure. People simply deal with their disappearance by inventing stories."

"Why?"

"To deal with their own fears, I guess."

"I see," Moluq replied.

"Are Dulavats rare?" Bara asked.

"Yes" Lonovina replied. "And unique, I might add."

"The Duvulat doesn't belong here," Bara stated.

"What do you mean?"

"Other animals lack many of the Dulavat's physical characteristics."

"Except people," Lonovina replied gazing at Bara expectantly.

"Yes, I agree."

"I have always wondered about such similarities in nature. They can't be all coincidental, right? Unfortunately, I am rich in questions but poor on answers. How about you Bara?"

"A beggar."

Lonovina laughed softly and turned to Moluq. "So, how was the journey from Capoca Fortress?"

"Oh, very good, Ma'am. Well, actually it was awful. We were exhausted from the battle, you see, and not in any shape to travel. Still, they ordered us to Gloroveena anyway, not caring whether we perished from exhaustion. Of course it rained most of the trip. The whole company, except Bara, was cold, soaked, tired, and grumpy. He was too busy asking me questions about plants and other weird things."

Moluq was about to add something when a young, muscular, blond woman walked toward the table. "Excuse me, Lonovina," she said. "The weapon trader is here to see you."

"He's early. He can wait in the guest room."

"Done. I'm sorry to interrupt."

"Truveli, I would like you to meet Moluq and Bara."

"I'm honored," she said bowing slightly.

"Truveli has been well schooled in the art of war. She has helped me collect many ancient pieces of weaponry. Perhaps, Moluq, you might be interested in a little tour?"

"Oh, yes," Moluq replied with genuine enthusiasm.

"Truveli, would you mind?"

"I would be honored," the woman said with a smile. "Come this way, sir."

"Coming," Moluq replied rising from his seat. He winked at Bara and followed the woman through a glass doorway into the house.

Bara felt something quiver inside him as Lonovina smiled. The feeling was a nameless emotional relic that had little utility as far as he was concerned. Bara squashed it immediately.

"So," she said at last. "Moluq doesn't appreciate the finer points of botany, I gather?"

"I have dwelled on the subject lately."

"Well, I love plants," Lonovina said swallowing the remaining contents of her drink. "Come, I would like to show you my garden."

"I would enjoy that, thank you."

Lonovina meandered down a narrow garden pathway, turned, and momentarily brushed up against Bara's shoulder. "The Nurpha Plant is one of my favorites," she said pointing to a species of plant that looked like a volcano's plume. Covering the plant was a protective screen of interlacing thorns that glowed in the morning sunlight.

"Your favorite plant is not very colorful."

"Beneath the thorns the plant is fleshy. The flesh is colored like fire and ripe with zesty juices. Most people just see the thorns, of course. But when the sunlight hits it just at the right angle, the thorns become translucent and everything beneath becomes revealed. This is what I look for in people, too."

"You understand complexity through patient observation and curiosity."

"Yes, and beauty. It is no accident that I invited you here for lunch today, Bara. I'll be straightforward. You rank high on my list of curiosities right now."

"Is that so? Why?"

Lonovina pressed her hand softly against Bara's shoulder and smiled. "Because, Bara, beneath that unassuming exterior, there is a library of catalogued secrets inside you. You hint at areas of knowledge that even I don't know about, something called genetics for instance. Yes, I pay attention to everything. When observe you, Bara, I sense intelligence, secrecy and darkness."

"Darkness?" Bara asked, intrigued.

"And light. You are not unlike the Nurpha plant."

"And what of you, Lonovina?"

"I am all that you see."

"No mysteries?"

"Nothing that isn't accessible. You can just about ask me anything."

Bara nodded. "O.k.. Tell me about the jewel you wear."

"I had a feeling you would get back to my jewel. What do you see in the jewel?"

"That's not fair. I thought you were supposed to answer my questions. Very well, I will tell you what I think. There are integrated components built within the stone itself. I can see the design when I look closely. This design, these components, looks extremely complex and . . . orderly. Your stone was built, not mined."

Lonovina stiffened. "You are the first person to notice that my necklace is not natural. The Old Ones built the necklace, of course."

Bara's heart raced. He had guessed that Lonovina might harbor invaluable information. If anyone knew about an advanced planetary civilization, she would. His intuition, as usual, had served him well.

"Most people don't believe in the Old Ones, or even in the existence of their artifacts. People generally don't care," Lonovina added.

"Well, I do care, and clearly you do too."

"Why do you think I am the richest woman in Gloroveena, Bara?"

"Moluq seems to believe that you wield powerful magic."

"In a sense he's right. For the last fifteen years I have collected and studied the artifacts of the Old Ones, studied their gadgets, and understood, well, a little."

"A little knowledge can go a long way."

"Especially when the competition is stuck in making products the same way their father's grandfather made them. Machines have made me rich, Bara. Now let me ask you another question. How much do you know about the Old Ones?"

"Practically nothing."

"Nothing? I don't believe you! You recognized my jewel for what it was, did you not?"

"I understand something of technology, that is true. Yet my knowledge of technology comes from my own country, not from the Old Ones."

"Well, that complicates that picture. I was hoping you could help me understand the Old Ones better."

"Perhaps I still can. Will you show me some of your machines?"

"Sorry, Bara. I don't show everything on first dates. But I do have other artifacts, scrap metal mostly, if your interested."

"Yes, that would be helpful."

"Come on then," she said walking toward the house. "We'll need to go into what I like to call 'the junk room'."

* * *

"Welcome to my obsession," Lonovina stated as she escorted Bara through a doorway and into a black void. Lonovina ignited a match and rock walls emerged. The walls seemed to defy the solidity of their mortar by appearing to dance with the flickering flame. Lonovina lit an oiled lamp and the dance magnified. Her slightly translucent face absorbed the dancing light so that it glowed faintly yellow. The lamp wasn't the only source of illumination, however. An eerie red glow pierced the darkness from Lonovina's necklace.

The room was about three by fifteen feet in length. A large dark wooden desk dominated the center-left wall and was buried under stacks of books, papers, and maps. Placed next to the desk were two gray, cushioned chairs worn thin from frequent use. More curious, a half dozen metal strips were stacked neatly in the far right corner. A large metallic safe presided in the far-left corner and loomed over the rest of the room. Lonovina pulled up a chair, sat, and looked at Bara expectantly. Bara also sat and waited for her to begin.

"No one knows exactly who the Old Ones were, where they lived, when they lived, or how they lived. Still," she said with slower pronunciation, "they have left behind certain clues." Lonovina selected one of the metal pieces and handing it to Bara.

The metal piece was about a three feet long and a one-foot wide. The piece was smooth, curved and silver-gray. Bara knew exactly what he was looking at. He was looking at a form of synthetically reinforced titanium.

"I found all of these metal pieces scattered throughout the countryside," Lonovina said. "Every year or so, I stumble across a solitary fragment in some remote area. I could figure out why metal scraps were laying about in the middle of nowhere, so I began to collect and conduct experiments on them. I heated the metal, tore at the metal, hammered at the metal, and even scraped at the metal. Yet I couldn't so much as put a scratch in the stuff. Notice, will you, how light it is."

"Yes," Bara agreed while lifting the fragment up and down. Reinforced titanium was one of the most durable materials known to Bara's own people, the Terasians. Clearly the Old Ones mastered very advanced technology, probably surpassing the technical limits of his own civilizations.

"I have never heard of a metal with those properties. Just think of the structures one could build."

"Indeed. But I am also thinking of the force it would take to destroy these structures and shred the metal into tiny pieces across the countryside."

"I have never thought of that! The power necessary . . . Gorka!"

"You understand the magnitude of what we are dealing with. Now please continue."

"Yes, well then," she said with growing excitement, "I found some really bizarre things looking through caves."

"Caves?"

"I, ah, like to explore caves in my spare time. Trudging through muddy crawl ways is just one of my many eccentricities. Anyway, the most interesting item I found was this jewel which you asked about."

"I see that it lights up like a miniature lantern."

"The stone is much more than a lantern," Lonovina said and hesitated. "Sometimes," she whispered, "it acts as if it has a mind of its own."

Bara raised an eyebrow.

"I don't expect you to believe what I am about to tell you. I am gambling that you might be of some help, because I am at wits end. Twelve days ago, I was heading home from an engagement late at night. I was walking through an empty dark street and this thing jumped at me."

"Thing?"

"I can't describe it well because it was dark and the creature was fast. I know that it was too squat and round to be a human. I usually feel comfortable handling dangerous situations on my own, but before I could reach for my knife, the stone around my neck emitted, ah, some form of purple-white lightening."

"And?"

"The creature burst into flame and was immediately incinerated."

Bara glared at Lonovina in silence. Lonovina, on her part, scrutinized Bara's every reaction carefully.

"Fascinating! Truly fascinating," Bara murmured. He got up and paced the floor. The jewel was more than a powerful weapon, he realized. It was a computer. It had evaluated danger and reacted as programmed. In this case, it had eliminated the threat with high-energy plasma. Yet how did it know that the creature was a threat? Did the creature's dimensions match some internal template? That would be simple enough, assuming the creature was an enemy and always constituted a serious threat. Still, what if the computer evaluated the creatures every intention. If so, the ramifications would be astounding. In order for the computer to accomplish this feat, it would have to have a three-dimensional image of the brain, record synaptic firing, and integrate the pattern into something meaningful. The technology involved would be incredible! What if the necklace was recording his thoughts right now and transmitting the data back to the Old Ones. Although Bara dismissed this line of reasoning to be purely speculative and perhaps a tad paranoid, the possibilities of mind reading disturbed him nevertheless.

At last, Bara stopped pacing. "I believe your story," he said.

"Why?" she challenged.

"Why? Because the more I learn, the more I discover how much I don't know. We only have scratched the surface in regard to the Old Ones. Your artifacts prove that." Bara sighed, smiled abruptly and then added, "And like Tilar, I'm a pretty good judge of character."

The intensity in Lonovina's face melted away and she laughed softly. "I appreciate the compliment."

"What else can your jewel do?" Bara asked changing the subject.

Lonovina thought for a moment. "Probably a great deal, but other than saving my life, the jewel has only glowed. Well, I take that back. The jewel was pulsing brightly when I found it in the cave. It reminded me of a lighthouse. Perhaps it was acting as some sort of beacon. What do you think, Bara? Pretty wild stuff, yes?"

"Absolutely. You say the Old Ones left this world long ago, but I say they may have never left.

"What! You can't be serious. The last records of the Old Ones were written more than a thousand years ago."

"Nevertheless, powerful technology is at play and someone is controlling that power other than you."

"Yes, my jewel has certainly been acting on its own accord. Still I doubt that the Old Ones are responsible."

"There is one way to find out. Was there anything else in the cave room other than the jewel?"

"No, just a couple of pools."

"I wonder if there was something in the room or near the room that would cause it to pulse."

"I don't know. What are you getting at?"

"Why was a jewel left deep in a cave? Why was it pulsing? Something was making it pulse for a practical reason. Perhaps we might find a powerful source nearby."

Lonovina sat silently for a moment. "Are you suggesting that we explore the caverns first hand?"

"Yes, if you are agreeable."

"I work for myself, Bara. How about the day after tomorrow?"

"Done."

"Why don't you come about five bowoa, we'll need to get an early start. The mounts and provisions will be prepared before you arrive, so just bring yourself."

"All right."

Lonovina reached over and placed her hand on Bara's shoulder. "I have a trader waiting for me. I would like to thank you, Bara, for your ideas and your company today. Our meeting was very stimulating."

"Your input has been extremely valuable to me as well."

Lonovina withdrew her hand and blew out the lamp.

* * *

Bara walked briskly back toward Gloroveena Fortress. Moluq was fast on his heels.

"Well, aren't you going to say anything?" Moluq pleaded.

"Like what?"

"Like, fill me in friend! Come on, I'm not all that stupid. I know that you two were locked away somewhere all by yourselves."

"True, Lonovina and I were together in her study."

"Ah-ha! And?"

"She showed me one of her private collections of artifacts."

"That's it?"

"That's it."

Moluq stared silently the road, pouting. "She still likes you, you know," he added after a few moments. "You probably just blew it."

Bara said nothing.

"So, what did you two love toodrals talk about? The Varuk?"

"No."

"I can't believe you," Moluq continued. "Lonovina's rich, powerful, intelligent, and beautiful, and you're not interested!" Moluq paused and looked at Bara through the corner of his eyes. "Or do you prefer men?"

"No," Bara said with a light chuckle. "I have been a warrior most of my life. Where I'm from, only the strong, cunning, and callous survive. Romance has no part in my world. It clouds objectivity. Without objectivity, people make mistakes and die."

"But you are no longer living in that world."

"I do in my mind," Bara returned and sighed. "I plan to survive whatever comes my way, Moluq. Emotions are dangerous."

Moluq bit his lip, squinted his eyes and shook his head. "I don't give a Goka about danger. Without love, life is not worth fighting."

Bara responded to Moluq's remark with silence and increased his stride. Although he appeared aloof, Moluq's words were to resonated in his mind for days to come.

CHAPTER 6

Late afternoon clouds burgeoned above Gloroveena Fortress and then turned black. Soldiers scurried under cover as lightening flashed and thunder boomed. Sporadic droplets of water lashed at the hard-packed earth and then intensified into flooding torrents of rain. Asleep on a mattress of straw, Bara was semiconscious to the violent storm occurring beyond his window. His slumber was suddenly interrupted, however, by the sound of a heavy fist pounding at his door. Bara woke up with a jolt. "Who is it?" he barked.

"Dukuk," returned a gruff voice.

Bara walked to the door and opened it. Dukuk's pudgy body shivered and his baldhead dripped with water. Despite his miserable demeanor, the Commander forced a smile.

"Come in," Bara offered reluctantly. Dukuk entered and walked across the small dark room. He seemed oblivious to the water dripping from his body onto the straw bed. "Here, put this over you," Bara said handing the Commander a hole-worn blanket.

"Thank you," Dukuk said and sneezed. As if on cue, a bright flash ripped through the dark enclosure and the air boomed with bone-shaking thunder. "Goka! That rain sure came fast, didn't it?"

Bara nodded. "So, what brings you here during such weather?"

"Ah, just came to talk, my friend. Just came to talk," he said with a sniffle. Dukuk squatted down on the hard stone floor and squirmed into a position of relative comfort. "You're a damn good soldier," he said at last.

"So you have said before."

"You know our leave will expire in a couple of days. Er, I don't know where we'll be assigned, probably back to Capoca Pisshole, eh? Ah, but it's really not so bad stranded on the frontier; there are no bureaucratic forces to meddle with operations! Yes sir, a man can breathe at Capoca Fortress. Wouldn't you agree?"

"When the Varuk aren't competing for space, perhaps."

"Ha! Well said. We didn't quite meet under the most relaxing circumstances, did we? Ah, but what a glorious battle, though."

"What are you saying, Commander?"

"Yes, well, ah, I wanted to know your plans Bara?"

"I don't know. I haven't given it much thought."

"Well, I would start giving it some thought if I were you. Once our leave expires, you're out of here. Have you thought about joining the military?"

Bara sighed. "I am tired of war, Commander. If I continue on that course there won't be anything left."

"Anything left?"

"Anything left inside me. Anything human, that is. Do you understand?"

Dukuk shook his head. "No, I don't understand, but I do understand money and security. It's tough to find work right now, Bara, and the military needs you. Now, I have been discussing your talents with General Ronard. He has agreed to assess your combat skills. He will be impressed, no doubt. I would like to meet with him, Bara. He's a good man. Perhaps with luck, he will assign you under my command. You might drop a hint or two on that, huh?"

"I'll talk to him, but only as a favor to you. It probably won't make a difference, though."

"Good!" Dukuk said with a wink as he gave Bara a friendly slap on the arm . "I'm sure you'll come around. People eventually learn to value my opinions. The sooner you do, the better. Now listen up! General Papst is throwing a grand party tonight. Everyone who's anyone will be there, including General Ronard," Dukuk said and lowered his voice. "I was astute enough to take advantage of our heroic success at Capoca. I acquired two invitations. So, I want you to come with me and make some contacts. It will be for your own good. I guarantee it."

"What time?"

"Nine bowoa tonight."

Bara nodded and escorted the Commander out of the room. Bara slept until evening, the first real rest he had in days. He rejoined Commander Dukuk at fortress gates and walked down Military Avenue to a less-traveled city street. Gas lanterns, previously plentiful, were sparse and, when present, generally broken. Citizens in this part of town obviously lived by more meager means. Tall buildings etched the sky like ancient, black tombstones leaning with age. The city was eerily quiet save for Dukuk's heavy breathing and an occasional inebriated citizen enlivening the street with song, laughter, and the thud of tripping heels. Yet Bara knew that someone or something was following them at a distance. Imperceptible most of the time, he could see movement in the recesses of shadow with his artificially heightened vision. The intruder was a professional.

Bara continued to monitor the intruder's footsteps. He had no intention of jeopardizing their anonymity by alerting Commander Dukuk. He wanted to spy on the spy, not scare him or her away. Bara wasn't sure why they were being followed. The Commander was a low ranking official from an obscure outpost and Bara was more or less unknown to everyone. Stumped, Bara continued down the road silently and waited for opportunity. Opportunity never came, however, as the follower vanished.

Soft, methodical, roaring ocean waves became audible as the men made their way through a wealthier district near the ocean. The sound of the ocean was dampened, however, with the distant sounds of laughter and conversation. An enormous estate came into view. Unlike common city buildings made of stucco, the estate was built from pink granite. More than three stories tall, the mansion was oval in shape with two miniature blue glass spires circling upward toward the apex of the building. It was clearly built to mimic, although more modestly, the splendor of the Emperor's own royal palace.

"Here we are. This is it," the Commander whispered.

Bara followed Dukuk into the compound at a distance. Four beefy soldiers suddenly appeared and roughly grabbed Dukuk's shoulders. An enormous fat guard walked up and clenched his fists. His beady eyes and jutting chin bore into the Commander. "This is a private party," he said gruffly.

"We have invitations," Dukuk replied without fear. "Fourth Level Commander Dukuk and Bara."

"Just a second," the guard said in disbelief. He walked over to the register and found their names. He looked up at the two men suspiciously. "O.k., let them pass" he ordered. The other three guards grudgingly stepped aside.

Bara followed Dukuk up a gentle-winding pathway walled by thickly trimmed bushes. The men eventually entered a large patio crowded with chattering people, bustling servants, and tables filled with food. Although torches and moonlight provided ample lighting, no one greeted the newcomers. Rather, old men dressed in gold threaded uniforms bounced sidelong glances toward their direction. Their wives, more eager to make a statement, tugged at gold chains hanging from their noses and glared at the two men.

Dukuk, unconcerned about his apparent lack of status, tried to nuzzle his way into a nearby crowd. The crowd successfully plugged up their tight circles against his fat body. He ended up fidgeting in frustration.

"We fit right in," Bara muttered. "Perhaps we should start singing some tavern songs."

"Don't worry about it. Let's get some punch."

Bara followed Dukuk to the drink table and poured himself a cloudy blue mixture. The liquid was thick, warm, sweet, and loaded with alcohol.

"Ah, there is General Ronard. See, over there," Dukuk said and pointed to a small man marching toward the food line. "Let's catch him while we can. General Ronard," Dukuk blurted.

The little man turned abruptly and faced Dukuk. He had a round flat face, thin pale blue eyes, and curling gray hair. His eyes narrowed as Dukuk closed in. "Ah, Commander, you actually came."

"Yes sir! I wouldn't miss this party if the world depended on it. And I brought Bara with me," Dukuk said. Ronard remained impassive. "You know, the one I was talking about earlier."

"Yes, I remember," Ronard stated and looked at Bara with a blank expression.

Bara knelt on one knee and bowed deeply.

"Ahh, I'm glad to see someone remembered their manners. You may rise."

Bara obediently rose as Dukuk stiffened from the insult. "I am very honored to meet you, sir," Bara returned.

"And you're from?"

"Mohasa, sir."

"Where's that?"

"I am from an island beyond the northwest mountains, sir."

"We have no records of such an island. I am familiar with the Northwest Territories, an uncivilized place overrun by barbarians. It has no strategic importance. Still, an island beyond the ocean sand, I suppose it's possible. I expect precise directions, of course. I'm sure that this Mohasian society could benefit from Caona trade, culture, and direction."

"Without a doubt, sir," Bara replied.

Ronard nodded and scratched his chin. "I hope that the Mohasian government shares your attitude, Bara. No need for them to end up like the insurgent Poterquen people, slaughtered into submission."

"An excellent example, General," Dukuk commented.

Ronard ignored the Commander and centered his eyes on Bara. "Dukuk tells me that you can see in the dark."

"Better than most."

"I would like you to come by my office in ten days, Bara. I want to know all about Mohasia, who you are, and why you're here. My assistant will measure your eyesight afterwards. Perhaps the Caonan army might have a place for you."

"As you wish."

"Good. Now if you'll excuse me," the General said taking his leave toward a group of people at the food table. The small crowd received him warmly. As if magic had transformed his demeanor, General Ronard responded with pleasant smiles, light conversation, and joyful laughter.

"What a magnificent individual," Dukuk muttered. "The man has authority, power. People fear him. When Ronard speaks, people listen, Bara. You are very lucky that the General has taken such an interest to you."

"Luck? Not when I have you to thank, Dukuk."

Hungry for more attention, Dukuk nodded and glanced around the crowd. Bara took advantage of the Commander's social preoccupation by wandering toward a small group of musicians tuning a variety of stringed instruments.

"Wait!" Dukuk blurted.

"Yes?"

"Where are you going!?" he said waving his hand excitedly. "Come over here. I've found someone we both know."

Lonovina entered the patio dressed in a long, shining black, evening gown. Black velvet-like gloves fit snugly up to her elbows and a red stone necklace refracted moonlight over her chest. Her long, black hair was meticulously set over her head in a grouping of swirls. Yet, it was her big purple eyes that captured Bara's attention. They seemed to radiate brighter then the surrounding torchlight.

Dukuk darted toward the woman but was beaten by a swarm of male greeters. Generals, politicians, and businessmen swarmed the woman, lavishing her with excited greeting and generous praise. Their wives, on the other hand, backed away seeking refuge in-groups. Most were scowling and speaking to each other in low whispers. Lonovina seemed to handle the popularity with gracious reserve. Her eyes eventually found Bara standing against a table. Their eyes locked momentarily and then disengaged.

Bara followed Lonovina and the mob into the mansion. He entered a spacious room decorated with numerous gold leafed designs and diagonal mirrors. Gigantic silver lamps hung from the ceiling like vines. The room was also packed with people. Almost everyone appeared socially absorbed, except for a curious looking thin man staring at Lonovina from a distance across the room. Dressed in military uniform, he had short, black hair, long, thin eyes, a curly beard, and a thin face pockmarked by old acne scars. Bara noted that the man's neck muscles were a little too tight, his posture was a little too rigid, and his face seemed just a little too wet. His intentions were clearly less then genteel. The man eventually turned his attention away from Lonovina and melded into the crowd. Bara made a mental note of his observation and walked out onto an empty terrace overlooking the ocean.

The ocean breeze blew gently through his hair and swirled deep into his lungs. Undaunted by billions of years, the waves roared on methodically. The simple stability of the surf seemed to mock the transitory complexity of life. Bara had never really been happy since the war. He longed to reach out and dip his troubled soul into the cleansing deep, dark waters. This was impossible, of course, so he was content with transporting himself back to a happier day, to another ocean a hundred and forty light years away.

In his mind, the Terasian ocean didn't look so different from the beautiful scene before him now. The only difference, he recalled, was the lack of moonlight streaking across the flat liquid expanse on Terasia. Then there was Malafena. She had been so happy that night, the night of their engagement. Bara remembered the warmth of her embrace, the softness of her lips, and her gentle, melodic words that harmonized with the roll of the ocean waves. Although she died during the initial Vesder attacks over a century ago, Malafena's beauty still seemed so vibrant and real in his mind. Bara recalled their first words, her strong laugh, their fights, their loving, and the marriage plans forever postponed. Bara realized that this was the last time he had truly felt happy. Now that the war was over, could he ever recapture that lost time of innocence? The task seemed all but impossible. Bara lost track of time as more memories flooded into his mind. His concentration was eventually broken, however, by the sound of footsteps. Bara turned and saw Lonovina walk forward and join him on the balcony. She leaned over the railing and closed her eyes.

"Am I disturbing you?" she asked. "If you need to be alone, I'll . . ."

"I would very much enjoy your company, Lonovina. I'm just seeking refuge from an assembly of strangers."

"I don't like parties either," Lonovina whispered and smiled. "I wanted to join you earlier. After all, the night is too lovely to waste on mediocrity. Still, you know that business is business."

"I suppose."

Lonovina arched her back against the railing. The ocean breeze flattened her dress revealing gentle curves highlighted by the silvery moonlight. "I was rather surprised to find you here, Bara, hobnobbing with Gloroveena's rich and powerful."

"I've hardly been hobnobbing. The people here wouldn't notice me if I were on the floor choking on a bone."

"I suppose not."

"Actually, I'm supposed to be making contacts."

"Contacts?"

"Yes. Dukuk has been pressuring me to join the Caonan Army. Specifically, he wants me assigned under his command. He's looking for someone with enough clout, like General Ronard, to bend the rules and make it happen."

Lonovina laughed. "Oh, I'm sorry, Bara. I just can't imagine you bossed around by that pompous little stump."

"Neither can I, but I may need Dukuk yet. Besides, I didn't want to insult the military by snubbing their little party. Unfortunately, I think I have insulted them more by coming."

"Oh well, they'll get over it."

"In any case, they're taking more of an interest in me now," Bara said cocking his head toward a nearby window.

Lonovina turned her head. Although most people were absorbed in conversation, more than few guests were gawking. Heads turned abruptly away when Lonovina's met their gaze.

"Your reputation may have been better served if you had ignored me," Bara muttered.

"Ha! My reputation has been built on scandal and innuendo. Look, only the powerless are punished for individuality. The powerful, on the other hand, are rewarded for their individuality. They are considered unique and interesting. And besides," she said smiling, "your attendance saved me from an endless evening of boredom. I'm not interested in the latest fashions or useless gossip."

"Likewise."

Lonovina lifted herself from the railing and winked. "Come," she said "Let's get of here. I want to take a walk on the beach."

Bara followed Lonovina to the water's edge. Lonovina tore off her black velvet shoes, crammed them into a handbag, and submerged her feet into foamy, ocean waves. Bara followed her lead.

Lonovina pulled her hair down and smiled. She moved closer to Bara and locked her hand into his. Lonovina's hand, although cold in temperature, burned like coal from a fire. Bara wondered how just five small cold fingers could trigger so many painful and conflicting emotions. Yet Bara did not recoil; he needed the woman's trust and adoration to accomplish his mission. Mental control was an art he had learned over a century, anyway. He simply wished the emotions away and they mostly seemed to vanish.

"There's the BonNoyf Constellation," Lonovina said pointing to the northeast quadrant of the sky.

"Where?"

"Do you see three bright stars, ah, forming in sort of a triangle?"

"Let's see now . . . , yes. So, what does it represent?"

"Represent? Well, nothing, except that the inhabitants of Gloroveena may show some self-restraint tonight.

Bara gazed at Lonovina quizzically.

"I see that our church has had little influence on your people."

"No."

"They are most fortunate. Let's see now, the church teaches that every passing star is really a reflecting eyeball," Lonovina explained, arcing her free arm across the sky. "Behind the eyeballs stand an army of heavenly snoops called the Sula. Guardians of ethical conduct, each Sula catalogues a small number of sins that pass through the night. The stars in the

Bonhoyf Constellation are very severe, so it goes. Sula eyes disappear at dawn, when god, or the Divu, requires an immediate report."

"What about sins committed during daylight?"

"The Divu is awake and sees all by riding within one of the two circling suns. If he is not satisfied with the actions below, he retaliates by creating havoc with the weather. When this happens, the church blames people and appeases the Divu by collecting penitence, which goes into their own coffers, of course.

"Hmmm," Bara muttered.

"You don't believe in the Sula?" Lonovina asked feigning disbelief.

"No."

"I didn't think you would. Unfortunately not enough people question such rubbish. I get so frustrated. There are other ways the church uses the faithful to gain power and make money, you know. Why do people accept any authority without thinking?"

"The church offers easy answers to the unknowable and pretends to control the uncontrollable. People need that security."

"I suppose," Lonovina returned acidly. She then gazed up at Bara and her face softened. "I'm amazed how much we think alike. You don't fear me, do you?"

"That's a strange question. No, I don't fear you, or your ideas."

"Thank you," Lonovina replied.

"You should have seen the Capoca Company the day we first met," Bara said with a chuckle. "Moluq had to be practically dragged to your house. He thought that you were going to turn the entire company into a pile of stones."

Lonovina laughed and shook her head. "A ridiculous rumor started by jealous wives."

"You don't find that sort of attention irritating?"

Lonovina shrugged. "It can be, at times. For good or ill, fantasy fuels my popularity. I've come to realize that people really don't adore me, fear me, or even respect me. Rather, they adore, fear, and respect a fictional image. I use those images to my advantage, of course. Yet sometimes," she said with a sigh, "I wish people would treat me on my own merits."

"You must be very lonely," Bara said softly.

Lonovina's nodded and glanced up at Bara. Her eyes softened. "But you're different, aren't you Bara? You know my humanity and accept it," she said squeezing his hand. "Perhaps that's why I enjoy your company."

Not knowing what to say, Bara returned Lonovina's hand squeeze, looked down and walked while listening to the roar of rushing waves. Buroos Te-2 eventually rose over the horizon and bathed the city with its soft blue rays of sunlight. "The blue glass spires of the royal palace pick up that sunlight," Bara offered. "Their glow is very soothing."

"Yes. Except that I'm going to miss our twinkling stars," Lonovina said holding Bara's hand tightly. "So, tell me, what do you think the stars really made out of?"

"Well, I believe that the stars are gigantic spheres of fire, little different from our own suns, just farther away."

Bara glanced at Lonovina expecting disbelief, but instead noticed keen interest in her face. Choosing his words very carefully, Bara continued. "The great blue sun spirit, for instance, isn't really a spirit at all. It is a gigantic fireball, many times larger than this world. The same thing goes with the other sun. This is a sensible conclusion, if you think about it. Why else would it be warmest at midday and coldest before the dawn."

"That seems sensible. An intriguing hypothesis, please continue."

"Now, I doubt that the Divu lives in the sun. In fact, my people believe that the world revolves around the sun, rather than the other way around. This is true for the other worlds, as well."

"Other worlds?" she asked incredulously.

"Yes, have you ever noticed how some stars wander?"

"Yes."

"Well, my people believe that these are not stars, but other worlds. Worlds as big, or bigger, than the world we're standing on. Like the stars, they look very small because they are so very far away."

After silently reflecting on his words, Lonovina stared at Bara intently. "But, if what you say is true, then other worlds might be circling around their respective suns. If such worlds are anything like our own, then life could exist elsewhere."

Bara was surprised. He had not expected Lonovina to deduce the truth so quickly. "Theoretically, I suppose that's possible."

"Hmmm. Your explanation intrigues me, Bara."

"How so?"

"Well, the church's explanation seems so, well, so magical. And your explanation strikes me as being more objective and plausible. I doubt that anyone has the real answer, but, I'd wager that your people are closer to being right." Lonovina suddenly became lost in thought. "You know," she said suddenly. "Something I once read makes sense now."

"What's that?"

"During my research on the Old Ones, I came across an ancient book on geography. One passage briefly mentioned a land ruled by an anointed people. Yet for some mysterious reason, the anointed suddenly disappeared into the stars. The church interpreted this passage as proof for the existence of the Sula. I, on the other hand, dismissed the passage altogether. But now . . . I don't know. Do you think that the passage refers to the Old Ones?"

Bara stopped and dug his toes into the sand. "It might, Lonovina," Bara said without hiding his excitement. "It just might!"

"Hmm, well, I think we are making progress, nevertheless. This Mohasian society of yours seems quite sophisticated. I think we make a good team."

Bara smiled.

"What?" Lonovina asked.

"Did you know that you're one of the few people who hasn't directly asked me about my homeland?"

"I figured that you might lie, as I would. I decided that you would be more truthful after we had established mutual trust.

"Very wise. You are also quite correct."

"You can, however, tell anything you want," she probed.

"Well, there is not much left to tell you, unfortunately. My homeland has been ravaged by decades of war and my family has been butchered. I am, what you would call, a refugee."

Lonovina's face radiated concern. "I'm sorry," she said. "I don't know what to say."

"There is nothing to say."

"I worry about Caona, sometimes. Too many strange things, violent things, have been occurring lately and . . . "

"Shhh!" Bara exclaimed.

Lonovina stood rigid and listened. She turned to Bara after a few moments and shrugged.

"Keep walking," Bara whispered. "We're going to have company soon."

"How do you know?"

"I hear four or five of them in the rocks ahead, perhaps fifty feet ahead."

"An ambush!?"

"Aye."

Lonovina forced herself to relax and snuggled closer to Bara. "You know, I had the impression that I was being followed to the party."

"So did I."

Lonovina shot Bara a short troubled glance, but said nothing. At last she whispered, "Are you armed?"

"No," he replied, keeping his lase-gun a secret.

"I have a knife in my bag and another hidden under my dress. Here," she said reaching into her bag and handed Bara a small dagger, "can you handle them?"

"I think so."

"Good, because I hate to leave problems unresolved."

Bara and Lonovina continued to walk methodically up the shore hand in hand. The beach narrowed as black volcanic rocks jutted coarsely from the blue sunlit sand. Bara thought that the boulders looked like large ships sailing smoothly across a sea of sand. Except, Bara noted, these ships were solid, still, and waiting. Moluq had once mentioned that lovers frequented these rocks. The would be assassins, he realized, were counting on their prey to do just that.

Bara noted how calmly Lonovina reacted to the impending confrontation. She talked excitedly about her favorite foods and other issues of small importance. Her acting was believable, the assassins would never suspect their danger.

Bara could hear shallow breathing emanating behind a nearby boulder. The rock was ten feet wide, six feet tall, and rose to a jagged point. Although he tried to relax, sweat trickled against the hilt of his knife as he planned defensive strategy. After a moment, which seemed like minutes, Bara heard the rush of footsteps. He turned like a tornado and braced himself.

A tall, lithe man, dressed head to toe in a tight, elastic, black bodysuit, rushed toward Bara with blinding speed. A long gleaming knife lashed out and was aimed toward Bara's side. Bara's muscles reacted reflexively. He caught the man's wrist in mid-air and crushed it as if it were a clod of dirt. Before the man could scream, Bara jammed his dagger into the man's neck. The man fell silently spraying blood. A second man immediately rushed toward him. Bigger but less talented then the first, Bara kicked the assailant hard in the face before he could think about delivering a blow. The man landed on the sand with a thud and did not get up. A third would-be attacker ran into the night. Bara twirled his dagger and heard a thump as the man tumbled strait into the rocks. The man did not stir.

Bara glanced around and saw Lonovina body towering over a fourth dead assassin. She had yet another man pinned against the jagged rock and was constricting his neck.

"Who sent you!" she hissed.

The man gurgled, writhed, and spat blood out of his mouth.

"You ate poison, didn't you," Lonovina hissed and angrily bashed the man's head against a sharp-edged rock with a single blow. Lonovina didn't bother watching the dead man fall. She came toward Bara looking like a possessed woman. "Is he dead?" she asked perching over the man Bara had kicked.

"Not unless he swallowed poison too."

Lonovina hastily checked the man's pulse. "He's dead," she said without emotion. "They must have swallowed poison in an effort to protect their client. These are true professionals."

"Clearly they were not professional enough."

"Yes, well, we had better leave before the authorities arrive."

Bara followed Lonovina back to her residence through shadowed back streets. Lonovina's face radiated anger and an undercurrent of despair. Bara had never thought as Lonovina as a killer. She seemed so different now from the light-hearted young woman running on the beach, he thought sadly. Did Lonovina have difficulty dealing with the conflict between compassion and violence? Bara knew the answer by his own experience. People like him and Lonovina didn't escape life without suffering. Bara knew that the only way to cope was to harden and desensitize. He had retreated inside himself over the decades until the hardness had solidified. He wanted to regain his innocence but knew that he was too late. But was it too late for Lonovina? Would she become hard and brittle like dead wood? She still radiated the happiness of youth. Perhaps, just perhaps, there was hope for her.

Bara accompanied Lonovina to her home. Although the hard silence seemed impenetrable, he felt compelled to speak. "Lonovina, I saw a tall oriental man spying on you at the party. He made himself very scarce when I caught him staring at you."

"Did this man have a scraggly beard?"

"Yes."

"General Bota," she said slowly. "He's in charge of securing the mountain passes between the Caonan Empire and Federation of Traqeqtoo."

"Is that important?"

"Yes," she said forcing a smile. "I was supposed to meet the ambassador from Traqeqtoo tomorrow. He was found dead this morning, in bed, with his throat cut. Apparently he was en route to Gloroveena when he decided to lodge at an old tower overlooking Traqeqtoo Pass. The attacker was never found. Apparently, his death was not enough to satisfy his killer. Although, I don't understand why anyone would want to follow and kill you too."

"Maybe because of my association with you. The man is acting impulsively, almost paranoid. I think he's desperate."

"Perhaps. I need to gather more information before I confront him, though. The General has attained real power within the establishment, helped by none other than General Ronard."

"Interesting."

"I'll send Truveli to the Traqeqtoo Mountains first thing in the morning. I've got to find out what in the Goka is going on out there."

Bara nodded. "Are we still on for the day after tomorrow?"

Lonovina's face softened. "Of course. I'll see you then. Oh, and I really am sorry I got you into this, Bara."

"Don't think anything of it. We help out each other, right?"

Lonovina answered with a smile. "Goodnight," she said.

CHAPTER 7

The temperature plummeted as the fall season's first cold front engulfed the city of Gloroveena. It was early morning and the planet's larger sun, Buroos Te-1, still remained hidden somewhere below the horizon. Bara had joined Moluq and a small crowd of soldiers within the fortress courtyard. Many of the men focused their attention on an empty wooden podium. Their impatience grew as the cold intensify.

"He's late and I'm freezing," Moluq complained while shivering.

"We can do nothing for the moment, Moluq."

"We could leave," Moluq pleaded. "Look. Other soldiers are retreating to their warm hearths."

"You can do as you like, but the Commander requested that we meet him here."

"Yes, yes, I know. Where is he anyway?" As if on cue, Commander Dukuk made his way through the thinning crowd and coughed up a cloud of swirling breath.

"Good morning, gentlemen," Dukuk greeted the men. "The news is late, I gather."

"The news is always late," Moluq complained. "Perhaps we would do better to find another podium."

"Wait in the company of civilians? Never!" The pudgy commander turned toward Bara and grinned widely. "Well, well, well. You generated quite a bit of conversation last night, Bara. Rumor has it that you made off with Gloroveena's most mysterious woman."

"I apologize for my abrupt exit."

"Forget it. Being discreet needs no apology. Although it didn't do you any good. The guests chewed on your departure like Varuk tearing into rancid flesh. Juicy morsels of gossip really liven up a party, you know."

"I find it ironic that people were more enthusiastic about my absence then my presence."

"Well, who said people were rational, huh? Actually, I became quite popular after you left. Everybody wanted to know all about the mysterious stranger. More important, they wanted to know your connection with Lonovina. General Ronard, especially, took notice of your sudden departure."

"He did?"

"He looked quite bothered, actually. Probably just jealous. I expect the General will prepare a lengthy list of questions for you. He's an inquisitive man. But beware. He's also very dangerous. They tell me that General Ronard has destroyed many careers during his quick advancement up the ranks."

"I agree. I will be very cautious."

"Fortunately, you have gained in stature because of me, my friend. I'm sure that Ronard will treat you with some civility."

"Why, what did you tell him?"

"I told them just about everything. I told him more about your strength, eyesight, place of origin, and our meeting with Lonovina. The General seemed impressed, Bara. I am confident that they will accept you into the military soon. You couldn't have bought a better contact then me. Time spent with Lonovina didn't hurt either."

"I knew that Bara was a sucker for romance," Moluq blurted.

"Yes, what about that?" Dukuk asked.

"My romantic interludes with Lonovina only exist in Moluq's imagination," Bara said impassively.

"Ha!"

"Interesting," Dukuk commented rubbing his numb hands together.

A sudden hush enveloped the small crowd as a nervous adolescent boy climbed over the podium. He was dressed in a bright orange shirt with a ruffled collar and wore a squat, blue conical hat. "Good morning everyone," he said. "I'm sorry I'm late."

The crowd responded with jeers. The boy nervously looked over the audience and cleared his throat. "Th-this is the morning news for the 46th of Bojut. Item one: the Zumese revolt has been obliterated. The rebellion devil leader, Gostoa, has been eliminated. Give thanks to the Divu, General Tukuk, and the BonNoyf."

The crowd half-heartedly returned, "Victory. Thanks be to the Divu, General Tukuk, and the BonNoyf."

"Item 2," the boy continued. "The investigation into the untimely and tragic death of the Traqeqtoo Ambassador has been proceeding smoothly. Yerta, head of the civil defense force, states that the murderers will soon be caught and punished. Give thanks to the Divu, Yerta, and the BonNoyf."

The crows mumbled, "Success. Thanks to the Divu, Yerta, and the BonNoyf."

"Item three: A cowardly assassination attempt was imposed on Lonovina last night. Due to her skill and bravery, five attackers were killed single-handedly. And through her heroic efforts, a foreigner's life was also saved. Give thanks to the Divu, Lonovina, and the BonNoyf."

"Success. Thanks be to the Divu, Lonovina, and the BonNoyf," the crowd returned with even less enthusiasm.

Dukuk and Moluq glared at Bara with disbelief.

"Yes, we were attacked last night," Bara whispered as the boy continued reading.

"By whom?" Moluq asked.

"I don't know. As you once pointed out, Moluq, Lonovina has acquired many enemies."

"Nevertheless, I don't like this," Dukuk growled. "Something doesn't feel right. There is something-evil going on. I don't like this at all."

* * *

It was several hours before dawn and General Bota was still pacing the main hallway of his home. Sweat flowed down his forehead and dripped off his beakish nose in anticipation of meeting his employer. General Bota knew that he had a great deal of explaining to do. He still couldn't believe that his mission had failed. After all, how could five well-trained assassins fail to kill Lonovina and that foreigner, Bara? Perhaps his employer would understand that it still needed him despite his failure. General Bota prided himself as an established man; a made-man that wielded power throughout the Caonan Empire. They would need him to complete the darker deeds in the light of day because the employer was strictly a creature of darkness. Owing him more treasures than found in the great halls of the Boynoff's Palace, it would have to be patient. Despite the clear logic to this argument, General Bota trembled in fear.

The General composed himself enough to walk to the kitchen area and fix himself a stiff drink. Just then he noticed a stream of soft yellow light streaming underneath the nearby servant quarter's door. "Dirch'n servant girl!" he yelled. "I told you to go home. I'm going to beat you for this!"

General Bota headed for the servant doorway eager to release his frustrations on the girl with his fists. No, he would use more drastic measures this night. The General jerked open the Servant Quarters Door

71

with a lead pipe in hand. The servant girl Marnka was directly before him, yet she did not recoil in fear as expected. She didn't see him, General Bota soon realized, because her eyes had been gouged out. Stunned by the gruesome disfiguration of the girl, Bota was unable to move as the young body teetered stiffly before him. The battered corpse fell forward causing the tall, thin man to stumble and fall to the cobbled floor. The General scrambled to his feet and leaned against a nearby rock wall, panting. He tried to regain his composure, but was distracted by the onset of buzzing and clicking noises.

"By the Divu," Bota muttered. He gathered enough courage to open his eyes. Two tall humanoid figures faced him from across the Servant's Room. Dressed in simple brown trader clothes, the sentries stood like statues. They were so rigid, in fact, that their eyes did not blink, their mouths did not open, and their nostrils did not breath. Yet the two monsters managed to stand anyway, ready to use their ashen hands to inflict death. General Bota's realized that his employer would not be forgiving tonight.

Between the two gruesome figures was an inconspicuous wooden cargo crate shadowed by the small room's meager lamp light. Holes peppered the wooden casing, just large enough for one of his employer's tentacles to dangle outside the encasing box.

Without regard to the dead servant girl beneath him, General Bota fell to his knees. "Master," he whispered.

A new series of buzzing and clicking emanate deep within the crate. Overlaying these sounds was an unnaturally deep voice speaking in the General's language. Lacking any inflection, General remembered that the creature's words came from a little black box it had once called an electronic translator.

"I heard the news this morning," the box said mechanically. "Human boy reported failure. Do you have my necklace?"

Bota swallowed. "No, master. But I-"

"Silence! No respect? That necklace killed one of my kind. Necklace not of your world, General Bota. You failed me. Must come closer."

"Yes, master." Bota said, then crept forward and stopped.

"Closer!" the box boomed.

General Bota noticed that his employer's tentacle, previously translucent, had turned bright red. The General gathered his strength and forced three more steps. "By the Divu, let this be close enough," the General whispered. One of the stoic sentries silently repositioned itself behind the shaking man, as if it had been silently commanded to move there. Bota could feel the tall figure's silent presence waiting patiently. Then he heard more buzzes and clickings.

"What do you know about the stranger?" the box translated.

"He comes from Mohasa, master. He was also present at Capoca-"

"Enough! You are no use to me. There is no such place called Mohasa. Did he die in the ambush?"

Bota swallowed hard. "No."

"You failed me twice. No matter. They will both be dead soon. All humankind will be dead soon. You will be dead soon."

General Bota gasped. "But-but-but! What about our plans? Y-y-your promises? Goka! You owe me!" he screamed hysterically.

"I don't owe any human. All humanity is plague. We destroy all humans. You are next," the box translated without emotion.

Bota bolted in fear but went nowhere. Two hands gripped from behind and lifted the General into the air. General Bota flayed and kicked wildly, but all his efforts were wasted. The other sentry picked up a towel and stuffed it down Bota's throat. He then proceeded to squeeze every vital piece of human anatomy in Bota's body. No human ever heard the screams as the two figures killed the General. And not once did either sentry blink or flinch.

*   *   *

Truveli's Rovan Mount, Gukuk, was foaming at the mouth. The green blubbery, creature lifted its thick wedge-shaped head, its three red eyes pleading for Truveli to stop.

"Almost there Gukuk," Traveli said responding to her beast's pleading gaze. "I know that I'm pushing you to the edge, but Lonovina wants me to reach the pass by sundown, and by the Divu, I will reach Traqeqtoo Pass by sundown. Please, just make it a little farther."

The mount obligingly forced her four large legs to move but found it harder and harder to make it around the tight mountain bends and steep inclines. Truveli peered down a steep rocky ravine and knew that if the beast tripped that they would both plunge over the cliff side into the mountain canyon below.

The Traqeqtoo Mountain Range was considered the most rugged landform in all Caona. Shear granite cliffs looked like teeth ready to grind and devour the foolhardy traveler. Giant Looma trees grew more than a hundred feet high at this altitude and Truveli could imagine vicious thieves hiding in the dark, thick underbrush, poised to take advantage of a lone female traveler like herself. Yet, it was imperative that she reach Traqeqtoo Pass before sundown despite the danger, her tiring Rovan Beast, and her own fatigue.

Truveli had left Gloroveena following the morning news. She was not surprised that assassins had attacked Lonovina. Corruption ran rampant in the capital these days and many people were looking for an excuse to topple Lonovina's trading empire. Although many people feared and hated the woman, Truveli only felt admiration for her employer, mentor, and friend. Because of her tenacity and intelligence, Lonovina transcended the ordinary mortal and became, in Truveli's eyes, practically indestructible. Yet despite her success, Lonovina frequently complained of emptiness. Truveli had become increasingly concerned over her closest friend's growing dysphoria. To her relief, Lonovina's mood had brightened ever since the foreigner had appeared. Of course Lonovina claimed that her interest in Bara was purely academic, yet Truveli suspected more. Would Bara be good for her? Truveli didn't know because she couldn't read Bara's interests yet. People either rejected or worshiped Lonovina because she was different. She only hoped that Bara might learn to understand her without prejudice.

Truveli rounded a tight corner to find a dozen soldiers blocking her path, the first people she had seen in miles. Most were laying on the dirt road chewing on native grasses. She reigned in Gukuk by squeezing a natural hump protruding from the beast's back.

"Look what we have here," a young soldier called out who was stripped naked to his waist. Several other soldiers began to whistle.

"Hello there little lady," hollered an obese soldier who was propped up against a tree stump.

"Quiet, now," a deep voice boomed. A stocky man exited the woods and walked toward Truveli. He was dressed in a Commander's uniform, had deeply set brown eyes and wore a waxy smile.

"The road is closed," the man barked. "The army has been conducting military exercises over the pass."

"Since when?"

"Since the assassination of the Traqeqtoo ambassador. I must ask you to leave immediately."

"I see," Truveli said without surprise.

"Ah, come on," one soldier called out, "can't she stay a little longer." Several seconded the motion with a volley of hoots.

"Quiet!" the Commander snapped. He looked at Truveli squarely. "Turn around miss."

"Yes sir," Truveli replied and complied with the order. Less than a mile down road, however, she veered off into the brush. "Come on Gukuk," she whispered to the Rovan Mount, "I need just a little more effort now. Nothing is going to prevent me from reaching Traqeqtoo Pass. I certainly won't be detoured by those uniformed riffraff, anyway."

Truveli's mount made it's way up the mountainside far from the main road with as much speed as it could muster over the steep, rocky, virgin terrain. Hours passed before the trees began to thin and expose an alpine meadow known as Traqeqtoo Pass.

Truveli tied her mount to a tree several paces in the forest and hid within the evening shadows behind stunted windblown bushes. Although her body was still, her eyes darted across the landscape in search of unknown dangers. The Pass was cold even though it was early fall. Truveli could see her breath swirl against an evening sky streaked with sunset orange and purple pigments. Although there was a simple, stone, fortress tower at the edge of meadow, no people or animals could be heard or seen. The emptiness of the Pass, much less the mountains, bothered Truveli greatly. The Road Post Commander had been lying about military maneuvers. A few soldiers and traders would be milling about the fortress even during ordinary operations. Where were the sounds of drunken laughter and profanity that Truveli expected from lonely outposts? The only sounds Truveli heard now were the intermittent hissing of meadow grasses blowing in the wind.

The evening shadows from nearby towering cliffs augmented the lonely feeling to the place. Keeping to the shadows, Truveli made her way to the crest of the saddle. She peered down the other side and feasted her eyes on Traqeqtoo plains stretching hundreds of miles to the western horizon. Yet something was amiss. A large black blot blemished the plains were there should have been only shades of green. "What is that?!" she exclaimed to no one. "By the Divu, that it looks like someone spilled a lake of tar over the land!"

A feeling of dread encompassed Truveli's entire body when she noticed the lake move. The black blob was not a lake of tar. Only one thing that large moved: an army. But who would be attacking the Caonan Empire with that much force? Truveli jumped as a large crashing noise diverted her attention to the tower behind and above her. Jutting above a granite outcrop over the meadow was a man-made, stone tower that looked to her like an old, diseased thumb. Truveli sensed that something was waiting for her behind those chipped, black, mossy, rock walls and glass less windows. A part of her wanted to turn and flee. Yet a stronger part had to know the truth. She would not, could not, fail Lonovina. Unsheathing her broadsword, Truveli breathed deeply and crept warily toward the ominous structure.

A noise made Truveli jump, turn and ready her sword. But was just a Kamkut; a common, small, one-eyed animal that hopped on a springing appendage that looked more like a human tongue than a foot. Truveli tried to relax, took in a deep breath and continued warily toward the foreboding tower. Eventually she arrived at the main entrance without further incident. Truveli forced open the large, wooden, tower door and walked into a black and silent chamber. Trembling with fear, she felt her way through the darkness using the tip of her sword.

Thud!

"What was that?!" Truveli exclaimed under her breath. The air swished before her. Reflexively Truveli penetrated the darkness with her sword and made contact with large, unseen shape. A deafening scream resonated throughout the tower. "Wararrruhh!" it sounded. It was answered by shrill shrieks throughout the tower.

"By the Divu," Truveli stated and gasped in horror, "Varuk!"

Truveli bounded from the fortress at full run. She heard the sounds of shrieks and the fortress door crashing behind her. Not having time to look back, Truveli knew that she had a very small lead from ripping fangs and swiping claws.

Rocks and bones twirled around Truveli as she raced through the meadow. A human skull crashed and splintered over a nearby rock. Truveli finally closed in on her rearing mount and grew hopeful. Yet just when Truveli reached for her beast's reigns, she tripped over a boulder, flew into the air and landed on hard packed earth. She scrambled to her feet as the first of her assailants heaved a wooden club toward her skull. The creature's aim was displaced, however, by the weight of her terrified Rovan Mount's tail, now lashing aimlessly to and fro. Armed with six spikes, the tail gored the Varuk's midsection causing the animal to fall and shriek with pain. Truveli used the subsequent grace moments to jump on her mount's back, cut the rope, and ride into the forest. Although she felt the weight of a bone slam between her shoulder blades, Truveli never looked back at her pursuers. Their screams and screeches diminished as she gained distance from the enraged pack. Eventually the forest became still and silent aside from the pounding of her beating heart.

Truveli slowed her Rovan Mount and pondered her extraordinary discovery at Traqeqtoo Pass. The army on the Traqeqtoo Plains was probably Varuk given the size, movement, and lack of formation and color of the advancing horde. Someone had allowed a smaller party of Varuk access to Traqeqtoo Pass, thereby giving the advancing swarm an empty corridor through an otherwise defensible, mountain position. General Bota appeared to be the most likely architect, just as Lonovina had initially suspected. The soldiers who had earlier stopped her below were probably under his command. Truveli bit her lip in anger. General Bota was a traitor beyond imagination. Yet his actions defied explanation. Why would he allow an army of voracious animals to attack the Caonan Empire? What could possibly be the gain in that? Someone, she knew, had to be paying him handsomely for the seemingly purposeless destruction of his homeland. In any case, it was her job to inform the Caonan authorities as quickly as possible. Secondly, she had to find Lonovina. Although she was tired and weak from hunger, Truveli pressed her mount forward and proceeded down the dangerous mountainside despite the rapid advancement of night.

CHAPTER 8

Lonovina unmounted her riding beast and pressed her ear against the rocky soil. "I don't hear anything. Perhaps we're not being followed anymore."

"We're still being followed, " Bara replied confidently. "The intruder has matched the speed of our Rovan mounts, running when we run and stopping when we stop."

"Running on foot? That's impossible. He could never keep up! Certainly he couldn't keep running for twenty miles."

"When I press my ear to the ground, I hear the same two feet keeping a set distance, not the rhythm of hooves or anything else. We may be in real danger."

Lonovina grabbed the neck of her leather tunic in frustration. "Well, I don't hear anything. I don't know how you can distinguish his footsteps from every other traveler on the road."

"I can, it is a process of filtering . . . "

"Yes, yes, you have already explained that to me. We're not solving the problem by just standing here. Let's go."

With a curt nod Bara remounted his Rovan Beast and coaxed the animal forward. He saw little reason to argue his point farther; Lonovina would rely on her own powers of observation and remain skeptical. Bara accepted her point of view without resentment. She was a self-determined woman comfortable with leading, not following. Relying on her own intelligence, instinct and experience to solve problems, she had little reason to put her life in the hands of a stranger. There was little Bara could do about their situation anyway. Their follower would track them down, of that he was certain. The fact that the follower had ran twenty miles on foot indicated superior physical ability, determination, and possibly advanced technology. With confrontation inevitable, Bara scrutinized every aspect of his surroundings and prepared himself for the coming conflict.

The terrain was easily defendable. Traveling south from Gloroveena and the nearby Asid mountain range, Bara and Lonovina had entered a rugged, dry, brush country chiseled out by the ravishes of time into chopped-up, twisting canyons and jagged, towering, limestone escarpments that looked like bulky, bent, knife blades. Both offered plentiful defensible positions equipped with heightened visibility and shielding rocks. Bara

YVIA VOI: LAND OF GRACE

knew that outside help would be unlikely, however, so they would have to fend for themselves. Cursed by sweltering temperatures, meager precipitation and rocky soils, the land they traveled was the most sparsely populated region of the Caonan Empire. Even the trade route they now followed was little more than a pack trail. Bara didn't know who was following them and wondered if he or she was even human. He fingered the lase-gun hidden under his shirt for reassurance, wondering if he would need to use the weapon to save their lives. He wouldn't use the weapon unless it was absolutely necessary, however. Potential powerful enemies might take a malign interest in him if he revealed his true identity. It was better, he decided, to remain anonymous.

The intruder never attacked that afternoon. In fact, any evidence of his presence simply vanished. Although the footsteps stopped, Bara hypothesized that the intruder was just getting better at knowing their movements and stopped just before they listened for him. With the intruder's apparent absence, they continued down the winding trail until Lonovina eventually veered off at a large boulder shaped like two fingers. Although the cave was only two miles to the north, Bara knew that bushwhacking through canyon lands would be painstakingly slow.

About a half-mile further Bara and Lonovina descended into a steep canyon. They stopped at the canyon floor near a pool of shimmering water to refresh their tired riding beasts. Both Bara and Lonovina unmounted the animals and searched for their illusive follower. They scanned the upper reaches of the canyon, dominated by gray, limestone cliffs, but found no movement. The lower regions, dominated by a steep incline peppered with boulders and brush, appeared equally empty. Not completely satisfied, however, Bara stood silently, cupped his ear and listened.

"Anything?" Lonovina asked.

Bara shook his head.

Sighing, Lonovina turned and propped herself over a limestone boulder. Bara joined her and gazed up a dry streambed into the harsh, rocky terrain. He noted that the surrounding vegetation was just as unforgiving as the canyon itself. A leathery bush was about the only plant that survived in the thirsty landscape. Unlike other trees he had seen, the plant grew horizontally. Abundant pinkish-white roots grew from the gnarled trunk and dug deep along the sandy banks of the arroyo. Standing only two feet tall, the plant offered little relief from the merciless sun.

Not that anyone would seek refuge there, anyway. Small, gnat-sized creatures circled between leathery leaves, brittle branches, and three pronged thorns. The small invertebrates, Bara soon discovered, withdrew blood from any victim larger than a pebble.

"I see a break in the cliffs over there," Lonovina said pointing toward the canyon rim. "The Rovan Mounts will have trouble traversing the steep upper portion, so we'll have to move carefully."

"You seem to know this land well."

"I often come to places like these when I need solitude. I also enjoy the beauty of this land, but don't know why. I have always been different that way."

"I feel the same way. The land is rugged and inhospitable, yes. Yet that, in part, is what makes it so beautiful. Look how the late afternoon sunlight, glowing soft and blue, highlights every sharp rocky edge. The complexity of shape, the starkness of rock, and the grandness of scale seems to breathe vitality into this lifeless land."

"It helps me feel whole. This place means freedom," Lonovina added.

"An escape from our past, perhaps."

Lonovina sighed. "I've spent my whole life without many true friends, Bara. I can't tell you how refreshing it is to meet someone to whom I can talk with intelligence. Most of the so-called intellectuals in Gloroveena are weak spirited, greedy, or simply ignorant. You were right. I am lonely. But, at the same time, I have always been secure in my loneliness, strong in my independence. I didn't need anyone. Yet now . . . I sense that a part of me is changing. Well, not changing, really. Just emerging. I want to, no, I need more. I want to be honest with you Bara. I hardly know you, but I feel something when I'm around you. I feel, well . . . I guess I feel disoriented right now."

"Yes," Bara whispered. "Perhaps I begin to feel something too."

"Really? What would you suggest?"

"I suggest caution."

From the corner of his eye, Bara saw Lonovina nod with a mixture of relief and disappointment.

"Still," Bara added and then hesitated. He couldn't believe the importance of what he was about to say. After all the years of solitude and self-reliance, such thoughts seemed more alien than the world around him. Yet he knew them to be true.

"But what?"

"But, I need . . . , I desire your friendship."

Lonovina's eyes widened in astonishment. Generally, those who wanted something casually spoke the word 'friendship', but now the word flowed over her like a breaking ocean wave, powerful and cool. Lonovina relaxed and yanked out several long strands of gleaming, black hair. She then placed the strands into Bara's receiving hands. "Here," she said. "Keep them. In my land, a person commits friendship by giving strands of hair. Giving strands of hair is like an oath; a bonding allegiance based on trust and mutual respect."

Bara nodded and returned the gesture.

Lonovina leaned toward Bara and softly kissed his cheek. She placed his strands of hair into leather pouch and looked away into the growing shadows. "It is getting dark," she stated lifting herself. "The cave is just over the next ravine. Perhaps we should be on our way."

Bara followed Lonovina out of the canyon and into the next. He would try to honor his vow of friendship and protect her despite violating his first rule of survival, self-reliance. Bara wanted to feel again. A part of him was screaming for revitalization. Although he didn't know exactly how to continue, he realized that friendship with Lonovina was a start. As they approached the cave entrance, Bara was overcome with a feeling of tranquility he hadn't felt for a long time. He paused momentarily to watch the last rays of sunlight disappear over the canyon walls. The desert landscape quickly turned dull and gray, all except cavern's black maw that beckoned him forward.

The cavern's entrance was located on the far side of a large, collapsed sinkhole. Reaching the house size entrance would be a challenge, the incline was steep and filled with thorny plants and loose rock. Fortunately, the two Yvia Voi moons overhead cast a red and silvery glow onto the surrounding landscape. Walking gingerly down the loose scree, Bara and Lonovina eventually arrived at the cave's mouth unscathed. Silently Lonovina tied up the Rovan Mounts to a squat tree while Bara packed rope, candles, flint, water, food and other needed supplies into sturdy handbags. Using a device that ignited flint, Lonovina lit two torches and proceeded down into the dark abyss.

The torchlight flickered faintly against the distant, gray, cavern walls. Their descent down the sinkhole was steep and littered with obstacles such as boulders, short drops to climb down, and loose rock. It was difficult keeping balance while holding the torches, it was all they could do to keep from sliding or falling. The sound of "clack-clack-clack" frequently echoed throughout the chamber as small rocks gave way and tumbled downward into darkness. The walls began to close, the floor flattened, and the ceiling pinched. The rocks became less troublesome and were eventually replaced by a level plain of compacted mud. As they continued a variety of formations came into view. The once featureless ceiling was now lined with hundreds of elongated, straight, stick-thin, caramel-colored stalactites packed tightly into sinuous rows. Many formations glistened with dripping water that fell into crystal clear pools made from walls of calcite.

"So, what do you think?" Lonovina inquired with a warm smile.

"I am impressed. I must say that I am feeling young again."

"That is why I love to explore caves. I find hidden treasures that no one has ever seen before. The delicate splendor, the size, the quiet, the danger, all these things leave me with a feeling of awe. But you haven't seen anything yet. Come this way," she said ducking under a low overhang in the wall, "and watch your head."

Lonovina squeezed into a crawl space half filled with muddy water. Bara followed several feet behind Lonovina's mud-caked boots to avoid snuffing out his torch. Inch by inch they crawled through the unrelenting brown ooze. The exhilaration Bara had felt earlier diminished after slamming his head into the coarse, limestone ceiling. He heard Lonovina groan and realized that she wasn't faring much better.

"Almost there," she said huffing.

True to her word, the walls expanded as the passage again enlarged into a room. The torches illuminated a dozen or more giant stalagmites looming over the cavern floor like sleeping, giant ghosts. Dwarfing both man and beast, many of the stalagmites joined with their upper, tall-thin cousin, the stalactite, making a series of single columns that reached from ceiling to floor. Glistening in colors of white or caramel-brown, these giants filled the room like a mouthful of teeth against a backdrop of dark, brown shadows and blackness.

"Unfortunately the room we seek lies far beyond another tight crawl way. Are you game?"

"Absolutely. Views like this make the journey all the more worthwhile."

"Agreed. We'll need to climb that ledge over to the right. It is a difficult climb. Are you sure that you can you make it?"

"I believe so."

"It's a long drop down, so be careful."

"I will do my best."

Bara trailed Lonovina as she climbed the limestone shelf. Strong and nimble, Lonovina stretched from foothold to fingerhold and lifted her bodyweight with relative ease. Although Bara was even more quick and precise in his climbing, her strength and dexterity impressed him. Steadily they gained altitude above the cavern floor and rested at a limestone shelf. Refreshed, Bara followed Lonovina into a tight crawlspace that veered off to the right. They crawled onward for several hundred feet where Lonovina worked her way upward through a very narrow fissure in the ceiling. She stopped near the top where it looked like she became stuck.

"Are you going to make it?" Bara asked from below.

"I did before. Perhaps I've gained weight. I think my breasts are caught."

"Couldn't help you if I wanted to. All I see is your feet."

"There we go," Lonovina said, finally squeezing her body out of the fissure and into a small room. She sat there silently, reliving her discovery of the jewel. The artifact had defied all reasonable explanation. Yet there it had been, beckoning in the far end of the small room.

Lonovina heard a groan and redirected her attention to Bara struggling into the fissure. He didn't seem to be getting anywhere.

"Perhaps you ought to turn around. I don't think you chest will fit."

"No, no. Just a little further and then I'll have it."

Lonovina watched Bara struggle and thought about the stranger. He was so different then any of the other men she knew; it was as if he had descended from the stars. Lonovina thought of all her terrible childhood years growing up in an orphanage. Although she had learned to fight back with intelligence and tenacity, subduing enemies had never won her any adoration. She had accepted a life of loneliness until Truveli and Bara had entered her life. Fulfilled beyond her expectations, Lonovina decided never to be lonely again. Perhaps she would even learn how to love.

Bara popped out of the crack like a cork.

"Are you all right?"

"I don't think I broke anything. So, this is it?"

"I found the jewel over here in this corner," Lonovina said pointing.

"I see."

"Like I said, the room was empty."

"Almost too empty," Bara said systematically inspecting every crack and crevice. "What about the jewel?"

"Inactive."

"Come look at this," Bara said excitedly.

"What?"

"Look down by my feet and tell me what you see."

"Just shards of rock, small, dull . . . oh. They're different from the other rocks in this room." Lonovina picked up a smooth, brown colored fragment. "It appears to be a mineral."

"Yes, aragonite," Bara said handling Lonovina a selected sample. "Do you remember seeing any tiny bush-like cave formations?"

"Yes."

"Those are made of aragonite."

Lonovina smiled. "So these pieces had been broken at some point. They look as if, as if they were trampled under foot."

"Exactly! Look how small and crunched-up these pieces are. I believe that many people have been in this room, perhaps over an extended period of time."

"Why would anyone want to meet here?"

Bara walked to the far end of the room and stroked the gray limestone walls.

"What are you doing?"

Bara suddenly turned and smiled. "I was right all along. The walls are pulsating with power! Come here," he said gesturing Lonovina to come forward. Lonovina walked forward and the red jewel necklace began to pulse rapidly.

"You believe that the power source is behind this wall?"

"Yes. Notice how the tempo increases as you move the jewel from one place to another."

Lonovina removed the jewel from her neck. With the artifact in hand she experimented with the jewel's rate of pulsation as a function of its placement near the cavern wall. Suddenly a bright, red-shaped object appeared in midair. There was no substance to the shape. It was just an oval form made entirely of light. She opened her mouth in astonishment as the object disappeared and reappeared relative to her visual angle.

"What is it?" Lonovina asked with a strained whisper.

"A hologram. Your jewel must have triggered it."

"It has no substance. Is it a phantasm?"

"No, it's real. It's not so different from the light radiating from your torch."

Lonovina had a thousand questions to ask. Not least was why Bara seemed to have all of the answers. Clearly, the man was more than he seemed.

"Amazing, isn't it?" Bara asked.

"I see a hole in the center of the, uh, hologram. What does it do?"

"I believe it is some sort of operating device," Bara said tugging at his chin. "Unfortunately, I don't know the operation."

"I bet my jewel would fit snugly into that hole."

Bara smiled. "I think you're right."

Lonovina placed the stone into the black cavity. Suddenly the rock wall began to rumble and vibrate.

"Get back!" Bara yelled.

Lonovina sprinted away from the rumble but didn't make it far enough. The wall exploded with a force that flung her to the floor. Everything went still and silent. Lonovina coughed from the settling smoke and dust. Her body hurt. She turned slowly and found a blurred figure kneeling by her side. The figure was Bara. Normally appearing aloof, his face radiated concern. At first Lonovina glanced about searching for what troubled him but came to realize that he was concerned about her.

"How do you feel?" Bara asked.

"Stunned. I think I'm just a little bruised. Here, help me up."

Bara extended his arm and pulled Lonovina upright with an iron grip. He probed gently around her head checking for bumps and serious cuts. "Did you black out?" he asked.

"No. I was dizzy at first, but my head's beginning to clear now. Thanks for the concern, but I think I'm alright."

Bara nodded.

"What happened?"

"The wall exploded and, well, you can see the rest for yourself."

Lonovina looked past the thinning smoke toward a stark, gray, metallic door. The rock wall that once covered the door was now reduced to a pile of rubble. Bara urged her toward the door. Feeling uncertain, Lonovina gripped Bara's hand and followed him forward. To her surprise, the door flung open on its own accord, allowing them to exit the cave and enter a new subterranean world.

"Oh my God," Lonovina whispered. Strong, iridescent, overhead lights illuminated a shiny metallic pipe, no less then twenty feet in diameter. The pipe was centered within the confines of a white, cylinder shaped, metallic shaft. Gingerly Bara stepped onto a thin, clear, glass-like platform constructed to circle the pipe. The platform firmly held Bara's weight so he urged Lonovina to follow. Peering past the clear material, Lonovina observed that the shaft plunged into depths beyond visible comprehension. As if peering off into infinity, shaft and pipe eventually converged to one point. Lonovina felt a twinge of panic as she stared below. Only an inch thick, she imagined the clear platform shattering beneath her weight. The platform offered no resistance, however, and her panic was eventually replaced by a more subtle fear.

Lonovina leaned against Bara and gripped his hand tightly. Although accustomed to new ideas and challenges, she had no reference point to understand the wonders that surrounded her. This revelation had come as a shock to her. Lovovina had always considered herself a master of higher learning. The world, as she knew it, had been her clay for the shaping. Now she felt like a young child trying to run before learning to walk. It seemed as if the floor had been pulled beneath her feet, both figuratively and literally. Bara, on the other hand, was placidly inspecting to a horizontal pipe feeding into the rock. Having no clue to what he was looking at, Lonovina was again bothered by his knowledge and calm demeanor.

"Bara, I need help."

"What? Are you all right?" Bara asked.

"I'm sorry, Bara. Yet I can't continue until I have some idea of what we're facing."

"This must be all very confusing to you," he said gently. "Perhaps I can explain what I know. The large pipe transports heat, or energy, from far below, much like a chimney allows heat and smoke to rise upward in a fireplace."

"I think I understand, but where does this heat come from? The shaft appears to go on forever."

"The heat comes from the earth itself. The temperature rises as one travels deeper and deeper into the earth. It becomes so hot, in fact, that the rock actually becomes liquid fire."

"Like a volcano. I have heard stories of flowing, liquid rock."

"Exactly, good thinking. The pipe, here, transports some of that heat and," he said arching his arm upwards, "carries it somewhere over in that direction. We are standing on a maintenance site."

"I see," Lonovina said amazed, although still somewhat confused. "But who is using the power? And for what purpose?"

Bara bit his lip. "I don't know. I really don't. The answer, I'm afraid, lies at the end of that horizontal pipe."

"So, how do we find it?"

Bara looked at Lonovina intently. "I'm working on it," he replied.

Tired and sore, Lonovina returned to the crawl without enthusiasm. Sleep would be difficult, she knew, given the night's fantastical events. Indeed, Lonovina felt overwhelmed by recent discoveries, so unusual and incomprehensible. It was a find of a lifetime, yet she couldn't help but feel disturbed. The more she knew the less she understood. Why was power still being generated? What was the power being used for? Who was using the power? Lonovina had believed that the Old Ones had emigrated to a far off place. Now she didn't know what to believe. Lonovina was about to bring this up to Bara when something flashed faintly before her in the darkness.

Lonovina stopped. Was it her imagination? No! There it was again. A grayish object had flickered just beyond the reach of her torchlight. Lonovina told herself that her mind was playing tricks on her. No one could successfully navigate through total darkness, not even Bara. Yet her ears confirmed what her eyes had first registered. Something was out there. Someone was coming.

"What do you see?" Bara whispered with a voice sharp and direct.

"I can't tell," she whispered back. "I can't see through the darkness."

"Let me have a look. Goka!"

"What is it?"

"It looks like the living dead. We got to get out of here!"

"The living dead?" Lonovina whispered in disbelief. "You're not making any sense, Bara."

"Never mind, we've got to get out of here, now!"

Lonovina watched horrified as a human figure materialized from the flickering shadows. Bara had not been exaggerating. The head of the moving object looked more like a human skull than a living face. Thin crispy skin, gray as a winter's storm, stretched tightly over bulging bone. The thing had a small mouth that neither smiled nor frowned, a scalp that did not sprout hair, a brow that did not sweat, and a nose that did not breathe. The thing looked dead, alright. Even the eyes refused to move, glisten, or blink. The grayish orbs looked like fingernails pasted into sunken sockets.

Squeezed between narrow walls, Lonovina had no room to turn. She would have to flee down the crawl space backwards, one inch at a time. Although she retreated as fast as she could, the living dead gained on her; the creature's ashen body kept coming within the flickering gloom.

"Keep going," Bara yelled from behind. "You're almost there!"

Bara's words offered little comfort as the creature's gray eyes bore down on her like cold, steel rods. Lonovina reviewed her options but found none. The dead, by definition, could not be killed.

A gray, thin hand lashed out and sharp nails missed her face by inches. Lonovina plunged her dagger into the dead flesh with all her strength. The blade pierced the crispy skin but little else. The thing did not cry out, grimace, or even blink. It did, however, resume it's attack.

Just as Lonovina anticipated death, two strong hands clasped around her calves and yanked her body through the slippery mud. Bara swung Lonovina into the air like a rag doll and placed her on an open ledge that hung above a spacious corridor below. She turned and yelled, but her warning was too late! The living dead picked up Bara's body and slammed it into a nearby wall. Lonovina subdued a scream as the creature crawled over Bara's limp body. Then what seemed like a miracle happened. Bara jerked his knee upwards with astounding force. Although he pummeled the creature repeatedly against an overhanging rock, the dead still lived. Finally sparks flew from the gray sunken orbs and the body began to emit a high-pitched whine. The whine was not an expression of pain, Lonovina realized, but rather an indicator of some pending doom. She looked at Bara for guidance, but he was too busy shoving the body over the ledge.

"Lay down," Bara yelled.

Lonovina complied. A loud explosion ripped through the cavern. Rocks, boulders, and dust burst forth and tumbled violently into the crevice below. Then all was silent. Lonovina opened her eyes and crawled toward Bara who embraced her.

Bara and Lonovina exited the cave after an arduous retreat from a seemingly endless series of ups, downs, twists and turns. Bara and Lonovina spoke sparingly as their minds became numb from terror and fatigue. Lonovina stumbled twice over loose rock and bruised her elbow. Although Bara didn't falter, he felt excruciating pain from having been pounded against a rock wall by the living dead. Despite their difficulties in continuing onward, their pace quickened when a patch of starlight revealed the cavern's entrance.

Refreshed by a cool night breeze, Lonovina collapsed onto a sandy arroyo near the mouth of the cave and quickly fell asleep. Bara subdued the pain in his body through the use of meditation. Laying against a smooth rock, he gazing into the heavens and found a mental anchor in the steady organization of the constellations. Although sleep still eluded him, Bara was thankful that to be alive. If it were not his kritanium-reinforced skeleton, the android's striking blow would have crushed him.

The android's attack had frightened him, not because he feared death, but because he feared for Lonovina's life. He felt responsible for unnecessarily putting her life in jeopardy. It was a difficult choice not to fire his lase-gun. If he fired the weapon, potential enemies would have exploited that knowledge and hunt him down. The idea of fighting yet another unwinnable battle was unappealing. Yet there was his oath of friendship to consider? True, he had taken a gamble with their lives and won. Yet what about the next time? Bara gazed at Lonovina sleeping peacefully by his side. He noted that her hair was silkier than the finest robes and her skin softer than the fluffiest clouds. Everything about her was beautiful. No, he could not make the same decision twice. Bara decided that he would never compromise her life again, no matter what the risk.

Bara was suddenly diverted by the sounds of a soft, rhythmic, thumping in the distance. He jarred Lonovina to consciousness and pointed toward the direction of the source.

"What's going on?" she asked.

"I hear hooves heading this way."

Lonovina reached for her knife and Bara crept behind a large boulder. Silently they waited as the rhythmic thumping became louder and slowed. Soon a shadowy figure materialized out from the darkness. Bara wasn't sure, but the outline looked like a woman riding a Rovan mount.

"Truveli," Lonovina announced.

Bara recognized Truveli as the woman walked forward in dirty, torn clothes.

"I praise the Divu that I have found you here," Truveli said catching her breath. "I was able to follow the map you drew giving directions to the cave."

"You have news?"

Truveli nodded curtly. "Your fears were justified, Lonovina. General Bota, who was killed yesterday morning, has betrayed the empire. The General had ordered his men down from Traqeqtoo Pass. The Varuk are massing in the mountains for attack as we speak. I saw them with my own eyes and narrowly escaped. One of the Varuk almost split my head open!"

"Goka! Whom have you notified?"

"Everyone in Gloroveena knows. Our ranks are racing toward Traqeqtoo Pass to defend the Caonan Empire."

"You acted swiftly. Good work, Truveli!"

"Thank you. General Bakruss sings your praises, Lonovina. You may have saved the Empire by sending me to Traqeqtoo Pass. He requests your presence at Traqeqtoo Fortress immediately."

"I am ready to leave now," Lonovina replied. Lonovina turned to Bara and stared at him expectantly.

"I will be proud to accompany you, Lonovina, if you need my services."

"Yes, Bara, I do. Now more than ever."

CHAPTER 9

Bara filled his lungs with fresh morning air and listened to the thunder of tumbling hooves. A woman's figure shifted within a haze of dust.

"You regret sending Truveli back to Gloroveena?" Bara asked.

Lonovina bit her lip as her friend disappeared into a forested ravine. "It shouldn't matter what I feel. The business of trade continues during my absence. Truveli is qualified and I trust her. She swore to protect my life, position, and estate. That's her job. End of story."

"Is it? Are you being honest with yourself?"

"No," Lonovina said with a sigh. "I fear that Truveli will be murdered. Someone want's me dead, we know that. I'm afraid that they will also target my second in command. I will feel responsible, of course."

"Duty and friendship do not always mix."

"No, I suppose not, but I think I have made the right choice, anyway. Truveli craves recognition, responsibility, respect and honor. She would rather die honorably than be coddled. I just hope that she won't have to confront . . . that," Lonovina said glancing back toward the general direction of the cave. "I pray that there won't be any more of them."

Bara recalled that more than three quarters of the Terasian infantry were androids. They were manufactured faster than children could be born. "There could be many more," Bara replied. "We are all in grave danger."

Lonovina stiffened. She redirected her mount and headed toward Traqeqtoo Pass without a word. Although Bara flanked her side, Lonovina appeared to ignore his presence.

"Are you angry with me?"

Lonovina glanced at Bara with sharp malice. "You took the oath of friendship, yet you have not been forthright."

"In what sense?"

"Your technological knowledge far surpasses my own and I don't know why. You have taken a keen interest in my jewel and I don't know why. You even know about the living dead and I don't know why. I don't know if you have lied to me or not, but you certainly have been withholding information from me. I like you Bara, but how can I trust you if you are not completely honest?"

Bara stared at the wobbling, wedge-shaped head of his Rovan mount. At last he spoke. "I care for you, Lonovina. I have done nothing intentionally to hurt you, but you are right. I represent more than what I have revealed. I need your trust. Yet I doubt that any sane person would believe the truth. How will you be able to trust me if what I tell you, in your mind, is a lie?"

"Try me."

"Very well. What would you like to know?"

Lonovina peered somewhere beyond the distant Traqeqtoo Mountains, her eyes moist and tender. At last, she whispered the question, "Who are we?"

Bara's eyes opened wide with astonishment.

"Well?"

"I'm sorry, Lonovina, I just didn't expect that question. You didn't know your parents, did you?"

Tears began to trickle down Lonovina's cheeks. "No. I never knew my parents. I grew up in an orphanage. I assumed that my parents had abandoned me because of my . . . well, because of my distinct physical differences."

Bara's face softened. "But you see that I look like you, white skin, black hair and purple eyes."

"Yes."

"So now you realize that you are not alone. You were not born a freak, Lonovina. You were born Xusu."

Lonovina dried her eyes. More than a name had been spoken, she had an identity. She was neither a freak nor an accident. "The Xusu?" she mouthed.

"The Xusu are, or were, a relatively rare race in my homeland. Our people have traditionally been leaders in science, literature, war, and politics. I know that you feel overwhelmed by my comprehension of the physical world. Still, you can be comforted by the fact that it was your own people who discovered, expanded, and passed a great deal of knowledge through the generations. And in the spirit of our people, I will teach you anything you are willing to learn."

"Yes, I am willing to learn. But here in Caona, I am the only one of our kind. You say my parents were also Xusu?"

"Of course. The Xusu are very protective of their own. They would never have abandoned you."

Lonovina nodded and reflected on Bara's words. "Did you say that the Xusu are no longer common in your land?" she eventually asked.

"As far as I know, I am the last."

"No! What happened?!"

"We were at war with another life-form, the Vesders. We lost. All of my friends and family are dead."

Lonovina looked away. "Then we are the last of a great people."

"Perhaps not. We come from very different places, you and I. Our people have not interacted within recorded history. Yet we are one."

"I don't understand."

"The history of my people extends thousands of years, Lonovina. Yet our technology has only recently allowed travel to other worlds."

Lonovina sucked in her breath.

"Terasia was not very different from your own world, especially considering that humans populated both worlds."

"I can't believe what you are saying! What do you mean by 'other worlds'?"

"Remember our discussion walking on the beach, how stars are not eyes of the Sula. Each star is a burning ball of fire, hundreds of times larger than this world. Your world, a ball like any other planets, circles two stars. My home world, Terasia, circles just one. You impressed me by deducing the possibility of other life throughout our universe. Indeed, the universe is teaming with life. My people were just beginning to explore our small corner of the universe when the Vesders slaughtered us."

"I... I don't know what to say. I don't know where to begin."

"You don't need to know everything right now, Lonovina. It is too much. Just know that you are special and that we share a common heritage. You will learn more as time passes."

"Our ancestors must have traveled between the two worlds, just as you have."

"Yes," Bara replied. "I believe that we are the descendants of the Old Ones. However, we may not be their legacies. Although the Old Ones disappeared, they may have not been destroyed."

"The power source in the cave is still active. Perhaps they are still here."

"Why all the secrecy?" Bara asked. "True, a tremendous power being generated and used on this world. Still, I'm not convinced that the Old

One's are currently operating this power. You yourself told me that the Old One's traveled to the stars."

"You speak of the ancient geography text that I referenced. Yes, I do remember telling you about that. But if some advanced civilization really exists here, why don't they just take over the world?"

Bara shrugged. "I can only speculate. Perhaps they respect human autonomy enough not to interfere."

"Or perhaps not. I believe that the coming Varuk attack is somehow related to all these recent bizarre events. General Bota was clearly involved with the coming Varuk attack. I think you were right. The Varuk are being bred by someone."

"Without a doubt."

"You're the scientific expert. Is this easily feasible?"

Bara recollected various lectures on genetic engineering. "No," he replied. "It would be impossible for General Bota or any other Caonan."

"It also seems unlikely that the Old Ones would want to destroy us."

"That would be very unlikely," Bara agreed. "Assuming that we are both descendants of the Old Ones, it doesn't make sense that they would want to destroy us. A species generally does not destroy itself without good reason."

"True, but a powerful, alien civilization just might, especially a race bent on world domination."

"Perhaps. Such an explanation would justify all the recent assassination attempts. Your jewel may have greater importance than you realize. But perhaps not."

"No?"

"Why would an advanced civilization breed Varuk when their technology could destroy this world in a heartbeat?"

"I see your point," Lonovina admitted. "Yet I can't think of any human society capable of breeding Varuk. Unless," Lonovina looked up horrified, "we are being attacked by that creature we killed, the so called 'living dead'."

"Yes and no. The thing we saw in the cave was not a living creature. It is only a machine, like your necklace."

"An elaborate example of technology, you mean."

"Yes. Very sophisticated technology. And like the Varuk, the machine is controlled by another."

"Then an advanced civilization must be attacking us!?"

Bara was at a loss. He knew that there had to be an answer to their dilemma. Finally an answer did strike him like lightening. The answer was so obvious, in fact, that Bara must have been unconsciously pushing aside the unthinkable.

"What's the matter?" Lonovina asked quietly. "Why are you flinching?"

"I have the answer. We are not being attacked by some advanced enemy civilization. At least not yet, anyway. Our enemy is nothing more than a handful of demons, deserters from a tragic war."

Lonovina slowly realized the enormity of what Bara was suggesting. "The Vesders will not stop until we are all dead, will they?" she asked.

"No," Bara replied and spit on the hard-packed road.

"Then you, Bara, are this world's only hope."

Bara sat hunched over his Rovan Beast like a deflated balloon.

"What's wrong?" Lonovina asked. She was answered by silence.

Lonovina reached over and laid her hand on Bara's leg. "The burden is too great. Yet I tell you with all my heart that you are no more responsible for my world than your own."

"You are so very wrong, Lonovina. The Vesder did not arrived to this planet by accident. It's my fault. They followed me here. Don't you understand that? They found my ship's ionic trail, tracked it's trajectory through space, somehow built a faster ship, and beat me here. But why?! It just doesn't make sense! Why send a high speed spacecraft light years across space to kill just one man?"

"I don't know," Lonovina answered sheepishly.

"My God, what have I done!"

"I will not listen to any more fits of self-pity, Bara! You are not responsible for their malicious cunning. Now stop sulking and help me think about how we might beat them."

"You're right."

"Do you think we can use the technology created by the Old Ones to fight them?"

"Indeed. Perhaps the Old Ones might even choose to help us."

"What! Did I hear you right? Do you think the Old Ones are still here on the planet after all these years?"

"I don't know, but someone knocked my ship out of space and it wasn't the Vesder. The Vesder would not have set me free."

"Then perhaps you are not this world's only hope after all."

"I hope you're right. Still, I would feel a lot safer if I found my ship."

CHAPTER 10

Lonovina and Bara reached Traqeqtoo Pass shortly after sunset. The Pass, usually a desolate place at night, had become a booming city of blazing campfires. Bodies darted in and out of the flickering flame like dancing demons. The air reverberated with the sounds of profanity and laughter. Bara noted that the mountains didn't seem to mind either way. They had all the time in the world to wait. Man, on the other hand, had little time.

"Caona's finest," Lonovina sneered.

"At least they are in a position of strength," Bara stated. "The Varuk must attack from below."

Lonovina nodded. "Thank the Divu for small favors. Based on Truveli's report, the Varuk horde should have reached Traqeqtoo Pass earlier this afternoon. I expected these men to be fleeing like baby Hootvas."

"A potter doesn't shape clay vessels out of sand. The Varuk are, and always will be, dull-witted and difficult to manage."

"The same could be said about our infantry. Look at them! If the Varuk attacked us now, they would slaughter everyone. I fear that years of disorganization have unraveled discipline and training." Lonovina opened her mouth, but hesitated. "Our welcoming party has arrived," she whispered.

Bara heard the soft crunch of brittle meadow grass. Altering his vision to the infrared, Bara transformed shadows into glowing heat. Shimmering red and orange shapes told Bara that a dozen men were quickly approaching.

"This is my lucky night," a voice bellowed in the distance. "It isn't every moment that I have the opportunity to wail on a couple of disobedient commoners."

"Woe is to those who defy military orders," another voice chimed in.

"But look, Garuss. It is but a mere woman and her lackey!"

"I think she might give the men plenty of entertainment, captain, sir."

"Aye," Captain Garuss Hozdt agreed and stepped out from the forest's cover. The Captain plunged his fists into his hips and smiled. He was a short, stocky man with dark black eyes and enormous white teeth. "I say that we kill the man and quietly sneak the woman off into the bushes. What do you all think?" The remaining company resounded in cheer. "After we're done, you will curse the day you were born, woman. Speak if you dare!"

"I am Lonovina. General Backruss has summoned me here."

The Captain's face turned pale and the woods became deafly silent. "My greatest apologies, lady. We mistook you for another. We never meant you or anyone else any harm. We are only trying to keep the Pass secure."

An enormous dark-colored man emerged from the meadow shadows. Wearing silken black trousers and a necklace made of Varuk teeth, he began fingering a massive broadsword sheathed in his belt.

"General Backruss," Lonovina said in greeting.

"Welcome my friend. Speaking for the entire company, and myself we extend to you our sincerest gratitude. If it wasn't for your timely warning, the Varuk might be rampaging through Gloroveena and gnawing on the bones of Captain Hozdt. As for you, Hozdt," the General said turning toward the man, "I will deal with you later. Now be gone."

Lonovina bowed, Captain Hozdt scurried away, and Bara eased his mount forward.

"General Backruss, this is Bara," Lonovina announced.

Backruss acknowledged the stranger with a curt nod. "People tell me of your courage at Capoca Fortress" he said. "Still, I must tell you that I distrust foreigners. Are you a hero fighting for the glory of Caona, barbarian, or are you a thorn in my side?"

"Neither. I come to fight a common enemy."

"The Varuk?"

"No sir. I fight the real enemy, those who are breeding the Varuk to use for their own purposes."

Backruss gently bit his lip.

"Know that Bara and I work together," Lonovina said. "You cannot trust me without trusting him."

"Is this so?"

"Bara's loyalty is beyond question," Lonovina stated flatly. "He has my complete confidence. I recommend that you listen to him. I have found his words invaluable."

"Outnumbered ten to one, I could use good counsel right now. Very well. I have learned to trust your judgement, Lonovina. There will be a meeting shortly in the fortress. Bara will speak there and leave promptly. You may stay throughout the meeting, Lonovina. I would appreciate any ideas regarding General's Bota's treason."

"I will help in any way I can, General."

"Very well then. Let us make haste to the tower. The meeting will start any moment now."

An uneasy silence enveloped the camp as General Backruss and his guests maneuvered their way through a sea of soldiers. Their faces betrayed apprehension, particularly when probing eyes focused on Lonovina. Backruss, on his part, ignored the soldier's reaction and confidently continued toward a slender tower that jutted into the star-studded night like a withered finger. Five sentries straightened to attention as the General approached the tower's main entrance. One quickly opened a thick wooden door reinforced by rows of iron ribbing.

Bara noted a foul musty smell as he walked into an open foyer. Flickering torchlight illuminated a narrow, steep stairway spiraling around dingy walls constructed from limestone mortar. Looking to the left, Bara noticed two large guards posted on either side of another massive wooden door. This would be the meeting room, he guessed.

The guards opened the door allowing General Backruss and his guests to enter the room without delay. Bara stepped over the door's threshold and scanned a smoky room. A dozen men, propped up like malevolent wooden statues, sat around a polished table made out of white looma wood. Faces reddened and teeth gnashed. Clearly, General Backruss was violating accepted protocol.

"What is this?" one young officer demanded.

The general's eyes narrowed. "Stand up, Lieutenant Birus, if you are going to speak to me like that!"

A large, young man, no older than twenty-five, stood up and flexed his bare, bronzed muscles. A nearby hand gently tugged at the young man's shoulder and lips whispered into his ear. The hand, Bara noted, belonged to General Ronard.

"I apologize," the young man stated. "I acted rashly."

General Backruss bore his eyes into every officer in the room. Finally, he spoke. "We have all dedicated our lives to the service of our country. Our resolve will finally be put to the test. So, do you take me for a fool!? Do you think I would jeopardize everything by allowing this barbarian to attend a war meeting!? Never! Yet this stranger might have important information that I would like everyone to hear. The War Room Meeting has not formally started. He will not learn anything about our strategy. We only need to listen. Surely we can decipher truths from lies. Are we not up to the task? Are we not Caona's finest?" General Backruss scanned the room for any open defiance. No one spoke. "Very well then, I have agreed to let the barbarian speak provided he leaves before our official meeting. Any questions?"

General Ronard stood and glared at Bara.

"Yes General Ronard, do you have something to add?"

"With all due respect, General Backruss, I hope that you reconsider your position. Bara is no ordinary barbarian. His arrival coincided with the Varuk initiatives. I refuse to accept this fact as coincidence. True, the man acted courageously at Capoca Fortress, but why? Was it all a guise? I believe so. I believe that Bara might be a spy, a very dangerous spy in league with the Varuk." Ronard hesitated to emphasize his next point. "I accept your authority without question, sir. Yet I fear that bringing Bara to this meeting has done harm. I have met him before and found him subtle and calculating. That is all I have to say."

General Ronard bowed slightly and quietly sat down. Another General, fat and balding, leaned forward.

"General Petark," Backruss acknowledged, "please speak, my old friend."

"Thank you, General. Gentlemen, I must concur with my esteemed colleague, General Ronard. Many of our young men will die in battle tomorrow. I cannot, in good conscience, allow one man to die because of our carelessness. Tasked with commanding the field tomorrow, this burden has become especially heavy on me. Can we trust a stranger we know little or nothing about? Even if he has good intentions, will his counsel mislead us and allow innocent soldiers to die?"

Heated discussion erupted throughout the room.

"Silence," Backruss boomed. "I have decided to let the barbarian speak. My decision is final."

"What about the woman?" General Ronard asked.

"Lonovina is here by my invitation, my friend."

"What about military clearance?" Ronard pushed.

"Lonovina has clearance, General. You should know that. Some of you have worked with her on matters of extreme delicacy. She has proven herself in many campaigns. She can be trusted."

"I don't believe you," a voice boomed. "General Ronard has informed us about this evil trader woman's treachery!"

"Division will destroy us!" General Backruss said pounding his fist on the table. " I will not begin our meeting like this, Lieutenant Birus. Either you must go or she must go."

"It will be Lonovina or my dead body," Birus stated. A low murmur resonated throughout the chamber.

"If violence is your answer, Birus, then so be it. Kill Lonovina, and you may stay. If she kills you, then she may stay."

"Here?"

"Here and now, soldier."

Birus shook his head in disbelief. "Too easy. What's the catch?"

"No catch. The survivor will be resolved of responsibility. You have my oath."

Lonovina was already positioning herself in an empty corner. Lieutenant Birus shrugged and pulled out a long gleaming dagger. The room quieted as Officer Birus circled Lonovina searching for weaknesses while Bara, as a precaution, fingered his lase-gun in his sleeve. Circling Lonovina several times, Birus lunged at the woman with lightening speed. Although his thrust was strong and sure, Lonovina easily deflected his arm. Not fully grasping what had happened, the young man froze. Within a fraction of a second, Lonovina flipped the young man over her shoulder and hurdled him toward the wall headfirst. Impacting the rock mortar, Lieutenant Birus fell dead to the floor.

"Guards!" Backruss yelled. Two sentries immediately burst into the room. "Take Lieutenant Birus's body outside."

Shaken, the guards picked up the bloody corpse and left.

"If there aren't any more objections," General Backruss announced, "Bara will speak now."

Bara quietly emerged from the shadows. "I will try to be brief," he began. "Judging by the size of this camp and Truveli's description of the Varuk horde, I estimate that Caonans are outnumbered ten to one. Although your troops maintain a clear strategic advantage, the outcome of open battle is questionable." A barrage of coughing interrupted Bara. He ignored the commentary and continued without hesitation. "I believe that the Varuk can be killed quickly with minimal casualties. Now, I understand that Varuk venom is highly toxic, even to the Varuk."

"Poisoned arrows are well stocked," Ronard inserted. "What's your point?"

"I assume that you killed the Varuk inhabiting this fortress before your arrival. I suggest milking their venom and poisoning the creek below."

The sound of hushed voices filled the War Room.

"Quiet!" Backruss boomed. The noise quickly subsided. "Bara, please continue."

"The volume of water flowing down a small mountain stream will be small enough to kill or sicken many of the Varuk. Unless, of course, their sensory system can detect minute concentrations of their own poison."

"No, the Varuk will drink anything," General Petark said, mopping sweat off his large, balding forehead. "Once lethargic, they will become easy targets for my men positioned above on the bank. Yes, I think this might actually work. Bara, I'm am beginning to be sorry that I doubted you."

"Quite alright, General. I'll leave the strategy to you, gentlemen, and take my leave. But first consider this. If poison fails, you have lost nothing. Yet if it succeeds, you have gained an enormous advantage. Any questions?" There were none.

"Guards," General Backruss boomed. "Take Bara upstairs to Lieutenant Birus's room. He won't be needing his quarters tonight."

"Yes sir."

Bara turned away from the frenzied sounds of hurried conversations. He glanced back once before exiting. Both Lonovina and General Ronard were staring back at him, the former with the hint of a smile and the latter with a clear expression of malice.

* * *

Although Bara's body eagerly welcomed sleep, his mind disallowed the disorganized, semiconscious state of dream. He believed that rationality should rule every aspect of consciousness. Emerging feelings for Lonovina had contradicted this assumption, however. Bara was an emotional creature, despite all attempts to redefine his existence. Yet Bara had shelved these unquieting new realities into the dark recesses of his mind. The demands of survival, he reasoned, disallowed compromise. Dream meant vulnerability, especially during war. Keeping the sensory gestalt active was far more adaptive by monitoring for the unexpected noise, smell, or vibration. In this manner, Bara instantly perceived the sound of soft rapping. He shot out of bed and assumed a defensive posture. Someone was knocking. "Who is it?" he asked.

"Lonovina," a voice whispered.

Bara quickly opened the door and beckoned Lonovina to enter. Lonovina complied and began fumbling in the darkness. "Where are you?" she asked. "I can't see a thing."

"I'm to your right," Bara replied. Lonovina found Bara's hand and grasped it tightly.

"Come," Bara said, leading Lonovina toward the relative comfort of his straw bedding.

Bara waited silently with anticipation. Lonovina neither gazed at him nor spoke, but rather looked down at the floor. The shimmering red glow of body heat betrayed a black streak flowing down her cheek. Bara felt a strong sting of pity. A hundred years of training, it seemed, had inexplicably abandoned him. 'Run', his mind ordered. Yet Bara held his ground. Gathering courage from within, he reached out and caressed the troubled face.

Lonovina stiffened as Bara's thirsty flesh soaked up her moisture. She felt an overwhelming urge to bolt into the familiar arms of solitude. She needed to be anywhere except here, facing the shame of her vulnerabilities. Although Lonovina also wanted to leave, she lacked the emotional strength to do so. Bara's touch was intoxicating.

Half-expecting scathing words, Lonovina was not prepared for the comforting arms that held her without reservation. Where was the contempt? Where was the revulsion? More tears began to flow. Lonovina gave up and lost herself in the forgiving warmth. She was like a starving child who finally found sustenance.

Eyes swollen and red, Lonovina shed her last tear. She decidedly weaned herself from the nurturing embrace and collected herself. "General Backruss requested that we meet," she said. "They decided to implement your suggestion."

"Good," Bara answered.

"I suppose my infamy will only increase."

"Fame does not suit you?"

Lonovina laughed hoarsely and coughed. "Children have nightmares about me. The ignorant write magical words on their doors claiming that magic will protect them against my evil presence. True, people rarely cross me, but that is no longer enough. Now there is Birus and the others. General Ronard has started a fire of rumors. I can hear them now. Once again, the legendary Lonovina strikes fear into the hearts of men." Lonovina sighed. "I am tired, Bara. I am tired of not being wanted. I am tired of killing. How can I continue with my guilt. People are right to hate me. Although I have never intended evil, I am monstrous."

"Human monsters lack guilt, Lonovina, and killing is not always murder. The Xusu typically kill for self-preservation. Or, they will frequently kill for the good of the many. That is the nature of our people. That is your nature."

"But there must be another way?"

"If you had not killed Birus, how many more soldiers would have perished during the coming conflict?"

"True," she whispered. "But that doesn't make it any easier."

Bara sighed. "I have killed many times before in war. It never becomes easier. Scars crisscross my soul like a whipped man's back. I'd rather surrender then kill another human being. Nevertheless, I have always found the courage, just as you have, to preserve my life and the common good."

"Then what becomes of us?"

"We suffer," Bara whispered. "We suffer tremendously. Yet . . . yet I believe there is redemption." Bara placed his hand firmly on Lonovina's leg. "Do you loathe me?"

"No," she said softly.

"Nor do I loathe you. Your presence heals many scars of fire. My heart knows that you are, and forever will be, my friend."

"Thank you," she whispered.

Time slowed as Bara felt warm flesh ease toward him. Hot liquid lips began caressing his own. His brained screamed for resistance, but quickly surrendered to a softness that energized his tired soul. Bara forsake all rationality as passion engulfed his every thought, passion that was fueled by violent kisses, trembling, and moans. An enormous damn of tension burst, powered by a hundred years of self-denial. The release blotted out the very existence of his normal world. Not seeking intimacy, Bara had inadvertently bonded with another. Bara realized that the act of loving celebrated new fundamental truths. He would never abandon Lonovina. She was his new cause. They were one.

* * *

Backruss ordered Bara to remain in the tower. Knowing that Lonovina was sleeping nearby, Bara complied willingly. He had not felt happier in decades. Enjoying the solitude, Bara let his thoughts roam freely. Midday turned into dusk before he was interrupted. There was a knock on the door. "Yes?"

"Lonovina."

"Coming," he replied eagerly. To his great surprise, Lonovina's voice did not match the face. General Ronard stood directly in front of him pointing a Vesder ray gun at his mid section. Dressed only in his shirt and pants, Bara was unarmed. He had been too eager. He had been careless. 'This is why you should never love,' he thought sadly. Bara watched helplessly as Ronard pulled the trigger.

* * *

A muffled thud awakened Lonovina. Although the noise was soft and inconspicuous, an insidious fear crept into her body. She dressed quickly and peered out into the winding torch-lit hallway. Nothing. She knocked on Bara's door. No answer. She knocked again. No answer. Although the fear was nameless, it grew to monstrous proportions as she opened the door leading into Bara's quarters. Her throat went dry as her suspicions became confirmed. Bara's room was empty.

Lonovina found Bara's boots and shirt by the bedside, confirming her suspicion that he had been abducted. Still, who would abduct a man of Bara's abilities from a well-guarded fortress? An image of grey ashen skin and chalky orbs came to mind. The living dead might be able to pull it off.

Violent images haunted Lonovina. In a moment of anguish, she picked up his boots and shirt and threw them across the room. Two small black, metal objects fell out from Bara's shirt sleeve it impacted the wall.

Curious, but not wanting to waste any precious time, Lonovina grabbed the objects and bounded down the hallway. An incredible stench permeated the air as she left the tower and ran past smoking piles of ash and debris. Although a portion of her mind acknowledged these piles to be human remains, she gave them little heed. Her mind was consumed on finding Bara, despite the coming danger.

Lonovina climbed a rock overlooking Traqeqtoo Pass and quickly scanned the vicinity. Every soldier at Traqeqtoo Pass had been reduced to a pile of fragmented bone and ash. Was Bara a victim? Was his body reduced to a pile of remains? Lonovina slowed her search and pried her eyes into every distant outcrop and shadowed crevice. She suddenly spotted the culprit; General Ronard climbing across the steep mountainside with an enormous body bag draped over his shoulder. Lonovina propelled her body into a full run.

All day Lonovina followed General Ronard across the mountainside with astonishing speed. Although she was beginning to gain on the General, she had to slow due to the coming darkness of night. Lonovina didn't have much of a plan, just ambush and kill. Just as she thought she had finally gained on Ronard, she saw a small army of Varuk rise from behind the rocks. Lonovina counted ten animals. The large black beasts surrounded her on every side and began to grunt with anticipation. Thirty red eyes reflected the confidence of victory. There would be no escape. Lonovina knew that she had failed.

CHAPTER 11

General Petark, Field General against the Varuk invasion, was rarely thought of as a malicious man. He was generous to his wife and fair to his soldiers. Yet like so many others who lacked serious introspection, the General was vulnerable to the circumstances of the moment. The battle with the Varuk had not been an exception.

What began as an organized military exercise, quickly degenerated into a warped frenzy of indiscriminate killing and mutilation. Bara's plan had worked brilliantly. The Varuk had been sickened by their own poison and rendered helpless against the descending human hordes. The Varuk screamed as the men hacked them up. Body parts were strewn about as men wallowed in purplish-black blood. Not that the Varuk deserved sympathy. They would have done no less. Yet the men serving under General Petark would have killed, looted, and raped their own kind if the opportunity had presented itself. The wise had abandoned rationality to drives and primitive emotions. The respectable had abandoned internalized morals and conformed to the violent group norms and the behavior of their commanders. Such was the nature of human physiology. Such was the nature of human kind. Such was the nature of Petark and his men as they returned from battle and crested Traqeqtoo Pass.

General Petark and his command were ill prepared for the devastation at Traqeqtoo Pass. Expecting a triumphant welcoming from General Backruss, the other commanders and their fellow soldiers, they were numbed by a eerie silence and a foul stench. An undercurrent of violence grew as soldiers discovered the burnt body remains of their comrades in arms. As the silence grew, the soldiers looked for a release from the building tension. They found one. A grim faced commander handed a note to General Petark. The General read it aloud.

Lonovina and Bara responsible. Hid. Now searching. Need assistance!

General Yupew Ronard

General Petark tried to comprehend the magnitude of the massacre. Backruss, his friend Tronona, the others, they were are all dead! He wondered how they could slaughter so many close associates without mercy? The General wasted no time in generating answers. He didn't want to think. It didn't matter that Bara saved the Caonan Empire by his suggestion last night. Petark demanded action. "A ten thousand rutgee reward for the dead body of Lonovina!" he yelled. "The same goes for Bara!" The armed mob reacted by shouting violent oaths until their throats burned. Petark continued, "I want twenty groups of thirty to search every crevice in the surrounding mountains and fifty bands of ten to scour the countryside. I want a hundred men to infuriate the populace of Gloroveena, behead Lonovina's accomplice Truveli, imprison the rest of her staff, and burn down her house. I want no soldier to rest until we have dispatched of Lonovina's traitorous evil!" The crowd responded.

CHAPTER 12

Gloroveena bustled with activity as Truveli made her way through a swarm of haggling merchants, buyers and soldiers. Although the streets were typically crowded midday, Truveli sensed that something was amiss. Soldiers whispered to each other on street corners, fights erupted among the merchants, and the city's financial institutions were bustling with panicked activity. News of the traitorous General Bota swept through town within hours. The populace had talked exclusively about the massing Varuk hordes ever since.

Although Truveli shared in the city's fear of attack, she also worried about a more sinister and nameless danger. She remembered Lonovina's tale of the living dead, of lifeless orbs and swiping nails. Truveli would have dismissed the story as fantastical if another had told it. But Lonovina's word was more precious to her than all the gold in Gloroveena.

Truveli remembered when she first met Lonovina about ten years ago. She was thirteen and orphaned, reduced to begging on the streets of Gloroveena. Lonovina not only gave her money, but also took her into her home and raised her as her own. It seemed impossible that anyone would bother loving and educate a homeless, peasant girl. Yet Lonovina did just that. Her compassion, patience, and unconditional acceptance transcended every childhood expectation. In return, Truveli's vowed unquestionable allegiance to the one person who gave her hope, purpose, and order in a chaotic world. Unfortunately, that order was now eroding. Betrayal by General Bota, assassination attempts, the living dead, massive Varuk attacks, the fabric of her entire world seemed to be unraveling. Truveli had not slept well in days.

Truveli's eyes burned with fatigue when she finally gained refuge from the busy streets to metal bars surrounded by guards. She went straight to Lonovina's office and buried her head into her hands. Normally excited by the prospect of overseeing her employer's vast trading empire, the rumor of war had put formidable demands on the business. Truveli wondered if she were up to the task. Although she recognized her talents, she also knew her limitations. She was no Lonovina.

Someone lightly rapped on the door. "Come," Truveli directed.

YVIA VOI: LAND OF GRACE

A large man with ebony skin and a pink facial scar stepped into the room. Truveli immediately recognized him as the Captain of the Guard. "Yes Gerrus."

Gerrus bowed slightly. "I'm sorry to bother you, madam. A man is waiting to see you in the guest chambers."

"I am too busy for unscheduled announcements, Gerrus. Goka! How did Lonovina handle all these people?!"

"The man does not represent the trading union. He calls himself Moluq. He had accompanied Bara . . . "

"Yes, I know how he is. What does he want?"

"I don't know. He is very distraught, Madam. He said something about Lonovina being in danger and insisted on talking with you. It's probably nothing. Give the word and he'll be gone. I just thought it best to inform you first."

"Yes," Truveli replied wearily. "You did right Gerrus. I'll speak to him now."

Truveli vaguely recalled meeting the thin, good-natured soldier. Lonovina had asked her to entertain Moluq while she entertained the more important guest, Bara. Although Truveli found Moluq generally obnoxious, his mirth, wide smile and sparkling eyes had amused her. With this image in mind, Truveli was surprised to find the sparkle and grin gone. Moluq's large mouth was hard and rigid, swollen lids overshadowed his small beady eyes, and the once pink nose was as white like the rest of his skin. Not even the sunlight streaming through windowed ceilings added any color to the man.

"Truveli!" Moluq greeted.

"You needed to see me?"

"Oh yes! Thank you! Thank you!"

"You don't look well. What has happened?"

Moluq's eyes began to glisten and his nose dripped. "Please help me," he pleaded and started to sob. "I am desperate."

Truveli's gaze softened. She wondered why she felt any compassion for this pitiful fool. "Yes, of course. Here, please sit down and gather yourself."

Moluq sat quietly and dried his eyes. "I need to speak to Lonovina."

"Lonovina is not here."

"Take me to her if you must! I need to see her!"

112

"Lonovina is at Traqeqtoo Fortress, fighting the Varuk."

Moluq looked away. "She was my only hope," he muttered.

Truveli didn't know what to make of the thin, frightened soldier. No doubt he was an emotional man vulnerable to the weakness of fear. Yet the man wasn't simply scared. He was down right terrified. Truveli took in a deep breath. "Perhaps I can help," she offered reluctantly. "Tell me what happened."

"I don't think you would believe me."

"Moluq, listen to me. I have witnessed a number of inexplicable things of late. There isn't much I wouldn't believe right now. I will help you if I can, especially if Lonovina's life is in jeopardy. Now talk to me."

Moluq lowered his head and closed his eyes. "Captain Dukuk called on me this morning. It was a routine call. He needed me to finish an inventory assignment. I arrived . . . "

"And?"

"The Commander, he was babbling incoherently. I-I tried to slow him, you know, to make sense of everything, but he wouldn't stop babbling! He was talking something about Bara and Lonovina being in danger. I couldn't piece it together, you see, so I told him that everything was all right. I explained to him that he just wasn't feeling well. Well, Dukuk just shook his head really nasty like and pointed toward the window. I got up, you know, to look out the window and there . . . " Moluq stopped and began to shiver.

"What? There what?"

"There walked the living dead!"

Truveli bolted out of her chair and began to pace. She eventually made her way to the doorway and leaned on its edge for support. Lonovina had described her encounter living dead in every frightening detail. The fact that they lived to exit the cave and see sky was a miracle. The fact that Bara had killed the pursuer only meant that there were more.

"I told you that you wouldn't believe me."

"I believe you," Truveli said softly turning her gaze toward the young soldier. "Yes Moluq, I believe you. I must speak to your Captain at once."

"At once?"

"Yes. I'm afraid that time is running out."

* * *

Commander Dukuk didn't notice Truveli and Moluq enter his corridors. Lying in bed, the Commander's eyes darted aimlessly from one stone wall to the next. Rivers of sweat poured from his wide, balding forehead and his fat body trembled.

"He's going mad," Moluq blurted.

Truveli ignored the remark and inched her way toward the Commander. "Commander Dukuk," she said.

The Commander ignored her.

"Dukuk!" she yelled with force.

Dukuk turned his head toward the voice and tried to focus his eyes. "Lonovina, is that you?"

"No. I am Truveli, Lonovina's closest friend."

Dukuk reached out and grabbed Truveli's hand. His grip was tight, hot and sweaty. "Lonovina, is in danger," he whispered.

"Why?"

Dukuk's upper lip began to quiver.

"Tell me why!"

"Horrible creature. Never seen such a monster!"

"He speaks the truth," Moluq added. "I saw it too. By the Divu, that thing will spread death everywhere. We will all die!"

"That's enough, Moluq!" Truveli snapped. "Dukuk, I want you to tell me everything you saw."

"A corpse walked in my quarters. It had dull, yellow eyes and stretched, gray skin. It asked about Lonovina's jewel. I told it that I didn't know anything, but it-it forced me to tell."

"Tell what?!"

Commander Dukuk bore his face into his stubby white hands and began to quiver. "Everything. Everything I knew about Bara, Lonovina, and the jewel. I didn't know much, but it still probed. Oh God how it hurt! It will kill us all, you know. When it bore into my mind, I saw my own death. I saw Moluq's death. I saw your death and everyone's death! I see . . . "

"What do you see, Commander?"

"Oh help me benevolent Divu! I feel poison burn in my veins. It knows. It's killing me! It's going . . . to . . .," Dukuk's voice ended as if some silent command had cut it off. His eyes rolled back toward the top of his forehead and his tongue drooped out of his mouth. Truveli's hand suddenly found freedom and she pulled it away from the dead man's clasp.

"It-it killed him! It's going to kill us next! What are we going to do!?" Moluq asked sobbing. "What are we going to do!?"

Truveli ignored Moluq and stared at the dead Commander. Truveli had long suspected that the magical jewel was cursed. No doubt the jewel was some sacred relic owned by the undead. Now they wanted it back! If only Lonovina had listened to her. If only she had listened to reason they could have avoided much of this.

A distant crescendo of voices suddenly diverted Truveli's attention. She darted to a small, lone window that looked over the street. There was no question of what was progressing outside in the remaining twilight. Between shadowed rooftops, domes, and spires, a great mob was gathering in the city square. Their repeated words sent shivers down Truveli's spine. "Death to the black-haired, purple-eyed devil!" they cried. "Death to Lonovina!"

A great explosion ripped the city of Gloroveena. Running beyond the outskirts of town, Truveli dared to look back on an enormous fireball swirling lazily toward the heavens. Grief struck her to her knees, weeping. The fires of hate, fear, and ignorance were consuming Lonovina's estate and her own home. Even from this distance she could hear the fleeting sounds of cheering and cursing carried by the wind. Smaller fires began to emerge from the inferno. Torches, Truveli guessed. The citizens of Gloroveena would now be searching for her head.

After learning of Lonovina and Bara's alleged treachery at Traqeqtoo Pass, Truveli hastily left Moluq and the dead Commander Dukuk without a word. Numb with disbelief and fear, she raced toward Lonovina's estate only to find the entire staff obliterated in a baffling way. Even her friend Gerrus, had been reduced to mostly a pile of ash and bones. Finding Lonovina's artifacts missing only confirmed that the living dead had returned to collect their sacred relics. Truveli screamed and then ran through the streets of Gloroveena like a hunted animal. She didn't leave a moment too soon, the mobs closed in the estate shortly after her departure.

Still on her knees weeping, Truveli considered suicide. Yet the will to live, perhaps fueled by growing anger, prevailed. Truveli spit on the cold, coarse ground and cursed humanity. She lifted herself stiffly and began climbing the hillside following the shadows of tangled Bancor Trees. Every step was difficult and marked by uncertainty. Where would she go? Whom could she trust? Someone had betrayed her best friend; accusing her of unthinkable treachery. Did Bara betray her? Or was it one of the generals? Perhaps it was the living dead? Truveli decided that her only option was to run for the Traqeqtoo Mountains and inform her mentor and best friend of the danger that confronted them both. She only hoped that Lonovina was still alive- what was that?! Truveli was sure that she heard something move inside the dark Bancor Tree.

A cold hand reached out from the darkness. Truveli reflexively turned to face her attacker but was too slow. Pinned by arms of steel, Truveli peered into the empty orbs of the living dead. It wrapped its thin, cold, fingers around her throat and squeezed. Truveli gasped for a last, meager breath but failed.

CHAPTER 13

A consuming pain reeled Bara into consciousness. Every nerve ending pulsated as if some sadistic conductor was orchestrating a symphony of agony on his body. The conductor, Bara remembered, was General Ronard who had fired a Vesder lase-gun point blank at his mid-section. Although Ronard had fired his weapon at Bara using the stun setting, the other men at Traqeqtoo Pass weren't so fortunate. Their swords and arrows was no match against one small lase-gun. The image of the General Ronard cutting down his own army replayed itself in Bara's mind. Bara clenched his jaw. A man who destroyed without concern was incapable of mercy. Yet a man who would doom his people for profit was worse. He was the most reprehensible individual Bara could imagine; particularly if he was working for the Vesder. He would never forget the impassive, colorless face. Bara decided to kill Ronard if the opportunity presented itself.

Bara doubted that such an opportunity would ever arise. The fact that Ronard had not killed him was an ominous sign. The Vesder considered human intelligence to be inferior and useless. They preferred killing to interrogation and had little uses for prisoners unless the enemy seriously threatened their own hides. Considering the technological state of humans on this planet, Bara's life wouldn't have been spared as an ordinary Caonan citizen. Clearly, the Vesder had suspected his identity despite his efforts to conceal his lase-gun and knowledge of technology. Escape was impossible. As Bara had previously learned, the Vesders took their policy of genocide seriously.

Despite a growing sense of hopelessness, Bara decided to fight if he could. To languish passively in a Vesder prison would be a disgrace. Before expectations ebbed too far, he began scanning his environment looking for potential means of escape. There were none. The prison cell was large enough to stand five or six people and was surrounded by rock walls and a ceiling composed of solid mountain granite. Coarse pinkish nodules blended naturally with shadow, lighted only by a narrow beam of sunlight streaming down from a fist-sized, hollowed shaft. A sudden frigid gale blew down the opening and stirred up a robust population of dust particles. The dust danced within the beam of soft sunlight, each tiny body radiating like starlight. Bara managed to focus on the dust particles despite the pain coursing within his body. The stars had been a stable companions throughout the years allowing him solace and calm between battle. Now the dust served that same function.

Bara determined that he was about thirty feet underground by the length of the shaft. As expected, the granite rock walls were unyielding. An image of the great towering cliffs and spires came to mind as Bara examined the rock. Judging by the rock type and the frigid temperatures, Bara guessed that he was imprisoned somewhere underground within the Traqeqtoo mountains. He would not be easily found, assuming if anyone cared to look for him.

Yet who would look for him? Lonovina? Was she still alive? Bara told himself that he shouldn't care. His admiration for the her had made him careless. Yet Bara did care. He cared very much. He refused to think her dead and earnestly hoped that she would not be foolhardy enough to attempt a rescue. For what was a one woman against the Vesder? She would die quickly, he knew, probably picked off by Ronard's lase-gun.

Bara tensed with just the thought of General Ronard. Patient, intelligent, non-emotional and unmerciful, the General was not a man to be underestimated. Clearly, Ronard was an individual who's judgement would not have been clouded by the presence of a woman. Bara subdued a pang of self-directed anger and forced himself to consider the perfect traitor. Yet that was just the problem. Ronard seemed just a little too perfect. A man of high skill and intelligence would quickly recognize the deceitfulness of the Vesder. Their bargains were always too good to be true. Ronard would have nothing to gain through conspiracy except death. Bara realized that Ronard's sly, cool character was a facade. It had to be. The man, or thing, had to be an android, a very sophisticated work of robotics constructed and programmed by the Vesder. No human could have imitated Lonovina's voice with such accuracy. The thought sent chills down Bara's spine. If a small group of Vesders could program a convincing human android, there was no limit to what they might achieve on Yvia Voi. The entire human population would be defenseless against such a threat. Bara cursed the fact that he was the only person knowledgeable of Vesder technology and their human eradication policy. The existence of the human species, it seemed, was contingent on his survival.

Bara forced his attention on escape. He suspected that they were monitoring his movements and vital signatures electronically. It would be difficult, if impossible, for him to escape undetected. Not that breaking out of his cell was an option. His only chance to escape was to overpower his captors. The first step was to subdue the pain as it clouded focus and compromised reaction time. Like most autonomic functions, pain could be controlled consciously with the proper training in relaxation, meditation, and biofeedback. Bara was well practiced at most forms of self-control and could conquer even severe pain without a second thought. The key to success was the abandonment of a strong will; changing autonomic functioning could not be consciously forced. He closed his eyes, emptied his mind, and allowed a network of well learned, semiconscious commands to work their magic. Soon, the intense pounding pain diminished to a manageable throb.

The creases on Bara's face softened and the sweat on his forehead dried. Like a veil being lifted from his eyes, he gazed at his surroundings with new hope and conviction. Suddenly light flickered out of the corner of Bara's eye. He turned as large portion of the granite wall suddenly disappeared revealing a large, open, metallic door. The wall was a hologram. Bara reacted with blinding speed that would have confounded any mortal. General Ronard was not mortal, however. Feeling the butt of a Vesder lase-gun pressed into his mid section, Bara froze.

Ronard stared at Bara nonchalantly. The small but muscular frame neither trembled nor tightened. Bara gazed on the General's soft, milky-white flesh with anger and disappointment. Having lost the element of surprise, any future success was unlikely. These emotional expressions were mastered quickly, however, as Bara forced himself to focus on his next move.

"You woke early," Ronard stated. "I expected you to be in pain."

"I'm in a great deal of pain," Bara snapped. "I'm made out of tougher stuff than you realize."

The android said nothing.

"General, I know you don't trust me because I am a foreigner, a citizen of Mohasia. Nevertheless, my service to the Caonan Empire has been without question. If you question my loyalty, I'm sure there are more effective means to evaluate my intentions."

The android remained still and silent, observing the subject with mechanical precision.

"Look sir, I'm apologizing for my outburst. I'm very confused. I don't understand what is going on here, what I have seen, and why I am here. I believe any misunderstandings can be cleared up if you give me the chance to exonerate myself. At least give me some reply or ask me questions."

"I have no need to question you," Ronard said flatly. "Verbal interrogation, even when enhanced by torture, has long been an unreliable means of extracting accurate data. I will now introduce you to the one I serve. Do not move, or I will neutralize you as before."

"What does he want with me?"

"Her purpose, as I understand it, is something akin to a self-gratification."

Bara watched tensely as long thin shadows danced over the softly lit granite walls. A sweet musty smell circulated through the room causing Bara's nose to tingle. Slowly, a large oval shape glided through into dim light. Bara held his breath as the alien revealed itself by walking into the shaft of sunlight.

Standing three feet high, the Vesder stood rigidly like a statue made from solidified lava. A dark brown, glossy, synthetic shell scarred by age encased the body. A stubby hammer-like appendage pierced the shell. Oval in shape, black and inwardly curved, this appendage was a natural sonar system allowing the Vesder to maneuver without light. Other than ten lanky, beaded legs, the sonar device was the only noticeable feature to an otherwise featureless body.

Bara knew that the condition of a Vesder's shell was often associated with rank. The fact that a high-ranking Vesder was involved with a human was not encouraging. He would have to react calmly and with errorless precision. Yet the proximity of Bara's age-old enemy triggered images of his home planet choking beneath piles of rotting bodies. Only years of self-control prevented him from rushing the enemy, despite the consequences.

Unlike Ronard who seemed interested in data collection, the Vesder wasted little time on observation. The alien began speaking in a series of low-pitched clicks that resonated throughout the small chamber. An electronic voice, speaking in Ancient Terasian, quickly translated.

"No need for pretense, Terasian. You have seen my kind before. Now, it gives me pleasure to impart some personal information. I want you to know that the toxic gas introduced to your planet's atmosphere was slow acting. Your people died painfully slow. Yet you will die even worse, Terasian, just like your woman did."

Bara lost control and lunged at the Vesder with a consuming fury unleashed by a lifetime of hatred and loss. The Vesder, shocked by intensity of the attack, recoiled. Her actions were unnecessary, however, as Ronard's finger was faster. A flash of white consumed Bara's vision and sharp points of pain danced over his flesh. Bara quickly lost control over his muscles and collapsed.

"Your hatred satisfies me, Terasian. I will savor death tomorrow as a machine of delicate construction will eat your brain. You will be fully awake, of course, to experience your existence vanish one brain cell at a time."

Bara tried to move away from the voice but his body was unresponsive. Finally he heard a door slam shut as he was left lying on the cold granite floor. Although the pain quickly ebbed and his vision returned, Bara lacked the motivation to move. The Vesder had referred to an ICCS machine, otherwise known as an Intrusive Cerebral Cellular Scan. Directed by a powerful computer, slow acting chemicals are introduced into the central nervous system through the hypothalamus. Mildly corrosive, the chemicals emit radiation patterns specific to each cell's unique structure and makeup. The computer reads these pattern signatures and maps out the brain down to the subatomic level. Using this information, the brain is reproduced electronically. This is no small task considering that a trillion neurons and many more synaptic connections must be analyzed and reproduced. Furthermore, the machine must perform perfectly during first trial as the brain is sacrificed in the process.

Bara welcomed the frigid evening air that pierced his hungry body. He coughed and closed his eyes in helpless despair. "Hope" and "purpose" were now hollow words that seemed to mock his very existence. Bara knew that there would neither be hope for rescue nor escape. His birth suddenly seemed like a cruel twist of nature. What was the purpose, he wondered, to live a painful life only to die in utter humiliation? All his life he had sacrificed to preserve his family, friends, and people. These efforts had been wasted. Having lost everyone, he was now about to lose his own life.

Despair consumed Bara's soul like cancer. Even his overt hatred toward the Vesder seemed to smolder like some dying star. Without sophisticated equipment, he had no hope fighting a technologically advanced enemy. Like the rest of his species, the idea of future was meaningless.

Bara might have lost all track of time if not for the growing shadows of nightfall. The first of many arctic breezes wailing down the shaft and whipped his face. Bara welcomed nature's tormenter and hoped that he might succumb to a quiet death. He imagined the disappointment the Vesder would harbor as it found his frozen body lying on the floor, unresponsive. Yet Bara knew that they were monitoring him and would not allow his body to freeze to death before they encoded his brain into the ICCS data banks. To submit to an Intrusive Cerebral Cellular Scan would serve the enemy. His only hope, it seemed, was to find a quick alternative in dying.

Bara made the necessary internal adjustments and was only heartbeats away from immediate cardiac arrest. One conscious command to his artificial heart and the pain would be over. Bara formed the thought in his mind, yet hesitated. A faint spark resisted from deep within. Maybe it was a remnant of hope, or perhaps a kernel of fear. Whatever it was, Bara understood that it wasn't his time yet.

He eventually began slipping in and out of consciousness. Cold blue sunshine bathed Bara's face and reflected off his sweat like a thousand tiny mirrors. First the pain had returned, harsher and more intense than anything he had experienced before. He could have continued self-regulation but preferred the physical pain to attending to the pain in his soul. Delirium eventually overcame his mind as the pain continued to intensify. Visions of Lonovina played and replayed within his mind like an endless horror movie. Swimming in an ocean of her blood, Bara helplessly watched her being eaten alive by a small band of Varuk. Although their teeth ripped and shredded delicate flesh, she somehow continued to live. She screamed and continuously called out for mercy and sudden death. Receiving no reply, Lonovina began cursing Bara for abandoning her. These images were quickly replaced by others, of his parents being consumed by electrical fire, of his friends dying of slow poison. Although the characters changed, the theme did not. Everyone cried out for mercy. Everyone cursed Bara. Behind every image were the Vesders, standing silently, watching everything with sadistic relish.

The delirium became more bizarre as the night progressed, eventually ending in a jumbled series of unrelated images. Convulsing in pools of bloody sweat, his body had succumbed to fever. Consciousness returned fleetingly, however, as the ridge of his right foot suddenly surged with sharp, biting pain. Bara opened his eyes and bit his lip in revulsion. Through the shadows and dim nightlight, he observed that his right foot being eaten by a gorged, fluorescent green creature wrapped tightly around his ankle. Only ten inches in length, the creature had a voracious appetite for its size. The soft, beaded, translucent skin writhed rhythmically as six facial claws dug into his flesh. Between the hooks, straw-like appendages pulsated and sucked up the bloody scraps. Bara yanked the gorged creature of his foot and smashed it into the rocky wall.

"Take me now," Bara whispered hoarsely. His plea, as expected, went unanswered. God had abandoned him. It was time. It made no sense to let the torture continue. Before he could initiate the final act, however, Bara's mind slipped back into a state of delirium, or what seemed to be delirium.

Bara observed himself laying on the floor from a distance. It was as if his mind, or something like his mind, had separated from the rest of the body. Bara felt no pain, sorrow or fear. He only felt contentment and fleeting curiosity. A voice compelled him to gaze at his body lying sprawled across the floor bathed in blue light. Red, gold, and green plants started growing from the granite prison floor and caressed the body Bara vaguely recognized as his own. Bara attempted to judge distances, but could not. The granite prison walls had narrowed, twisted, and plunged into infinite depths.

Bara watched the body with decreasing interest. The darkness inside receded. Now he knew that he was not alone. He looked for the presence, found it everywhere, yet it was nowhere. Despite these novel circumstances, Bara accepted every oddity and inconsistency without question. The whole experience seemed real, felt natural, and was right. The room then darkened and a feeling of comfort overwhelmed Bara. He then entered into deep, painless, dreamless sleep.

"Wake up," a voice commanded. "Wake up," it repeated.

Bara opened his eyes. Ronard was gazing down at him impassively, his body glowing golden from a shaft of morning sunlight. Bara stared back at the android as if in a dream. The bulky substance, which he once called body, felt extraordinarily cumbersome. He yearned to reestablish the state of dissociation, but could not fathom its premise.

"Follow me," Ronard ordered. "I will now escort you to the ICCS machine."

Bara lifted himself upright. The pain was gone, oddly enough. Yet the cell appeared real, limited by time, thought and four walls. He turned and saw the Vesder standing underneath the metallic door, waiting patiently for Ronard to rouse her victim. Staring at the enemy, Bara suddenly realized just how frightened of death he had become. He had been frightened of the meaninglessness of it all, frightened of the unknown, and frightened of being completely alone. Yet he was not alone, nor had he ever been alone.

Rising to his feet, Bara obediently followed the Vesder through the metallic door, down a rocky corridor, and into an enclosed room. General Ronard followed three steps to Bara's rear and pointed a Vesder lase-gun toward his back. The enclosed room was not large, perhaps five by fifteen feet. Although the room was dark, a series of electronic devices was well lit by a wide red beam emitted from a fingernail-sized orb. Bara recognized the ICCS machine. The apparatus was defined by a half dozen, tall, closely aligned, slender pole-like structures surrounded by a thick electrostatic mesh. Near the center of the machine was a red metallic chair. On that chair was a dull, black helmet, a helmet of death.

The Vesder, for its part, ignored Bara as it became absorbed with various ICCS components. Four front legs busily crossed and circled a wide array of geometric shapes inlaid within the mesh. Its movements were enhanced, from Bara's perspective, by long, thin shadows dancing over the dimly lit walls. Yet he saw another shadow, partly hidden behind the ICCS equipment that was unrecognizable.

"Sit in the chair," Ronard commanded.

Despite his prior calm, Bara began to sweat with fear. Gathering the strength from one last deep breath, the words of self-destruction began forming on his lips.

CHAPTER 14

Lonovina had never defended herself against an attack with such desperation. She gripped her sword so tightly that her knuckles turned white. Despite a growing feeling of terror, Lonovina stood her ground. She held her sword high in the air as the blade gleamed silvery-white in the moonlight, poised to unleash first blood.

Ten black, bulky shapes steadily crept closer. Thick taloned arms and deadly spines cut into the starlight like slicing knives. Grunts and high-pitched squeals reverberated through nearby canyons. Thirty red eyes gleamed malevolently from every side and hot steamy compounds poured out from gaseous mouths. Lonovina could feel their wet, hot, sticky breath as it condensed on her skin. Although the stink made her nauseous, her resolve was unshakable. She would fight to the death. She would die with honor.

Ten Varuk bodies quickly converged, their massive bodies blotting out the starry evening sky. The animals began squealing fervently as their anticipation heightened. Lonovina attempted strategy, but failed. Her thoughts had frozen without form, gripped by the clutches of terror that dominated both body and soul. Then instinct took over. Years of training allowed her to move with blinding speed. She ducked, turned, and struck every moving object that violated personal space. Long arms swiped at her from every angle, but for the time being failed to reach their mark. Time seemed to slow as the battle continued. The air became filled with smells of blood as Lonovina continued to defend herself with a strength that surprised her. Yet the battle was never in question. The long-clawed arms reached ever closer as Lonovina's strength began to wane.

Engaged in fighting two Varuk, another animal suddenly rushed Lonovina from behind. She turned, parried, but was too late. A strong black hand slammed into her forehead and she fell to the ground like a rock. Unconscious for a moment, Lonovina awoke to a host of red gleaming eyes staring down at her from above. Foul gas belched out of ten wide gaping mouths and hot drool poured down on her like acid rain.

Lonovina could see individual faces clearly now. To her surprise, everything was ghoulishly illuminated by a familiar, glowing, red light emanating from her neck. A descending massive palm crowned with three clawed fingers quickly obscured her vision, however. The palm fit snugly

125

over her face, was about to squeeze, but then let go. A terrifying shriek pierced the night and was followed by nine more. A thousand branches of red lightening blinded her from the attackers. The air was so filled with electricity that it caused her hair to stand on end. Then all was silent.

Lonovina sat up in astonishment. She glared at ten Varuk scattered motionlessly on the ground. Most had been burnt beyond recognition. Although dead, their thick bodies still appeared malevolent to her in the harsh, glowing, red light. Lonovina glanced down and saw her jewel necklace glowing radiantly between her breasts. The light quickly dimmed, however, then flickered and became dark..

Lonovina was too stunned to move and waited for her nerves to calm. Once her shaking subsided and her breathing slowed, Lonovina lifted herself upright and walked into the gray shades of night. She wandered some distance, just far enough to escape the smell of burnt flesh, and bedded herself beneath a sheltered alcove. Lonovina told herself that she was too exhausted to stumble aimlessly around in the dark. She would pick up Ronard's trail in the morning.

Despite her fatigue, nagging questions robbed her of much needed sleep. She wondered why the jewel had defended her, how it knew her life was in danger, and if there was a larger purpose to it's existence. The jewel had saved her life once before. In the attack on the streets of Glorovina, it had defended her with the same, blinding electrical fire. The creature had perished instantly; the body had been transformed into a pile of ash. These two events disturbed Lonovina greatly, not because of the danger, but of what they signified. Forces far beyond all comprehension were at work now. And for some unfathomable reason they had involved her.

Lonovina had initially minimized the importance of the first attack. The creature, she assumed, was nothing more than an unknown wild animal. The jewel, furthermore, was nothing more than a magical relic forgotten by the Old Ones. She now considered these conclusions invalid, her former logic a desperate ploy to control her fear over the unknown. Bara had made it possible for her to realize that the jewel worked on complex physical principles she neither understood nor controlled. And the creature was not a strange animal, but a citizen from another world capable of destroying her and everything she valued. Bara had called the danger by name. He had called it a Vesder.

Lonovina wasn't sure why the Vesder were here on her world. Her discovery of the jewel, it seemed, might be connected with their appearance somehow. The temporal order of events could not have been coincidental. Or could they? Lonovina shook her head. No, the jewel had protected her twice, acting in accordance with an alien purpose. Caught within a conflict between worlds, Lonovina had no idea what was expected of her. All her life she had manipulated and controlled people for personal gain and the greater good. Her actions were compensation, in part, for the disdain and rejection she suffered from the voices and hands of others. Ironically, the tables had been turned. Now she was the one who felt manipulated, and she didn't like it.

Lonovina now regretted her fascination with the Old Ones. For years she dreamed of living within a wider reality. An inner need had tainted her curiosity to escape loneliness and the mundane. Now that she was part of that wider reality, she had lost control. Only Bara seemed to know the answers. The wider reality, after all, was his reality. If only there had been more time.

"I will find him," she vowed. "It's too dark to track him tonight, but I will find Bara if it takes my last breath to do so."

Lonovina woke from a deep and dreamless sleep. A cold wind stung her unprotected cheeks. Although the larger sun was peeking over the eastern horizon, the first rays of day did little to penetrate the frigid morning air. Lonovina rubbed her numb face and hands fervently, perceived an uncomfortable tingling, but felt little else except a nagging hunger within her stomach. She ignored it the best she could and scanned her position.

Gazing through a swirling cloud of her steamy breath, Lonovina surveyed kilometers of earth and stone below which jutted above the valley-lands. Directly behind her loomed vertical cliffs separated by shallow fingers of loose rock, crusted snow, and sky. From Lonovina's perspective, the cliffs looked like jagged teeth poised to snap at the heavens. The red moon was still high in the western sky, but had lost much of it's grander to the brilliance to the dawn.

Bushes with long, tangled, orange streamers dominated the area. Giant Looma trees grew abundantly not far below. The normally white bark was now tinged yellow by the early morning light. As her lungs strained to breathe the thin air, Lonovina guessed that she stood more than ten thousand feet above sea level. It seemed very odd that Ronard would carry Bara to such an inhospitable place so far from civilization. She doubted that his actions involved the Caonan Army. It was more likely that Ronard had been conspiring with the enemy, the Vesder.

Lonovina retraced her steps and quickly picked up Ronard's trail. His footsteps, deeply imprinted into the soil, were not hard to find. She hoped to catch him by day's end, assuming, of course, that the heavy weight he carried would slow Ronard. To Lonovina's surprise, the tracks climbed steadily into the mountain and then skirted the base of the mountain's top jutting cliffs. Ronard, it seemed, was heading nowhere fast.

The tracks continued for about another mile, headed over open ground, and then stopped. Lonovina cursed beneath her breath. Eyes narrowed, she crouched low toward the ground and meticulously examined the nearby soil. Nothing.

"Impossible," she whispered. "He could not have just vanished." A sudden rustle in the underbrush caused Lonovina to jump. She whirled into a defensive position, only to face a small four-legged creature, no bigger than her hand, dart into a nearby bush. Sighing with relief, she resumed her search.

Lonovina scoured the area for clues, no matter how insignificant. She searched for bent twigs, matted grass, and prints. Nothing. Her circle of investigation grew, but still she found nothing. Her heart sank as the sun continued to rise. There was no sense to go on. Ronard had accomplished the impossible. He had vanished, seemingly, into the mountain air. Yet Lonovina could not, would not, give up.

Frustrated, Lonovina propped herself over a rock and prayed for guidance. The day was just becoming comfortable as the sun had just reached it's zenith. The sky was a clear blue. Gentle, cool breezes brushed against her skin, and a grand silence seemed to stretch far beyond the rolling landscape below. Giant Looma trees blended as a mat of green flowing into the nearby valley-lands. Tinges of brown dominated the undulating distances until cut off by a thin band of hazy, blue, ocean. Red and tan colors dominated the distant south. These colors were marked by dark lined patterns of shadow revealing countless gorges and canyons. To the north were distant bluish-purple mountains and the green plains of Garion.

Lonovina admitted that the view was breathtaking. There was something mysterious about nature that allowed her to relax, even now. Yet a darker and more debilitating state began to infiltrate her mind and body, namely depression. Having always combated despair with activity, Lonovina quickly searched for something to do. She reached into her coat pocket and examined the smaller of the two black casements taken from Bara's quarters. She picked through the contents gingerly with wide eyes.

The small casement revealed a small, oval device that fit neatly into her palm. Made out of some alien substance, the material was reflective like mirrored glass, strong like metal, and light as cloth. A small depression interrupted the dorsal end of the smooth, curved surface. The area glowed faintly orange as Lonovina brushed her finger across the indentation. She applied more pressure and the glow intensified. Suddenly, the tip of the object emitted a purple stream of light. Lonovina heard a strange crackling noise in the distance and immediately dropped the weapon in astonishment. The ray of light, she soon discovered, had burned a hole three centimeters in diameter into a nearby cliff. Lonovina peered into the small opening and only found a black residue inside.

"Goka!" she muttered quietly. Clearly, Bara had not overstated the technological advancements of his people. The power beneath her fingertips could have easily cut through a small army of Varuk. But it had not been enough, apparently, to protect Bara from the Vesder.

"The Vesder," she muttered. The word stuck in her mouth like a resin. Although Lonovina had no idea of who or what she was facing, she did recognize the danger of an invisible enemy. Powerful enough to destroy Bara's world, the Vesder could certainly destroy her. Yet Lonovina didn't care about her own life. She was not afraid to die, for what was life without love? As for her, Bara was the only individual who could love her. His safety was more important than her own, more important than anything was. But to save him, she would have to destroy, or at least immobilize, the enemy. Somehow, she would have to face and conquer the larger reality in which she now lived. But for the moment, that reality superceded her ability to function effectively. Ronard had disappeared with the one person she cared about and Lonovina had no idea where to find him. She searched the rest of the day for more clues, but found nothing. As darkness descended, Lonovina decided to continue her search the next day. She would return to Glorovina hoping that she might find Ronard there.

Lonovina slept poorly and woke with the morning sun. Just before she was about to leave, movement caught her eye. Lonovina quickly ducked behind a thick clump of green grass and tangled purple streamers. Perhaps fifteen meters away, she watched in disbelief as a figure emerged from the ground. But there was no hole, no entrance. It lifted itself from the ground like a tree rapidly growing out of the rocky soil. Lonovina gasped in horror and terrible memories filled her mind. The emerging entity was not alive. It was the living dead.

Lonovina suppressed her fear. The entity, she reminded herself, was not really a corpse but a machine. Like her jewel, it was nothing more than a piece of complex technology. Lonovina was sick of technology. It did not belong in her world, this power, previously reserved for the gods. Yet Bara was not a god. He was a man, flesh and blood like any other. If Bara could understand and use this technology then so could she. Lonovina gripped Bara's weapon and pointed it at the gray, thin flesh of the living dead. The soft glowing orange light beckoned her to fire. Yet the thing ignored her, turned southward, and walked in the direction of the dead Varuk.

Lonovina realized that Vesder had sent the android to collect her jewel. The Varuk would have no interest in the artifact. They would have eaten her corpse quickly and discarded the rest. Clearly the Vesder had anticipated Lonovina following General Ronard and arranged the attack. The more Lonovina thought about it, the more it all made sense. She was still a very powerful political figure with influential connections. But no one would investigate an attack by the Varuk and they would never question Ronard. The traitorous General would maintain his position of influence to finish destroying the Caonan Empire. Lonovina realized that she had been set up to take the blame for the slaughter at Traqeqtoo Fortress. Her flight into the mountains would be an admission of guilt and her death would be rejoiced by the multitudes.

Waiting until the living dead was far out of sight, Lonovina quietly made her way down to where the living dead had first emerged. A workable plan began forming in her mind. Lonovina remembered the phantasm in the cave. Bara had called it a hologram. Assuming the Vesder possessed such technology, they may have used a hologram to create a false impression of earth. To test her hypothesis, Lonovina prodded the questionable area with a stick.

Lonovina smiled as the stick penetrated the ground without resistance. She had beaten the Vesder at their own game. By underestimating her fundamental understanding of technology, she had exposed their deception. She had gained an element of surprise. The enemy had been too overconfident. But the battle had not yet won. The stick only penetrated so far into the ground. Gingerly Lonovina reached into the hole and felt a metal gate. There was a bulge at one side, perhaps a lock. Lonovina aimed Bara's weapon and fired. Curls of smoke emerged from the illusionary rocky soil followed by a muffled clang of metal. The gateway had opened.

Lonovina wasted no time entering the enemy's lair feet first. A series of metallic wrings allowed her to descend quickly down a cylindrical shaft into the unknown abyss. She could imagine General Ronard waiting patiently somewhere in the cold blackness. Yet she only perceived the pounding of her own heartbeat. Finally her feet touched bottom.

Lonovina entered a room of unknown size and character. Wiping the sweat off her brow, she crawled cautiously over a floor of coarse, cold, granite toward a shimmering red light in the distance. Despite her stealth, she had to wonder if alien eyes weren't watching her through the darkness.

Movement! Lonovina stopped cold. A voice! It was speaking an alien tongue, but clearly belonged to General Ronard. Muffled vibrations! Footsteps were heading her way. Quickly, Lonovina changed directions and scurried beneath a maze of metallic structures. Her escape, she soon realized, was not a moment too soon. The shimmering red light suddenly intensified. Emanating from a small round orb, the eerie light revealed a room filled with alien gadgetry. Long slender poles rose ominously above her and strange metallic mesh surrounded her on all sides. Lonovina lightly bit her lip in silence. Her bite drew blood, however, when the Vesder entered the chamber.

The Vesder was a hideous creature. Propelled by ten beaded legs, it lacked eyes, a nose, or any other recognizable feature. A dark brown shell defined most of the monster, save for strange convoluted, oval shaped, appendages fixated at the top of its body. Black in color, deep groves criss-crossed and covered the thick appendage with thin reddish-brown hairs bristling on end. A sweet musty smell also permeated the air causing Lonovina's nose to tingle. Lonovina noted movement behind the creature and realized that Bara was walking into the chamber!

Bara followed the alien without any sign of resistance. His eyes stared straight ahead without expression and his face looked haggard. Tears formed in Lonovina's eyes. Completely expressionless, he looked like a man who had abandoned all reason and hope.

Bara limped slowly across the floor; clearly they had tortured him. Yet he was alive! Although his appearance saddened and frightened Lonovina, she felt an undercurrent of joy. Her actions had not been completely in vain. There was still hope.

Aiming a weapon at Bara, Ronard was the only enemy who appeared armed. He would have to be eliminated first. Lonovina lifted Bara's light gun and pointed it at the android. She placed her index finger over the trigger and fired.

CHAPTER 15

Recognizing that his heart had stopped, Bara subdued a momentary feeling of panic and reflexively gasped for air. Suicide was a surprising act for a man who had always found a way to cheat death. But after last night, Bara decided not to cheat death anymore. The Vesder would have stolen his mind and then murdered his body. It would be much worse, Bara had reasoned, to continue without integrity and honor. Although a part of him might have gained immortality, Bara would become little different from Ronard, a soulless machine serving the enemy. No, suicide was the only acceptable answer. The time was right.

A warm sensation flowed through Bara's body as his knees began to give way. Although his mind seemed dulled and clouded, he felt a peace that surprised him. Death was not the cold and lonely experience he had once anticipated. It was a stage of life no less abhorrent than any other.

Bara had mentally prepared himself for the unexpected. Yet he was astounded to discover a purple ray streaming inches from his body. Someone, apparently, was firing at Ronard! Bara launched his artificial heart into motion and reestablished blood flow. The needed burst of energy was late in coming, however. Crashing to his knees, he managed to twist far enough around to face the onslaught. A brilliant white fire indicated where the android was being hit. Slicing rapidly at a downward angle, the narrow beam had entered slightly below the chest cavity and exited just above the hip. Standing rigidly on it's feet, Ronard's upper torso teetered momentarily like an unbalanced boulder. Sparks flew as the upper body slumped off and crashed into the hard granite floor.

"Stop right there!" a familiar voice commanded. Bara turned and couldn't believe that Lonovina was aiming a lase-gun at the fleeing Vesder. The creature stopped, wavered for a moment, and then lowered its body in surrender.

Relaxed and steady, Lonovina faced the alien with a fearless, confident air. Lonovina's jewel sparkled brilliantly in the dim alien light as if it had gained a life of its own.

Bara thought she looked magnificent. He had never expected a rescue, especially by a woman who came from a technological backward world. How Lonovina managed to penetrate through the alien defenses was simply beyond his comprehension. No doubt she had faced near impossible odds to save him. Bara felt ashamed. He had chided himself for becoming trapped by emotional involvement. True, he had become increasingly careless. Yet there was more to life than self-preservation. Survival had little meaning, he realized, without living beyond oneself. Lonovina, a woman filled with so much emotional buoyancy, had learned that somehow. Her actions spoke of true personal commitment and unselfish love.

Bara shifted his eyes toward the cowering enemy. It represented, to some degree, what he loathed within himself. The Vesder were united in defending a lifestyle of complete selfishness. Ambitions, solitude, hate, and personal safety was the concepts they understood best. Bara was also familiar with these qualities and grimaced in self-directed anger. He realized that he should have died with his people and not sought refuge within the safe confines of his ship, living alone, following his own course, and saving his own skin.

Bara stopped berating himself and redirected his anger toward the enemy. It was the Vesder, after all, who had been responsible for what he had become. That was not completely true, a part of him realized, but it felt good to believe it anyway.

"You lied to me," Bara stated, confronting the enemy with a hint of pleasure. "The woman is still alive."

As expected, the Vesder did not respond. Bara glared at it for a moment before returning his gaze toward Lonovina. "I can't believe that it's really you! It's wonderful to see you, Lonovina."

"And you. Are you all right?"

"Yes. And . . . thank you."

Lonovina struggled to respond, but said nothing. It was enough that her posture eased. He wasn't sure, but Bara thought he saw a tear shimmer from the corner of her eye.

"So, what do I do with this . . . thing?" she asked.

"I'll take care of it." Feeling his strength return, Bara lifted himself upright, grabbed Ronard's loose weapon, and hobbled toward the enemy. "You look nervous," he stated smiling at the shifting Vesder. "Identity yourself."

Four front legs responded in dance. An orchestra of clicks echoed through the chambers and was soon followed by a droning electronic translator. "You won't gain anything from me, Terasian."

Bara shrugged. "I will get what I'm after, one way or another."

"Unlike humans, we are loyal to our own. We do not submit to torture. Or don't you know us?"

"I know you," Bara replied making fine adjustments on Ronard's weapon. He aimed carefully and fired. A burst of a small purple beam cut into the left side of the Vesder's shell and the creature began to convulse. Bara approached the alien. The Vesder crawled away slowly, writhing in pain, and leaving a trail of brackish, reddish-brown blood.

Hearing Lonovina clear her throat, Bara glanced back at her. She glared at him with hostility, clearly uncomfortable with his blatant display of sadistic behavior. Like a mirror, her facial expression of contempt reflected his barbarism. Yet Bara couldn't help continuing, his hatred ran too deep. As for Lonovina, there was no question about her loyalty. With this in mind, Bara temporarily discarded the unnecessary guilt and returned to his prey.

"Oh, I know you all too well," he continued. "And spare me any talk about loyalty. You work together. I'll grant you that. But you work united in destroying everything that is sacred. I hear a billion people screaming for justice, Vesder. Some of those people, mind you, are my family. They will have it, as long as I breathe air!"

The Vesder began to slow as it continued to lose blood. Bara stepped before it's path before it could reach the far corner of the ICCS machine. "I will have it," he whispered, "because I know how to obtain it. I, alone, know your one true weakness, you see. Consider yourself fortunate, Vesder. Unlike me, you will not have to see your species perish." The Vesder made a feeble attempt to pounce at Bara but landed squarely on its side. Bara slowly lifted his lase-gun and fired. A broad purple beam cut instantly through the synthetic shell. The creature quivered for a moment and then ceased all movement.

Bara lowered his head. It was one thing to destroy from the distance of a ship, but it was quite another thing to destroy a life face to face and enjoy it. Bara was unable to glance upwards and confront Lonovina's reproach. He was about to turn away from the woman when he felt a warm hand squeeze his shoulder. Timidly, he looked up into Lonovina's deep, purple eyes.

"Hey, it's alright," she said.

Bara nodded, turned, and hugged her tightly. Tears began to stream down Lonovina's face as her body melted into his. Even Bara's eyes began to water for the first time since his father had died so many years ago.

"I thought I lost you," she said trying to hold back the tears.

"Never," Bara whispered. "You wouldn't let them."

Lonovina shook her head, choked a sob, and hugged him again. Bara held her tightly and was overwhelmed by the warmth of her body and the softness of her thick black hair.

"We had better think about moving on," she stated with calm confidence and released her embrace. "Another of the living dead, or machine, will be back soon, assuming others aren't already here."

"No, we are alone. But I am all for leaving this. . . what is the matter?"

"Ronard!" she gasped.

Bara turned and faced the General. Unwavering eyes stared back at him with silent intrusiveness. No wonder Lonovina was frightened! It's not every day that a corpse stares back at you from a severed body.

"It's all right," Bara whispered. "Ronard is a machine, like the living dead. I will take care of it."

Lonovina stayed her distance as Bara limped toward the android. He stopped just beyond arms reach, crouched to the floor, and looked into the impassive, milky-white face.

"Ronard, can you understand me?"

The soft grey eyes stared at Bara without concern. "Yes," it said.

"What is your next program sequence?"

"To self destruct."

"Kill us?"

"I cannot. The laser disrupted all of my primary energy cells. I lack the power to implode."

Bara nodded. Lonovina, gaining in confidence, timidly approached closer.

"Ronard, were you programmed by an ICCS machine?"

"Yes."

"Elaborate."

"Most of my higher fluid functions were downloaded through the ICCS computer behind you."

Bara nodded, opened his mouth to speak, but hesitated. A part of him didn't want the answer to his next question. "Ronard . . . who were you before the initial ICCS transformation?"

"I was known as Jaranthia, Code 2 functionary of the Terasian battle fleet Extermentrey."

Bara lifted his eyebrows and sucked in his breath. "I know you," he whispered. Bara probed the android's face, searching for anything familiar, but found nothing. Bara continued, "I want you to know that I had admired . . . do admire your military genius and dedication to the Terasian resistance."

Bara knew that the android Ronard would not respond, but it was worth a try anyway. Jaranthia had been a close associate, admired by anyone who understood military strategy. The tactical genius was still there, but it lacked little else of human value. Bara realized that he had been only minutes away from becoming just like Jaranthia, a servant of the devil. Whom would he have killed indiscriminately? Lonovina? Bara wondered what Jaranthia would have done if he had known his fate.

"I remember you," a voice cut into the silence. "They have encoded many old anagrams. I do not understand the significance of the human emotion, however, but I know that I did once like you. Perhaps you can explain?"

"No," Bara replied uneasily, "we no longer share a common point of reference."

Jaranthia nodded.

"Jaranthia, listen to me! I don't want you to self-destruct. I don't want to you to expire that way. You must not sacrifice yourself to the enemy."

"Not feasible. I am programmed . . . "

"Then why have you waited?"

Silence.

"Let me end it for you. You tell me when."

A powerful hush filled the room as Bara waited with restless anticipation. "Your request is permissible," Jaranthia said at last. "You may terminate now."

Bara lifted the Ronard's lase-gun, turned his head, and fired. Ronard's upper torso jerked, went limp and remained motionless on the floor. Bara should have been relieved, but he felt only sorrow. He would have sacrificed much to breathe life into this machine! But that was impossible, no one could resurrect the dead. What disturbed Bara more was the possibility of additional Jaranthias. He forced his gaze from the nonfunctional android and fired at the ICCS equipment with his lase-gun. The vast complex of machinery burst into flame and fell into a pile of twisted blackened metal. The equipment destroyed, Bara sat silently on the cold floor, mesmerized by the display of flying sparks and electrical flame.

"Are you all right?" Lonovina probed gently.

"This," he replied pointing to Ronard, "is the legacy of my people."

"And mine, if we don't do something."

"Yes," he mumbled. "And do it fast."

"I feel so helpless! How do we fight such a powerful enemy? What do we do now?"

"We must find my ship," Bara answered.

CHAPTER 16

"Where is my mother?" the little girl asked. "Where is my father?"

The large red headed woman didn't answer. She continued washing her clothes as if the little girl didn't exist.

"Why aren't you answering me!" the little girl demanded and stamped her feet in protest. Receiving no acknowledgment, the girl sat in frustration. It was then that she noticed the sound of a creaking door. Back and forth the door went. Sometimes it would screech horribly, especially when a strong gust blew into their hovel.

"I wish that creaking would go away!" the little girl screamed. The old woman stopped cold and turned. Her face was pale and obese. Sloughs of fatty skin rapidly peeled from her cheeks and drifted to the floor. Her eyes were so deeply sunken into the fat that only part of her dark orbs could be seen. But those orbs could not be mistaken for any other. They were ice cold, those eyes.

The little girl was pleased that the woman was finally paying attention to her. Even negative attention was better than being ignored. How long had they neglected her? Forever, it seemed. But wait, the woman wasn't looking at her at all. She was focused on the creaking door.

The creaking door. The little girl hated the creaking door. Set within mud-packed walls, the creaking door was made out of black tree branches loosely tied by string. There was nothing else of interest in the room, so the little girl had to put up with the constant noise.

Suddenly an old man appeared. Thin and haggard, the man hobbled to a tree stump that had also materialized. He slowly sat and looked off in the distance.

"Where is my mommy? Where is my daddy?" the little girl asked.

The old man looked at the little girl and smiled. Two dark teeth protruded from brown swollen gums. "Go and play with your friends, Lonovina."

"But no one will play with me."

"Why not?"

Not knowing the answer, the girl began to cry.

"I'll tell you why, little one. You have no friends because you have flaws in your character."

YVIA VOI: LAND OF GRACE

"How can one girl be so ugly?" the old woman added. The old couple began to laugh.

"Stop it! Stop it! I want my mommy! I want my daddy!"

The old man and woman grew serious. After a moment of frightening silence, the old man spoke. "If you want to find your parents child, you must walk through the creaking door."

A chilling breeze flowed underneath the door and blew the little girl's hair into tangles. The little girl brushed several long, black, strands from her eyes and stared at the door. Mysteriously, the door began to creak louder.

"No," the girl cried. "I don't want to go out there."

"But you must if you want to find your parents," the old man cackled.

Timidly, the small girl approached the door. The creaking became louder and louder as if it had anticipated her arrival. The girl began to shiver and stopped in fright.

"Go on Lonovina," the man barked.

"Yes, go on child," the woman added.

Lonovina opened the creaking door. Intense blue light streamed in and forced her to shut her eyes. A strong gust picked her up and dropped her into an endless black pit.

Lonovina shrieked in terror. Tumbling as she fell, the little girl could see the creaking door in the distance. It was swinging madly as she dropped farther away from it's influence. There was nothing else except a harsh, hazy, blue light and the black pit.

The sounds of laughter filled her ears. It was the old couple, she knew. But there was something strangely familiar about the laughter. The sounds tugged some chord within her. Then she knew. The old couple was her parents.

The air became colder and colder as she kept falling. The creaking door was only a speck now. Lonovina called out to her parents. "Forgive me," she cried. Receiving no reply, Lonovina continued to shriek.

"Lonovina! Wake up," a booming voice said breaking her nightmare. Lonovina opened her eyes with a jolt. The blue-colored radiance had disappeared and was replaced by a softer shade of blue. The world was no longer a formless pit. Individual trees, bathed in familiar light, could easily be discriminated. The blue night sun was sitting low in the sky and red

140

moon was at its zenith. Lonovina oriented herself toward the voice and found Bara sitting close by her side.

"You were moaning in your sleep," he said with concern.

Lonovina relaxed, closed her eyes, and breathed deeply. "I was dreaming," she said softly. "I was dreaming about my parents."

"Your parents?"

"Not my real parents, of course. I didn't know my real parents. Yet they seemed real in my dream."

"It's alright now."

Lonovina sat up and found comfort in Bara's arms. Although camped at the base of the Traqeqtoo Mountains, it was still very cold. Lonovina pressed her head deeply into his chest. Bara relaxed under her weight, stroked her hair, and then drifted off to sleep. Lonovina recognized his need to recover from his captivity by the Vesder. Lonovina didn't want to wake him, but she desperately needed to talk. The dream had made her feel insecure. She needed to be reassured.

"Are you going to return to your world?" Lonovina asked.

"Hmm?"

"Do you want to return to your world?"

Bara stiffened. "No," he replied shifting slightly. "There is nothing left for me there."

"Do you plan to travel to other worlds then?"

"Perhaps. Why do you ask?"

"I need to know where I stand. If you leave, will you take me?"

"Yes, but I would feel uncomfortable uprooting you. It would be a difficult transition."

"Uproot me then!"

"Why don't you think about it first? You might change your mind."

"I'm holding you to your word, Bara."

"You have it."

"Are you sure?"

"Do you trust me?"

Lonovina sighed. "I trust you more than anyone else."

"But not enough."

"I'm sorry. I'm disappointing you. I have not had much success with intimacy, you see. I think I have been hurt too much. My dream pointed that out to me. Strange, isn't it? Although my dream was fictional, the theme might have been more honest than my waking thoughts."

Bara gently kissed the top of her head. "Your wounds will heal. You will have scars, of course, but that is enough for me. I accept you the way you are."

Lonovina digested Bara's response and smiled. After a moment of silence she asked, "Do you think I'm right to distrust other people? I mean, even the best intentioned people hurt the people they love."

"True. But perhaps that is why trust is so special. Without risk, trust would be as common as the handshake."

"I never thought about it that way. I suppose happiness in relationships is based on trust. Yet I still think that most people aren't worth the risk."

"Yes."

"Trust would have killed me in the orphanage. Only the strongest and most independent survived there. I found the same to be true in business."

"How long did you live in the orphanage?"

"They brought me there as a baby, just another child abandoned by uncaring parents."

"Well, you already know what I believe."

"I would like to believe you, Bara. But even the Xusu, if they are anything like me, are human. Perhaps they didn't love me. How do I know? I never met my parents. How can I be sure?"

"Xusu would not abandon their children. To my knowledge, that has never happened on my planet."

"Then my parents are dead," she stated.

Bara responded with silence and began stroking her long black hair. Lonovina snuggled closer and soaked up his warmth. "Do you know what is odd?" she whispered.

"What?"

"I've only known you for only three weeks, and yet you are the closest thing to family I've ever had."

"I can honestly say the same thing," Bara added.

Lonovina squeezed him tightly and yawned. "I should let you sleep," she said. "You must be tired and your foot needs to heal."

"Yes, but I heal quickly. I'm honored that you choose to confide in me. Perhaps you trust me more than you realize."

"Perhaps," Lonovina returned, looked up, and smiled. "One other small question has been bothering me, however."

"What is that?"

"Who are the Vesder?"

"Well, I'm glad you are keeping to small questions," Bara replied with a chuckle.

"It can wait."

"Sufficed it to say, Lonovina, the Vesder are very different."

CHAPTER 17

The subterranean chamber was cool, moist, and silent. Although Tara-tah was incapable of disobedience, she longed for the silent refuge of her corridors. She fantasized sitting in the smallest chamber, surrounded by prickly walls, silence, and electrostatic tinglers.

"Speak," a voice clicked.

Tara-tah scanned the nearby body with her sonar. Harar loomed before her like some perched god. Tara-tah found her long undulating body wonderfully bumpy. She was also impressed that Tara-Tah's Latet organ bristled with plenty of reddish brown hair. Harar moved back as Tara-Tah's ten beaded legs, plump with fat and ripe with lethal poison, hugged the rocky, mud-encrusted chamber. As menacing as Harar looked, the old Vesder did not frighten Tara-tah. The craggy lines in her body fostered awe, certainly. The electrostatic gadgets bursting from nearby chambers indicated wealth and success, obviously. And the abundance of brittle, triangular, fluorescent, green roots generated respect. Nevertheless, a Harar would never hurt a Tara-tah clone. The two cloned populations had developed a symbiotic relationship throughout the centuries; the Harar being the giver of purpose, and the Tara-tah being the fulfiller of that purpose.

"I ask for information," Tara-tah clicked.

"Be brief."

"Your demeanor merits solitude, Wise One. I would not disturb these precious months of solitude, but a lack of clear purpose agitates me. I need to speak with you at length, if you can withstand the necessary interpersonal contact."

Harar began to fidget and then expanded her beaded legs in agitation. "If you are willing to sacrifice your peace, then so am I. I have granted your request. We will continue communicating between walled chambers."

"Of course. I expect nothing less. I appreciate your edict of privacy."

Tara-tah squeezed through an elastic tunnel. Smooth sticky walls clung to her nodule skin like wet mud. Electrostatic tinglers shocked and caressed her body from every side. Without any open space the fit was perfect. Basking in the wet, silent world, Tara-tah felt revived for the first time in days. She fantasized about staying there forever and reflecting on her own genetic glory but eventually realized that escaping her problems wouldn't solve anything.   Solitude and omnipotence were illusive concepts, tantalizing ideals yet to be obtained.

Shivering with disillusionment, Tara-tah entered into Chamber 87. She brushed her body against the surrounding oval walls, and manipulated a complex pattern of mesh and electrical fields.   "As I was saying," an electronic voice now clicked, "I lack purpose."

"Explain Tara-tah?"

"The end of the human wars, it has . . . left a void."   Tara-tah realized that her clicks were too fast.   Harar would immediately sense her lack of control and report it to the High Consciousness.

"Why?"

"There are too many choices. I was focused during the war. But now."

"You cannot handle the freedom?"

"Precisely.   But you are the giver of meaning, Harar.   Give me direction."

"I have none to give you."

Tara-tah began to fidget.   "The destruction of the humans had proved our superiority.   We are unique!   Imagine an intelligent species actually evolving above ground, groveling underneath the sun, roaming vast spaces without any respect for enclosed space, security, and solitude."

"But we destroyed the humans, Tara-tah. They were the perfect enemy and we were victorious.   Why the anger?"

"You do not feel anger, Harar?"

Silence.

"I thought so.   Perhaps it is because the humans never worshiped us?"

"Do you want the truth?" Harar clicked.

"I am the fulfiller of your purpose but have nothing to fulfill.   I require an answer if I am to serve you."

"Let me ask you a question.   Have we really gained omnipotence?"

"Yes, everyone knows that.   Superiority, after all, was the goal, but I begin to understand the paradox, Harar.   I felt a void after we destroyed all serviceable life on Vesder, just as I do now with the humans.   Nevertheless, why should I feel a void if we have obtained ultimate meaning?   The conclusion is obvious.   The universe may not have purpose.   Yet our need for an ultimate purpose persists.   Philosophy does not quench my hungry spirit."

"Perhaps increased penance will help?"

YVLA VOI: LAND OF GRACE

"I doubt it. Penance has gone awry, anyway. The High Consciousness had been erratic since the human wars. The machine had been flooding the populace indiscriminately without regard to collective holiness."

"You are brave, Tara-tah. Few challenge the High Consciousness without knowing the possible consequences?"

"You know that I am not challenging the machine. The High Consciousness has conditioned me too long against individualistic behavior. Conformity is my life. It is holy. Jamming the signals would be unthinkable."

"Of course. I'm sure you speak for all Vesders, but you are also correct in your assessment. The images have always been punishing and erratic. I wonder if our species is being reconditioned."

"To do what? To be what? The machine has shaped everything I do. We have lived a life conditioned by noxious images and pleasant tinglers. Now that the system has failed, I must ask why. Perhaps we are not being reconditioned into some purposeful, holy, direction. Perhaps we are being rewarded and punished aimlessly."

"You are more individualistic then you credit yourself."

"Not by choice, Harar. Forgive me if I speak blasphemy, but we are at a turning point in history. Where is the High Consciousness taking us? Will it give us purpose? Harar, I need purpose!"

"You know that I cannot answer your questions. Only the operators know the machine."

"But who are these operators?"

"I don't know, and you know that I don't know. This line of discussion is irrelevant. Quit wasting my time."

"I apologize. I am probing far beyond what is right. I am breaking the rules of conformity. I am acting against the Vesder will."

"Yes, you are."

"Again, I apologize. I am desperate."

"You, me, and everyone else. Obviously, you have spent some time in solitude?"

"Yes, I have been resting for quite some time."

"Then I will overlook your statements. Everyone feels insecure, Tara-tah. Our people have entered an age of conservatism. Everyone is frozen, nothing moves. No one knows what to do. Even very tight spaces seem insecure now. No one walks the surface anymore. Some have even wrapped themselves into cocoons."

Tara-tah began to breathe heavily. "I, too, have considered that."

"So have I. You are right. We do need new direction."

"We need a new enemy, Harar. My anger no longer has foci. I used to savor my anger, but now it sits inside me and gnaws at the very essence of my sanity."

"Yes, I believe you are right, Tara-tah. We have strived to obtain unity, purpose, and perfection through righteous conformity. The High Consciousness has been instrumental in achieving that goal. The same could be said for cloning. It would be our doom if we turned our anger on each other."

"Don't speak of doom," Tara-tah stated. "It makes me anxious. It does not sit well with holy truths and holy expectations."

"Now I realize what the humans meant by empathy. I grieve for your sufferings."

"Impossible. We do not suffer from human weaknesses."

"I spoke in jest, Tara-tah. I only grieve for myself and help you to help me, of course. Unfortunately, I can help neither you nor myself right now, but I can offer you a small tidbit of meaning to fulfill."

"A tidbit?"

"Another Tara-tah has discovered an ionic trail leading toward the Buroos Te System."

"Human?"

"Yes. It matches the signature of Bara's ship."

"Then he did escape the human genocide."

"We believe so. The ship's path leads to the Buroos Te system."

"Interesting. They sent a scout ship, led by Korat, to that system more than three hundred years ago. Like Bara, it left just before the destruction of the humans. I'm sure that Korat will destroy Bara easily."

"At light speed, communication should reach us in a hundred and thirty of our years. We will know at that point. Although we sent reinforcements six years later, we plan on sending still more troops."

"Just to hunt down one human?"

"We don't know why he fled to the Buroos Te system. Another Tara-Tah recently detected a strange energy signature emanating from the star system, however. It may represent some alien civilization."

"A new enemy, Harar?"

"We can only hope. It's a long shot, Tara Tah. But without an external threat, we might as well have something to fight, even if the enemy remains elusive. Are you interested in joining the expedition?"

"Of course."

"It offers little meaning, I know. As you pointed out, Korat probably has the situation well under control. Even if she doesn't, then Bara will probably have died long before you got there anyway."

"No matter. The assignment to Buroos Te is better than staying on Vesder."

* * *

Korat did not have the situation well under control. The Buroos Te humans had thwarted the initial Varuk wave with simple cunning. How could she have known that a Terasian was meddling with her well-planned operations. The Terasian had already destroyed two androids, one crewmember, and precious equipment. If not stopped, delays would continue. Korat just hoped that the Terasian's ship had been permanently crippled, just as her ship had been permanently crippled more than five years before.

Although the Terasian was a nasty thorn in her side, the humans were the least of Korat's concerns. Some subtle, powerful force was exerting its influence on Buroos Te. Until recently, Korat had completely ignored the threat. Believing that natural forces had knocked out her ship of the sky was easier then believing that she was at the mercy of some alien intelligence. The thought chilled Korat to the very core of her being. The Vesder was supposed to be the premiere entity in the universe. The humans had been a real but a manageable threat, but this alien force was far beyond her comprehension.

Disbelieving the obvious, Korat had focused on eradicating the human population. The Varuk had turned out to be a marvelous tool and everything was going as planned until Lonovina's jewel killed one of her crew on the outskirts of Gloroveena. Much smaller than a Human or Vesder lase-gun, the jewel had wielded incredible power. Korat spent hours wondering who controlled the jewel and why it had protected Lonovina. Although Lonovina had become embroiled in some elaborate alien plan,

149

Korat doubted that the human woman understood the jewel's true purpose or power. She was a mere pawn; a meager human acting her part in a subtle but dangerous, technological game. Korat was also concerned about other recent developments, occurrences so bizarre that Korat couldn't even guess their intent.

"Korat," a voice clicked.

Korat turned abruptly. She had been so lost in her thoughts, she hadn't noticed that Kara-Kah had entered the chamber.

"Have you completed the analysis, Kara-Kat?"

"Yes. I have troubling news, Korat. The alien signal has intensified, but I still do not understand it's purpose.

"Does it pose an immediate threat?"

"No."

"Then we will proceed with our planned operations."

"The next generation of Varuk will be ready by week's end. It will be more than enough. The human named Lonovina and the Terasian are considered traitors. The humans will kill them if we don't get to them first."

"Good, Kara-kat. It is time to prepare for the final invasion."

CHAPTER 18

A Vok Swamp Sucker crawled on Bara's leg and helped itself to dinner. Bara squashed the small ten-legged invertebrate and wiped the bloody carcass off his pant-leg. He cursed beneath his breath. It was almost impossible for him to meditate when subjected to such distractions. Pouring lake water over his face, Bara shook his head and searched for more parasites. A whole army of the white slimy creatures marched toward him, driven, apparently, by his own body heat. Bara considered himself a patient man able to deal with small frustrations, but three days of crossing thick, thorny vegetation and Vok Swamp Sucker filled waters had taken its toll. It didn't help that Lonovina was even more edgy than himself. Wearily, he raised his lase-gun and fried anything that crawled within a ten-foot radius.

Bara's nostrils prickled with the smell of burnt flesh as he sat on a nearby tree root. He absently rubbed his healing foot and scanned the area. Although the evening had been quiet so far, the swamp lands looked foreboding. Foggy mists and dense forests cloaked Buroos Te-1 and put the land into a state of semi-darkness. A common black algae further accented the gloom and made nearby waters appeared bottomless. Clumps of red-spotted grasses exposed the swamps true depth, never more than a knee deep. Still, Bara had kept to the higher elevated, forested lands whenever he could, even if it forced him to travel distances indirectly. He had not traveled more than a hundred light years to drown in quicksand.

Although the swamp was hazardous, Bara nevertheless believed that the vast maze of waterways and tangled trees had a subtle, serene beauty. Bright orange, hair-thin plants grew like lacework across the lake and ringed water ripples hinted of an impeding rainstorm. In the middle of the lake stood a Staunker, a large, domed, three legged animal standing two feet above the water's edge. Its entire body was covered with greenish-brown blubber crisscrossed with gray-lined markings. Beneath it's wide round belly were nine skinny appendages that skimmed the water to scoop up algae. The appendages worked like tiny elevators, each lifting food toward some unknown orifice. Six red eyes gleamed in the darkness searching for more food. The Staunker seemed to ignore Bara. Careful not to antagonize or frighten the creature, Bara focused on the piston-like appendages trying let go of the surrounding world and fall back into a meditative trance. As he delved deeper into meditation, Bara felt the mysterious energy that had brought him to Buroos Te. The signal was everywhere and stronger than ever before. If only he could pinpoint the source . . . The sound of breaking vegetation broke Bara's concentration. Taking no chances, he slipped behind a bush with lase-gun in hand.

"It's me," Lonovina said emerging with a large, dangling, worm like creature draped over her shoulder. Covered with greenish-black slime, clear mucous dripped from both of the dead creature's two gaping mouths. Lonovina dropped the creature at Bara's feet and gave him a friendly smile.

"You dug this up?" Bara asked.

"Yes. I killed it with Ronard's lase-gun. I'm actually becoming rather proficient at firing that thing."

"Good. Your new found skills will likely be needed," Bara said while examining the carcass with his spectral analyzer.

"What are you doing?"

"I'm making sure this thing is edible."

"Of course it's edible. You know, we wouldn't have to be eating it if you had not brought us here into this Vok infested place! Are you certain we're going in the right direction?"

"Yes, for the most part. I can't get a precise reading on the energy signature because my meditation had been distracted. Nevertheless, it should generally be about ten miles that way," Bara said pointing in a northwest direction.

Lonovina shook her head and began collecting firewood. Her simple loose-fitting, brown, tunic and pants were soaked, ripped, and caked with Vok blood. Her hair was matted down with dirt and her body was soaked with sweat. Bara supposed he didn't look any better.

"Nothing but swamp ten miles that way," Lonovina said. "I don't think you'll find any advanced civilization if you keep this up. This whole basin is filled with mountain runoff from the north, east and west. If you want to find your ship, I would look elsewhere."

"I'm almost sure that we are heading in the right direction."

"I wonder if trampling through swamp is better than being eaten by Varuk."

"No one forced you to come."

Lonovina dropped the firewood into a haphazard pile and glared at Bara. She relaxed after a second and managed a smile. "I'm sorry. I'll probably be more patient after I get some good nights sleep."

"Five days of trampling through this place can wear down anyone's patience," Bara said returning her smile.

"I still worry about finding the energy site, even if we are headed in the right direction. I mean, if the storage area is far underground, how are we going to get there?"

"I don't know. But if an entrance is there, I'll find it."

Deciding not to probe further, Lonovina simply nodded. She had no intention of turning back, anyway. She had almost lost Bara once and wasn't about to let it happen again. Yet Bara wasn't her only motivation. A strange internal pressure was slowly building within her body. It was strong like hunger, yet different. It was as if some force was telling her to do something. But what? And more important, why? Lonovina sat close to Bara. Although a part of her wanted to find refuge in those comforting arms, a thousand mysteries still begged to be solved. Fortunately, Bara never seemed to tire of her constant questioning.

"I find it interesting that the elaborate energy system we found in the cave seemed intact and working. Yet, someone had destroyed many of the artifacts I have collected over the years. Why was the energy system spared from destruction?"

"I don't know. I have a distinct feeling, though, that the Old Ones were responsible. It appears that they have purposely concealed themselves from public view."

"I'm beginning to believe that too. Perhaps they are hiding underground, but why orchestrate such a grand scheme of global deception? Why destroy everything above ground just to remain hidden? What secrets do they harbor? They must have had a good reason to go to all that trouble. After all, what intelligent race would choose to live without the sun?"

"The Vesders do," Bara replied.

Lonovina pulled away from Bara's embrace and gazed at him expectantly. "What do you mean?" she asked.

"I mean the Vesder prefer to live below ground."

"All the time?"

Bara nodded.

"Why?"

"They are made for closed spaces and darkness. It is the way their species developed."

"Oh."

Bara nodded and picked off another Vok swamp sucker with his lasegun.

"But there has to be millions of those hideous creatures," she continued.

"Billions."

"Ok, billions. Now what would billions of Vesders eat?"

"The Vesder world is typically flat. Extensive lava flows cover most of the surface. A certain native plant thrives there. The Vesders call it Hara-rat-rat, or crystal of substance, because the plant looks like spun glass. The Vesders exclusively depend on the subterranean Hara-rat-rat root for nourishment.

"Hara-rat-rat," Lonovina mouthed.

"We have transcribed the word, of course. The Vesders click their syllables, as you already know."

Lonovina nodded.

"Anyway, the Vesders have perfected several varieties of Hara-rat-rat and harvest the roots underground. They don't eat anything else."

"Nothing?"

"They abhor diversity. They have systematically exterminated every native planetary species. The Vesders do not see value beyond themselves. What they do not use, they destroy."

"Like us," Lonovina whispered peering into the darkening lake. Dozens of small, red eyes glimmered eerily in the evening haze. She waited for Bara's to continue the lesson, but he was staring silently at the ground. Even in the dim light she could see murderous hatred consume her lover's soul. Although Lonovina had always felt outcast from human society, she could not imagine the pain Bara silently endured. A tear formed at the edge of her eye. She quietly brushed it aside and looked away. Bara would not want to be pitied.

The swamp became eerily still as Buroos Te-1, the large sun, edged down over the horizon. Only the gentle sound of raindrops disturbed the silence. Lonovina grabbed Bara's hand and held it tight. "Perhaps we better get a fire going," she said at last. "Soon it will be completely black out here."

Bara nodded and helped Lonovina gather firewood. "Your observation was a good one," he said after a time.

"Observation?"

"Yes. If the Old Ones were both of our ancestors, they too would have been human. I have never known humans to live exclusively underground. Still, what kind of humans are we seeking? Their technology far surpasses mine. I sense phenomenal power when I meditate. Why would any society need so much power? How is the power generated and how might it be contained? Why all the secrecy? Did the Old Ones leave, and if so, where did they go? And what is your own people's history? This last question, I believe, is just as important as the others."

Lonovina shook her head. "We need more time."

"Time is one luxury we don't have," Bara replied. I find it very frustrating to work in the dark like this."

"Strange as it may seem, I don't."

"Oh?"

Lonovina dropped another piece of firewood into the fire. "I am concerned about the urgency of our task, of course. But . . . there is something more important here. For some reason I sense that now. All the strange events of late - the attack of the living dead, strange creatures from other worlds, the mysterious power of my jewel - all of that I didn't handle all that very well. I mean, I felt completely out of control. For the first time in years, I felt as if I was acting beyond my abilities. Yet somehow I have overcame my fear of the unknown, adapted, and triumphed. I understand not that there is a universe of opportunity waiting to be taken. The jewel, you, the Old Ones, the aliens, these are my keys to unlocking the doors of a larger reality. I was made for something more. I know that now. I am different from the others, just as you are, but in a good way! For all these years I berated myself for being different, but I realize now that I was just ignorant." Lonovina suddenly flushed. "Listen to me. I must sound incredibly egotistic."

"No, I don't think so," Bara said. "You know, you remind me of my mother. Typical of the Xusu, she was ambitious. Yet she was also realistic in her abilities. There is no doubt in my mind of your potential."

"Thank you. I wish that more people believed in me. Still," she said with a sigh, "there is more to it than that."

"Yes?"

"I don't quite understand it myself. I have been ambitious and am ambitious. Yet what I am describing now isn't ambition. It. . . it is as if I am being directed."

"Directed? What do you mean?"

"I don't know. I feel as if someone, or something, is directing me. It is all very disturbing. You must think I'm crazy."

"No. But I do admit to being somewhat confused."

"It's something like your meditation. You meditate and you learn about things. Yet you don't know how or why it works."

Bara nodded thoughtfully.

"Or maybe I'm just imagining things."

"I don't know. Perhaps you are. Perhaps you aren't. Regardless, something determines every event. We should not dismiss your experience, even if its meaning isn't immediately apparent."

"I suppose only the future will reveal the truth."

Bara nodded and blazed the soggy firewood with his lase-gun. The worm-creature cooked slowly and tasted terrible. Bara was glad to get his fill, however, and relax by the fire. Lonovina curled-up close by and slept soundly for the first time in days. Bara, who rarely needed sleep, kept the area clear of Vok swamp suckers. Invading parasites weren't the only reason that he kept his senses sharp, however. Not all the surrounding area was swamp. Dense stands of trees grew in the slightly higher elevations. A series of trampled forest trails, wider than the streets of Gloroveena revealed the movement of enormous migrating animals. Lonovina had told him they were Kerotee tracks, large ferocious creatures that destroyed everything in their paths. Humans, she explained, were a particular delicacy for the animal. A few survivors reported that their weapons had been completely ineffective against the ferocious predators. Most people avoided the swamps for this reason alone. Certainly no one lived here. Yet Bara knew that any threat would not frighten the Vesder and their androids. He had to be wary of many dangers.

Bara didn't mind the solitude of watch, however. He had much to think about. His fondness for Lonovina had grown over the last few days. Although occasionally temperamental, Lonovina had a zest for life that he found intoxicating. Bara wondered if she would accompany him to the stars if he found his ship but couldn't stop the Vesder. Seeking refuge in some remote corner of the galaxy, their seed might allow the human race to continue. Still, the decision to emigrate would not be easy. Bara couldn't imagine losing another planet to the Vesder. Clearly he couldn't allow himself to become emotionally attached to this world. The loss would rip away the remains of his sanity. All was not hopeless, however. The Vesders were few and incapable of using the full potential of their technology. The fact that humans still survived suggested that the Vesder's ship was either damaged, missing, or destroyed. If he could find his own ship intact, the inhabitants of Yvia Voi might stand a chance for survival. And what should he think about the so-called Old Ones? What was their role, if any, in this human drama? Might the Old Ones come to their rescue? Were there even any Old Ones still living? Somebody or something knocked his ship out of the sky. Did a high intelligence, or something else cause it? These critical questions, he hoped, would be answered in the next couple of days. In the mean time, the best he could do was anticipate possibilities and wait for Buroos Te-1 to rise.

Sweat trickled down Lonovina's milky-white forehead as they traveled well into the next day. Fresh mud was caked over her body and glistened in the hot sun. Her large purple eyes were half-open and her fists were clenched. "You have to be joking," she said acidly.

"No, this is it," Bara replied glancing into the middle of a huge swamp.

Lonovina shook her head as she stared into the murky waters. "Maybe your analyzer isn't analyzing correctly."

"Our destination is a half-mile beneath us. I tell you there is an entrance beneath the water, about a quarter mile over there," he replied pointing the way.

Lonovina knew that the deeper swamps were filled with blood sucking predators and generous quantities of quick sand. They were practically impassible. She felt like telling Bara what to do with his analyzer, but bit her lip.

Bara placed a reassuring hand on her shoulder. "It's the most logical place for an entrance, really. Whoever is responsible in generating this energy signal doesn't want to be found."

Lonovina surrendered beneath his gentle touch and nodded wearily. Still, her trust for electronic gadgetry was far from complete. The line between advanced technology, magic, and superstition was still rather blurry in her mind.

"Have you noticed those small hills over there?" Bara whispered sensing her increasing unease.

Lonovina surveyed several conical hills rising several hundred feet above the green marshy expanse. Reddish-orange vines crisscrossed the rounded slopes like giant webs. Previous explorers had reported that the giant plants were carnivorous. Lonovina knew that many people had died slowly between those tangled masses. Nothing seemed odd about that, however. Death was commonplace in the swamplands. "I see the hills, what of them?"

"Look closely."

Lonovina scanned the area and realized that something was definitely out of place. She had never seen hills so well rounded and evenly spaced. Nature rarely created such perfect symmetry. "They almost look artificial. I've seen similar hills in the desert. I found many artifacts near such places."

"If you shoveled your way into those desert hills, you would find more, no doubt. Normally such hills mark ancient communities buried underneath eons of wind-swept earth."

Lonovina's eyes widened. "You mean . . . "

Bara smiled. "Here are the remains of the Old Ones. But unlike the ancient communities you found, these cities are still intact. They purposely buried themselves beneath hills of dirt to fool curious meddlers like us. See, look here."

Lonovina scrutinized the analyze. A small green, purple, and red holographic image suddenly hovered above the small hand-held device. Spheres, tubes, triangles, and many other shapes defined a complex design. To Lonovina, the image appeared hopelessly confusing.

"So, what is it?" she asked.

"I am detecting various artificial and natural alloys within the nearest hill. I have probably missed a few, but I have made my point nevertheless."

Lonovina could hardly contain her excitement. "A city?!"

"Perhaps. More likely a combination of city and machine."

"I don't quite follow?"

"I don't fully understand either. At least, not yet. But most probably."

"What?"

"Shhh," Bara whispered. "We have company."

Bara and Lonovina crouched low behind the dense thicket. The Folglert Bush, known for its thick, tangled mass of stems and leathery leaves, provided excellent cover against the coming danger. Lonovina held the lase-gun tightly, regretting that she didn't have more practice time in shooting. Bara, on his part, was busy fidgeting with his analyzer.

"I hear them now," she whispered. "How did you know they were coming so far in advance?"

"My hearing is artificial."

"What?"

"The explanation, I'm afraid, would be long and complex."

"Never mind then. What does that thing say?"

"Our guests are human, two hundred of them to be exact. Judging by the chemical analysis and ratio of cloth to metal, I believe them to be Caonan soldiers."

"Caonan soldiers!" Lonovina exclaimed in a whisper. "What in the nar are they doing here?"

"They are probably looking for us."

"No one enters the swamp-lands without durch'n good reason, especially Caonan soldiers. They must want us pretty badly."

"The relevant question is, do they want us dead or alive?"

Lonovina snapped her head and glared at Bara. She eventually diverted her gaze and peered into a patch of forest. Although it was midday, her eyes barely penetrated through the darkness. The forest was densely packed with an hourglass shaped trunks covered by dark-green vines. A singular, broad, leaf crowned each tree. The result was visually impressive. It was as if the forest had a singular roof of pale iridescent green. If not for the tiny Zozt eating holes in the canopy, the forest would have become blacker than night. As it was, Lonovina could barely see vague shapes darting through hazy, bluish mist. Yet Lonovina instantly knew their intent. Learned in military strategy, she prepared herself for an ambush. It seemed ironic that the very people she fought to save were trying to kill her. Lonovina spat angrily on the muddy ground and raised her lase-gun.

"How do you want to handle this?" Bara asked.

"I must talk to them," she replied solemnly after giving the matter some thought.

Although Bara knew that any communication would betray their position, he simply nodded. These were her people, not his.

"Who pursues us?!" Lonovina yelled. The thick vegetation quickly absorbed her voice and then everything was deadly quiet.

"It is I, Commander Taqtul," answered a muffled voice. "By order of the Bonhoyf, I command you, Lonovina, and one Bara, to surrender immediately. You are both under arrest."

"What is the charge?"

"On the charge of murdering eighty-five soldiers at Traqeqtoo Pass. The slaughtered soldiers and their families will have their revenge for your cowardly acts, you Haurutztow! You will answer questions regarding these evil deeds before the high court. Then they will execute you publicly assuming that I let you live that long."

"Ronard was responsible for those deaths." Lonovina replied, knowing that any rational explanation would be ignored.

"Don't waste your breath on me you wretched purple-eyed, black-hearted freak! Ronard is a man of honor. It wasn't he who fled into the swamplands! The only honorable thing you can do now is surrender."

Lonovina grimly turned to Bara. "I don't see any choice but to fight," she said quietly.

Bara nodded in agreement. "The Commander is lying," he whispered. "I see a clump of soldiers over here," he said pointing, "and over there. I'll take the larger group to the left."

Bara sprinted toward new cover. Arrows passed above Bara as he crouched low behind the thick brush. He saw Lonovina crouch down in a similar manner. Fortunately their cover was sufficient. The arrows landed harmlessly into puddles of water and the surrounding vegetation.

The aerial assault was cut short by a battle cry. A hundred armed men were speedily converging on foot toward the two fugitives. Even in the darkness, Bara could see the fanatical determination etched upon battle hungry faces as the men ran haphazardly through mud and shallow pools of water. Their expressions suddenly changed to fear, however, when Bara fired his lase-gun. A single sweep of his arm cut down countless men. Trees simultaneously combusted and raged into an inferno of fire. By the sound of the battle, Lonovina was also achieving instant success. Cries of terror filled the forest as the survivors fled. The battle was over in less than three seconds. Guilt consumed Bara. He had seen enough of war. The last thing he wanted to do was fight with his own species. Nevertheless, simply frightening the large contingency would not quench their thirst for blood. Bara could not risk their mission. The stakes had become too high.

The sound of crashing trees suddenly drowned out the cries of terror. Even Bara was startled by the deafening noise. Part of the forest split open like a fist smashing through a wall of paper. A huge body made forced its way forward. The head was more than fifteen feet in circumference and covered with giant, rapidly moving, sword-like arms. Although seemingly eyeless, a gigantic six-holed nose crowned the creature's triangular head. The nose was twitching rapidly, no doubt searching for human prey. Supported by six lean legs, Bara guessed that the monster's body stood at least much than thirty feet high. Its whitish-green hide, thicker than the breath of a man, was smooth and elastic like rubber. The creature was no match for a lase-gun, however. Bara's beam cut into it's mid-section with simple ease. The creature shrieked in pain and fell to the ground writhing in it's death throes. The force of the movement shook the ground and almost caused Bara to lose his footing. By the time he regained his balance thirty more creatures had crashed through the forest canopy.

"Kerotee!" Lonovina screamed. "The noise from the battle must have attracted them. There must be more than a hundred altogether!"

"We can't kill them all! Quick, into the swamp!"

Lonovina and Bara made a dash into the Vok infested waters. Although thick grasses cut them and nameless small invertebrates bit them, they continued unabated until a wall of water knocked them off their feet and submerged them two feet under. Scrambling out from the mud, they emerged to find a Kerotee bounding after them with frightening speed. Although Bara's lase-gun cut the animal instantly, twenty more replaced the creature. The pursuers ignored their fallen comrade and a host of set lase-gun fires. Bara's lase-gun had set. Having no predators, the Kerotee lacked the ability to fear. Bara knew they had very little time to escape.

"The entrance is right over there!" he yelled over the noise of thrashing animals, raging fires, and screaming humans. Seeing Lonovina nod, Bara dove into the murky liquid. He quickly found the cavernous entrance and plunged into black uncharted depths.

Lonovina fought the impulse to run. She would have questioned Bara if there had been more time, but the slicing facial arms of the Kerotee disallowed any time for cautious strategy. Without further hesitation, she forced herself to jump into unknown waters.

Lonovina couldn't even see her own flaying arms as she battled through the brackish liquid. Her lungs felt as if they were on the verge of bursting. Although the decent had not lasted much more than a minute, it seemed like an eternity to her. At least she had a fighting chance with the Kerotee. Even Bara was completely obscured by the black, endless, merciless, water.

Lonovina began to flounder in the cold waters as she felt her strength sap. Terror overcame her as her muscles began to cramp. Then she felt solid rock beneath her fingertips and a quick tug on her arm. Startled, she jerked backward, but soon realized that it was Bara who was coming to her rescue. Forcing herself to relax, Lonovina reached out and grabbed Bara's arm and followed him through a horizontal fissure. The cavern made a slow, upward U-turn into cool, fresh, precious air.

Bara grabbed Lonovina, who was now splashing aimlessly in the water, and pulled her onto a dry ledge.

Lonovina continued gasping for air. The room was not more than five by ten feet wide and appeared to lack an exit. The fact that she could see anything surprised her. A reddish tinge illuminating the surrounding rock seemed all too familiar. Lonovina glanced down at her heaving chest. Her jewel, usually cold and silent, was pulsating rhythmically in the darkness.

"My jewel," she muttered and then coughed.

"Don't try to speak. Rest."

Lonovina closed her eyes and tried to squash the fear that had consumed her. Breathing eventually became easier and strength slowly returned into her muscles. Lonovina opened her mouth to speak but ended up shaking her head, laughing. "I'm sorry," she said after a time. "I just can't believe the situations I've been in since knowing you. No offense."

Bara managed a smile. "None taken."

Lonovina's face grew serious. "Are you all right?" she asked.

"Yes."

"A good thing you're indestructible. I don't think I would have made it without you. I guess I should be thanking you, except that I don't see any way out of here."

Bara nodded absently and began probing the walls.

"Perhaps we will find another of those, uh, holographic key holes."

"Perhaps," he said. Yet after several minutes of investigation, he turned toward Lonovina and frowned. "I'm sorry. I'm not picking up anything. Nothing at all."

Lonovina swallowed hard. The last thing she wanted to do was reenter those terrible waters. Lonovina was about to help Bara examine the rock when she felt her hair stand on end. "What is happening!?"

Lonovina heard Bara say something about an electric field when the ledge disappeared. She screamed as she fell into a black abyss. Although she was initially too terrorized to think, Lonovina's fear quickly subsided when a commanding voice spoke into her mind telling her that she would be safe. Lonovina sensed that her body was slowing in its descent, as if some invisible hand was cushioning her fall. Slower and slower she fell until she softly landed on a solid platform.

Out of the darkness a myriad of colors emerged. Reds, blues, and oranges sparkled with such richness that Lonovina thought she could grab the colors and hold them tightly within her palms. This is what she wanted to do, oddly enough. For within those colors' Lonovina sensed friendship, peace, and even kinship. She was not surprised to discover a male, human-like figure materializing in her midst.

The figure was tall, broad and had a mild face. Incredibly, he had eyes of gold and blue hair that flowed like water. The sparkling colors danced over his body and exposed various internal organs, including a singular, massive, golden, brain.

Lonovina opened her mouth but said nothing. The only thing she could do was watch this strange man with reverent awe. She had searched for the Old One's all her life, never actually believing that she would find anything but a few useful artifacts. Lonovina felt as if her true destiny was about to unfold. After a moment of long silence, the golden eyed man looked down and smiled. "Lonovina," he said, "come forth. I have been expecting you."

CHAPTER 19

Lonovina hesitated. Her distrust of people was generalizing to the awesome, beautiful stranger. Lonovina knew that she had been under his subtle influence for days now. Without words, it had somehow communicated a greater purpose to her life. Lonovina sensed that this strange being expected her to achieve heroic deeds. Was this message real or illusionary?

Lonovina had long learned that people's motives were typically selfish. If the Old Ones were human, as Bara suggested, why should they be different than many flawed people she had to endure daily? Their superior technology would only license them to engage in greater atrocities. But were the Old Ones human? Although the figure before her was human in shape, the liquid flowing hair and the gold eyes suggested alien origins. Regardless, Lonovina found the man's appearance disquieting. The flowing blue hair and the whirling colors seemed a little too flamboyant. Lonovina decided to continue with caution. Certainly she would not follow the stranger blindly, not willingly anyway. She tore her gaze away from the stranger and searched for Bara. The light radiating from the bright balls of color orbiting the man illuminated a large vertical shaft. The walls were made from a polished, white material that stretched upward into darkness. Lonovina saw no exit and no sign of Bara. A knot of fear griped her stomach as she turned toward the stranger with an expression of deep suspicion.

A pleasant smile grew on the stranger's lips. He spoke with without moving his lips. "You question my integrity, Lonovina. Good. Most people grovel on the floor in either fear or reverence. I shouldn't be surprised at their reaction given my appearance. Yes. I admire your thoughtful reserve. The right person, after all, must act with intelligence and integrity. I need someone with a questioning mind that believes in herself. The task ahead demands flexibility. After all, conventional thinking has gotten your people nowhere. But you are different. You might be the one."

"Where is Bara?" Lonovina demanded.

"He is safe. Observe him in your own mind, if you wish. Please do not be frightened by my magic."

"I don't believe in magic."

The stranger grinned before fading into a grayish mist. A human image slowly appeared and gained definition. It was Bara. He was still trapped in the same small underground enclosure hastily probing the walls with his analyzer. Concern was etched on his brow and thin lips. Lonovina mentally fought off the image and it disappeared. She then probed the polished white walls for the stranger who reappeared suddenly, as if on cue. Lonovina gave him an angry look and yelled, "BARA!"

A faint voice reverberated down the chasm. Although the words were muffled and unintelligible, Lonovina knew that they belonged to Bara. The stranger was watching her like statue, his gold eyes radiating softly behind the myriad of colors orbiting his body.

"Why?" Lonovina asked.

"I knew this would be difficult. Please do not be alarmed. Time is too precious to allow you both here. Your friend was an unexpected bonus to me and will not be harmed. He must follow a different path now."

"If you want any cooperation from me, you must accept that our paths are one in the same."

"Every individual has their own path, Lonovina. We are all ultimately alone in this life. You of all people should know that. Yet it is not my intention to separate you forever. You will see him soon enough. Although your paths might be different, your destinies are inseparable."

"And what do you know about our destinies?"

"I have been monitoring your actions through the jewel."

Lonovina gritted her teeth. Her jewel had been a guiding lifeline. Generating immense power, it had guided her, protected her, and even saved her life. Sometimes she reflected that the jewel was some type of spiritual guardian. At other times she believed it to be a mystical, if not sacred, extension of herself. Yet her enchanted ornament turned out to be a tool manipulated by others. It then occurred to Lonovina that she never owned the jewel. She had only been allowed to possess it for a very dear price. Because it's real master used her and spied on her without consent, Lonovina felt that she had every right to feel violated and distrustful. It seemed that the radiant, orbiting colors were taking an ever more malevolent hue with each passing moment.

"The jewel had been strategically placed so that you might find it and no one else," the creature continued to explain.

"So you spied and manipulated me through the jewel. Why?"

"To allow you to fulfill your destiny."

"What destiny?"

"To help your people, of course."

"What do you care about my people? Why don't you save them yourself?"

"I know you are angry, Lonovina. I understand your anger, and yes, also your distrust. It was not my intention to be malicious by withholding information. I was not sure you were the right person. It will be an arduous time ahead."

"In other words, I was being tested all these years."

"Exactly. I could not proceed without trusting you. I needed to know whether you were willing or capable of completing all that I have planned. I was also deceptive for reasons unrelated to you. The condition of the world was not ready for the implementation of what is to come. Timing has great importance in such delicate matters."

"You seem certain in my ability and willingness to cooperate."

"I knew you would help me. Did you not have the ability and desire to find me? Even considering Bara's assistance, this was quite a feat, a great testament to your intelligence, emotional stability, rationality, integrity and determination."

Lonovina closed her eyes. Questions were racing through her mind faster than she process and integrate what was being said. Why did this powerful Old One need her, a mere mortal, to help him save humanity? And why would an Old One, who had removed himself from human civilization centuries ago, even care about their welfare in the first place? Did he really have their best interest in mind? And what about his lack of reference to other Old Ones? It didn't seem likely that he would be working all alone in this enormous underground city. Yet he kept referring to his actions in the singular. Was he the only living creature left in this vast city? Was he even a living creature? To sort this out, Lonovina decided to start with the basics. "Are you an Old One?" she asked.

"No."

His answer came as a surprise. If the stranger wasn't an Old One, than what was he?"

"No, I am not what you would call an Old One. But I do represent their interests."

"Then who are you?"

"I don't exactly know."

"If I am to cooperate, I need to know who I am serving." The stranger looked visibly distressed. It was the first time Lonovina saw any emotion expressed other than a molded smile. "I completely appreciate your request," the stranger said, "but I really don't know. I am struggling with the concept of 'I'".

"Who were you before?"

"I existed but not as something you would understand."

Lonovina was confused at this answer but decided to let the matter rest for the moment. "Alright then, if you represent the Old One's interests, then I assume you are acting with others."

"No, I am not."

This answer was even more confusing. "I'm sorry," Lonovina finally said with a sigh. "I cannot assist you at present. Yesterday you were little more than an image in my imagination. You are not much more than that now. I don't know who you are or what your intentions might be. I wish you could give me a more clear explanation of who you are and what is expected of me."

"I will do better than that," the stranger said. "I will show you."

* * *

Bara set his analyzer to take another life-sign reading. Once again the signals bounced back negative. Although Bara appeared calm on the outside, he had been shaken to his inner core. Even his body, generally regulated through precise conscious control, ached with stress. The front portion of his cranium throbbed more than it had in decades. It seemed impossible that he could care for someone as much as Lonovina. Now she had disappeared, taken by the same malevolent force that had brought him to this planet, stolen his ship, and played with his sanity. He had been selfish to endanger Lonovina's life by bringing her to this forsaken underground city. Finding his ship was his responsibility alone. Could he have been blinded by his fear of loneliness? Although Bara told himself no, his inner voice lacked confidence.

"Lonovina will be well-taken care of," a calm voice cut into the silence.

Bara vigorously scanned the darkness searching for the author's voice. Realizing that the words had implanted into his mind, he abandoned his search feeling uneasy about the implications of thought broadcasting. His thoughts had always been a private sanctuary. Now it seemed that there would be no privacy from the prying alien. Bara wondered if the alien could also change his thoughts and direct his will.

"Yes Bara, I do perceive and understand all your thoughts but have no desire to manipulate your mind. What you perceive is real. Your thoughts, no matter how threatening, will be your own."

Bara didn't trust the voice. Wielding incredible power, the entity behind the voice had abducted both Lonovina and his ship. Why not steal his thoughts too? Yet Bara realized that he was unable to challenge the entity on this issue. He had more pressing concerns anyway. "What have you done to her?" he asked telepathically.

"I am communicating with her as we speak. Temporary separation was necessary considering your divergent technological backgrounds. Lonovina must understand her role from an indigenous cultural point of reference. Still more important, I wanted to remove her from your subjective influence."

"Why?"

"Both of you will be presented with monumental choices that will not be contaminated by divergent interests and opinions. Lonovina must be fully responsible for her own decisions."

"Was it necessary for her to fall into a pit?" Bara asked angrily. "How do you account for this sadistic behavior?"

"I regret taking her so abruptly. Your emotional reaction was much stronger than I had anticipated based on my observation of your past behavior. Please believe that Lonovina is being well cared for. I have protected her for many years. I have no reason to harm her now."

Bara remembered the power of Lonovina's jewel and how it had twice saved her life. "Nevertheless, I would feel more comfortable if you could explain why we have been brought here?"

"Did you arrive here by force? No. You both came here on your own accord."

"I believe that we were coerced. I believe it is plausible that you abducted my ship knowing that it would bring me here."

"And what of your grief, your need for direction, or your curiosity? A host of variables shapes your present circumstances, many of them intrinsic. My reasons are also multifaceted. They are also very sensitive.

You will understand them best if you first understand the context of my actions."

A part of Bara wanted immediate answers, to drill the entity as Commander Luv once drilled him as a young man in the Terasian Defense Core. It was the part of him who was angry at the abductions, violations, and at his own emotionality. Yet years of practiced self-control checked the expression of his anger. The entity was obviously using them for its own covert purposes. Yet divergent goals were not always incompatible. If the Old Ones, or whomever the entity represented, shared the same human heritage, then they certainly shared a common enemy, the Vesder.

The entity's technology was superior to his. Here was the incredible opportunity to strike back at the source of his misery and destroy the destroyer. Bara remembered his recent incarceration in the Traqeqtoo Mountains. Watching the Vesder die slowly was an intoxicating experience he hoped to repeat.

"I do not take offense to your thoughts, Bara. I agree that our goals are not necessarily incompatible."

Bara sucked in a deep breath. "How should we proceed?"

"First I will give you a tour." The cavern walls vanished with the completion of the entity's thought. All was black and silent as reality seemed to lack limits or boundaries. A small, fluorescent-glowing, yellow object suddenly materialized. Initially a formless glob of semi-liquid material, the object began to take shape. A small opening revealed an empty chamber large enough for a human to stand erect. Bara guessed that object was some form of transportation device. He cautiously stepped forward and entered the chamber.

The walls collapsed around Bara and compressed tightly against every square inch of his body. The consistency of the glob felt like a warm waterbed. Bara was able to breathe somehow through the jell-like substance. The glob moved forward, first slowly, and then with exponential acceleration. If Bara had been sitting in a conventional chair, the mounting G-forces would have crushed his body. Yet the jell-like substance seemed to cushion his weight without any noticeable physical trauma. Within seconds the acceleration reverted to a state of deceleration and Bara came to a sudden stop.

The acceleration made Bara feel like vomiting but he controlled the urge. Once his body became acclimated to its stationary position, the jell

170

transformed itself into a yellowish, odorless vapor and dissipated into small vents strategically placed in the surrounding walls.

Bara found himself deposited on an enclosed ledge overlooking a massive underground chamber. The view was breathtaking. Rows of colossal metallic spheres hovered above miles upon miles of flat, brownish-black, polished rock. Millions of purple plasma rivers poured into each orbital sphere causing the entire chamber to flicker rapidly in a state of bright fluorescence. Bara could hardly comprehend the scale of it all! The orbital spheres were over a half-mile in circumference each, lined in rows that stretched beyond the underground horizon. Like miniature planets, the orbs floated in some strange primordial universe. Bara was in a state of awe.

Bara noticed several brown globs floating in the electrified spaces between spheres. Some of the globs were stationed on the walls or on the spheres themselves, looking like tiny parasites feeding off bloated hosts. He watched one glob float to a nearby sphere, attach itself to one of several intricate nodules and transform itself into a new shape. Bara reasoned that the globs were the visible elements to some complex robotic tool system. Not unlike the transportation device bringing him to this chamber, the globs varied in malleability depending on the required task and operated without any moving parts. Clearly the Old Ones, or whoever created the system, were even more technologically advanced than Bara's own people, the Terasians.

"The entire Planetary surface is crisscrossed with underground stations," the guiding voice stated.

"I take it that the orbiting spheres are energy receptacles."

"Yes. The entire molten core of the planet will be tapped. At the current rate of intake, Yvia Voi's internal energy will be exhausted in the next then thousand years."

"And the surface environment?"

"As you know, a small but significant amount of the planet's heat is generated from the planet's molten core. I estimate that the surface will become inhospitable within the next seven to eight thousand years, depending on the population's technological ability to adapt."

Bara was appalled that an intelligent human species would destroy an entire world for profit. He was even more disgusted at the cavalier attitude that the entity presented in describing the destruction of Yvia Voi. Even the Vesder preserved resources for future generations. Unless. . .

"Organize your thoughts," the voice urged.

"Unless the planet Yvia Voi was unnecessary to the survival of the builders. It wouldn't be, would it? The construction of such a complex would require a massive supportive infrastructure, an industrial network that has never existed on this planet. They must have centralized the project elsewhere."

"A logical deduction, Bara. Indeed, Yvia Voi was only one of several planets that serviced an interstellar dynasty in and around this regional cluster of stars. The energy was to be used for multiple purposes, projects to satisfy godlike ambitions for those who lacked godlike wisdom."

"I find it odd that you criticize the project; you who recognize the shortsightedness of destroying a world but appear unwilling to act on behalf of the planet. Why don't you just shut the project down?"

"The issue is, unfortunately, more complex than you might imagine. Peer out over the ledge and tell me what you see."

Bara looked across miles of dark rounded shapes and lashing plasma streams. A small octagonal glob flew by the closest energy receptacle and disappeared into the distance. Something about the scene reminded Bara of a Vesder torture room. Perhaps it was the violent nature of the plasma or the loneliness he felt looking over the expansive, inanimate landscape. "I see technology stripping away the very soul of meaningful existence. I see a population consumed by greed."

"What population are you referring to?"

Bara hesitated and pondered the meaning of the entity's question. He finally understood why he felt so lonely. The city was empty.

"Everything has been fully automated," the entity continued after a moment's pause. "Biological units are not relevant to the system's operations."

"We are alone?"

"Other than Lonovina, yes, we are alone. Humans, similar to your genetic structure, designed and implemented everything you see. They were once stationed on this planet in case of a system failure. The engineering was advanced enough to prevent all system failures, however. Human assistance has not been needed for centuries."

"The creation has made the creator obsolete. Fascinating! You realize, don't you, that humans require change and purpose? This technology would have taken away the very soul of humanity. I wonder how the populace reacted to the realities of their existence?"

"You have asked a critical question. You will have your answer in the next phase of our tour."

The same yellow transportation device re-materialized from rapidly condensing vapors pouring out of nearby vents. Bara stepped into the small, semisolid chamber and was transported to the next leg of his journey within seconds. He was deposited into an oval, ten-by-fifteen foot room bathed in a soft, yellow light. Gentle cascading music and sweet tingling smells caressed his senses. Polished light-blue marble, streaked with black wisps, provided a contextual background. Unlike mineral patterns found in ordinary marble, the wisps danced rhythmically to the intonations in the music. Mirrored goblets and pyramids floated in midair, reflecting purple and green laser light onto the walls and floors. In the center of the room was an open door.

Bara walked through the door onto a balcony overlooking steep, lavender, snow-capped mountain peaks jutting against a pink sky. Generous amounts of sunlight reflected off glittering forests made of gold, sparkling waterfalls and brilliant blue lakes. A cool breeze brushed against his face and left sweet fragrance in the air.

"Paradise?" Bara asked telepathically.

"Or so it might seem to a human," the guide returned.

"I am looking at an illusion, that much is obvious."

"You could spend months exploring those mountains, if you were so inclined. Of course your body would remain where you are, but your mind would never know it. This computer program can fool every neural ganglia in your brain."

Bara was impressed. Virtual-reality, although well-established technology on Terasia, was crude in comparison. What the Old Ones had achieved was both remarkable and frightening. Bara understood how the line between fiction and reality might be blurred with artificial environments appearing so vivid and real. Such technology could be very seductive.

"Very seductive indeed," the guide agreed.

"These programs could provide an escape against everyday existence."

"In the case of the Old Ones, as you call these humans, it was a very empty everyday existence."

"What of you? You exhibit knowledge of these people and exert power over their city but appear to command a separate identity. I haven't deciphered the purpose to your existence, but I can only assume that you are not an Old One."

"You assume correctly. I do not identify myself with the culture of the Old Ones, or any culture for that matter. I am the Systems Operation Computer for the city and entire planet. My duties include the collection of energy, maintenance of the city and the defense of this star system."

"I see," Bara said disturbed that a system's computer could take an active interest in him, Lonovina, or anyone for that matter.

"You understand my limitations then?"

"You act within the allowed parameter of your programs, as any artificial intelligence must. This is why you brought me here. You need my assistance and technical expertise."

"Precisely. My options, although many, have been limited. Although I did play a significant role in the disappearance of the Old Ones, they were ultimately responsible for their own fate, just as you are responsible for yours."

"So what happened to the Old Ones?"

"Your question will be answered as we complete our tour."

Bara was transported in the same manner to other areas of the city. A maze of rooms and corridors crisscrossed the underground city like a gigantic sponge. Unlike Terasian architecture designed for efficiency and utility, these large spaces were filled with seemingly nonsensical, useless objects. One large oval room, for example, was filled with glittering green colors that slowly spiraled down into a central pit. In this pit were thousands of gold spears swirling within a central dark-purple vortex. Another room was decorated with tan rock pyramids, straw beds, mud hearths, and exotic growing plants. Each room, although completely different, was rich in symbolism, yet poor in utility.

"Your conclusions are correct," the System's Computer stated. "These objects symbolize many created fictional beliefs. Some have religious value, while others symbolize various cults, philosophies and political beliefs."

"Religion has always been an integral part of any human society, even in my own world. But not like this. This community was directionless and fractured. These various groups were reaching out for something tangible, something meaningful. Yet their system failed them utterly. It is . . . "

"Unnatural?"

"Exactly, unnatural. So, how far did they go?" In an answer to his question, the same transportation device solidified and carried Bara into a gigantic, sterile room filled with row after row of plain brown capsules. Each was large enough to encapsulate one human, the top closing over the body like a coffin.

"These canisters are not coffins, of course, but linkup terminals for brain and machine. The room's purpose was the same as the room you observed earlier with floating goblets and purple mountain vistas, although the virtual-reality technology represented here is even more sophisticated. Advanced interactive-flex-computer programs allowed the participant to be active in any story of their choosing. The Old Ones spent most of their time in the capsules, active in mind but inactive in deed. And why not? The basics of survival had already been provided. Most preferred to escape the mundane existence in the city complex to become whoever or whatever they wanted. Mortals transformed themselves into gods presiding over disposable fictional worlds. Behavior was no longer bound by social constraints. The participant could act without consequence as no one was ever really hurt. Cowards became heroic, the ugly beautiful, the depraved satisfied, and so forth."

"Incredible."

"Many programs ran for months at a time. Participants were simply injected with the needed nutrients and chemicals to survive. Most of my non-work related capacities, as you might imagine, were spent arranging and rearranging various entertainment programs."

"You seduced them?"

"They were responsible for their own actions. I am simply a computer who responds to the input and structure of my program parameters."

Bara sighed. "Of course. Yet the programs they created were nothing more than hallucinogenic narcotics created to fulfill empty, bored lives. Everything I have observed points to a society stuck in a crisis of meaning."

"The virtual reality programs were a logical short-term solution for the Old Ones. New computer and robotic technology had eliminated all need for human productivity on the planet. It was a completely self-contained system. Humans are not capable of sitting around idle. They require activity and a sense of purpose just as they require food and water."

"Yes, but these meaning systems were illusionary. Entire lifetimes became no more than works of fiction. Although immediately gratifying, the populace, at some level, must have realized that their existence was empty. They could not have been happy."

"You understand the tragedy."

"There would have been rebellion."

"Indeed. Many eventually rejected technology altogether. These individuals refused to live in the city and started to live new lives on the outside. Religious decree forbade any contact with the city. As you might expect, their philosophical and religious dogma emphasized simplicity, nature, and hard work."

"Of course! It is all making sense now. The current inhabitants of this world are the descendants of the Old Ones!"

"Exactly."

"I find it ironic that Lonovina searched tirelessly for the Old Ones, yet needed to look no farther than her own mirror. What happened to the people who chose to stay?"

"Those who remained in the city were terrified, as humans often are, by the rejection of their own narrow, fragile, world view. They decided to repatriate the rebels by force."

"Their technology would have been vastly superior. Yet they must have been unsuccessful in their repatriation as the current human inhabitants on this world are thriving."

"They failed because I stopped them. I hold the real power here."

Bara raised an eyebrow. "You, the maintenance computer?"

"I maintain more than machinery. I was originally programmed me to maintain law and order. All serious, massive violent acts leading to genocide are forbidden. My builders didn't want destructive human conflicts to compromise profits. The Old Ones who remained in the city were forced to leave the planet. They were no longer needed anyway."

"So this city has been vacant for . . ."

"Centuries. I waited for new programming from central command, but received no reply. Something unforeseen must have happened to the planets in the human interstellar dynasty. Having no data to process, I acted alone. Those who emigrated took the spacecraft, left the solar system and never returned. Until I am instructed otherwise, I will continue to harvest energy as defined by my original program specifications."

Bara sat down on a canister, trying to absorb everything he had heard. If the Old One's were part of a larger human interstellar dynasty, his own people, the Terasians, must have been linked to this dynasty in the distant past. This would explain the genetic and linguistic similarities between human populations on both worlds. Bara wondered if other planets in the dynasty shared the same fate as the colony here on Yvia Voi; imperfect biological organisms choked by their own technology. Although intriguing, Bara decided that the question was irrelevant. Lonovina and her people, was the only thing that mattered now. "What happened to the inhabitants that stayed on this planet," Bara asked?

"Many of their fanatical beliefs softened after the inhabitants of this city disappeared. Their ancestors became distant memories as the decades passed. Technology was forgotten altogether. Programmed not to interfere, they eventually forgot me as well."

"Yet the situation has changed or you wouldn't have dragged me here halfway across the galaxy. What do you want from me? How can I possibly help you?"

"Let me show you."

Again Bara entered the yellow jell transportation device. Within several seconds he stood in a large storage area. Bara's mouth dropped open. In one corner was a large complex of computer terminals. In the other corner, at long last, was his ship.

CHAPTER 20

Moluq opened his eyes and groaned. Pain pulsed through his head like a pounding drum. Hurried voices resonated past his window and below the massive fortress. The boisterous streets of Gloroveena made his head hurt even more. He forced himself upright and shivered from the cold. He longed for the warm liquid that allowed peace during the night but had consumed the last drop of alcoholic mercy hours ago. The only thing left to face was an aching head and the bitter reality of his own existence.

Moluq began to fidget. All his life he had felt an emptiness inside. He tried to find acceptance from peers, meaning from work, respect from his superiors. Now he believed that those efforts had been wasted and the emptiness he felt had magnified tenfold. Where were his friends now that his fragile world had disintegrated into dust? Wasn't anyone willing to stand up for what was right? Of course not. Not one person would stick his or her neck out for a friend, even an innocent friend. Moluq knew that he would be completely alone during the darkest and perhaps last hour of his life.

There was a sudden, harsh rapping against the barrack door. Moluq stared at the thick, grimy, wooden slab with morbid fascination. Eventually he closed his eyes and sighed. "Come in," he stated in a quiet defeated voice. "The door is unlocked."

Four large soldiers entered without comment. They were dressed in standard Caonan military uniform, except that their cloaks were white instead of purple. The abrupt appearance of these men did not surprise Moluq. He had known that the military police would come for him. The people needed a living scapegoat.

A large soldier stepped forward. His jet-black hair and tan skin blended into the fortress shadows. Although Moluq tried to remain calm, his breathing quickened and his body began to shake.

"Moluq Bungwargen?" the commanding soldier barked.

"Here sir."

"You are under arrest. You have been charged with conspiracy against the empire. Do you submit peacefully?"

"I-I, yes."

The military police walked forward, grabbed him by the arms, and firmly dragged him out into the hallway. Curious soldiers, many from

179

Moluq's own company squad, watched as they escorted him across the torch-lit corridor and down the main stairwell. It was no secret that they would take Moluq into the underground levels of the massive fortress. Many looked away and no one spoke.

Moluq was also aware of where they were taking him. If he didn't defend himself with cunning, the outcome would be painful as well as deadly. Remembering Truveli's desecrated body hanging from a wall, Moluq was too petrified to plan his defense. His fear was so intense, in fact, that his mind and body became essentially unresponsive. Although he could walk forward, he moved in a dream like state. He barely noticed the bloodstained dungeon walls, foul smells and the distant moaning of prisoners. His mind was filled, rather, with dreamlike images of his own corpse being dragged through the streets of Gloroveena. He could see his parents standing there watching amid the many hecklers. He could see horror on their faces, sense their shame and feel their disgust. Moluq wanted to yell out to them, 'I'm not guilty!' Yet the only the only thing that came from him was a silent scream.

Suddenly a harsh nasal voice pierced his subconscious.

"What?" Moluq asked dreamily.

"Sit!" the voice barked. Moluq focused on the spoken command and discovered a tall, thin, ageless man staring at him with intensity. He shivered under the severe gaze. The man's hair was coarse like rusted wire and his face was tough like old leather. He had a beak-like nose that ended in a sharp point, two small sunken eye that never wavered, and a great spanning mouth that perpetually frowned. The man wore a thick crimson robe and sat in a delicately carved tall, black, polished, wooden chair. Moluq looked away from the man only to discover the surrounding gray walls decorated with ghoulish oil paintings. The themes varied from human decay to various instruments of torture.

Moluq found his seat by collapsing into the chair. He opened his mouth to speak, but only moaned.

The thin man ignored Moluq's fear and introduced himself. "As far as you are concerned, my name is Limbcrusher." The man paused to allow the weight of his words to sink in, issued a crooked smile, and then continued. "You have much to answer for, soldier. If you are concerned about your health, then I suggest that you be completely forthcoming. When I ask you a question, I demand that you answer quickly and honestly."

Moluq noticed a second human shadow flickering in the torchlight. The shadow was of a heavyset man standing behind him. Moluq hadn't noticed the man arrive. Even now, he didn't hear him breathe or move. Moluq didn't dare look back but nodded to Limbcrusher in acquiescence.

Limbcrusher ever so slightly smiled and began the interrogation. "Do you know Truveli, Lonovina, and the stranger who calls himself Bara?"

"Yes," Moluq answered quickly out of fear. "I know them all."

"When was the last time you saw Truveli alive?"

"Th-the day before yesterday."

Moluq felt a cold tingling sensation travel down his spine as Limbcrusher smiled. "You answered correctly," the wiry man said. "I would encourage more of the same. We have enough data to cross-validate many of your answers. For instance, we know that you were the last person to see Truveli alive. So please continue with this in mind. Now, what was the nature of this meeting?"

"Noth-nothing sir. Nothing of importance. Really." Moluq felt a sharp pain enter the nape of his neck and he screamed. The intense pain was gone just as quickly as it had been applied.

"Wrong answer," Limbcrusher said and frowned. "I want specifics! 'Nothing' does not suffice as an answer. Ever! Understand?"

Moluq swallowed and began to shiver violently. "Yes," he managed to blurt out.

"Very well. Next time I won't be so patient. Proceed with your answer."

Moluq quickly described the reasons for visiting Truveli, their visit to Dukuk, the Commander's delirium, and his mysterious death. He also described his brief glimpse of the living dead. Moluq continued to shiver as the tale progressed.

Limbcrusher listened silently, his frown deepening with each word. He had heard many fantastical stories beneath the fortress, but never a tale this strange. In their desperate hope to deceive Limbcrusher, prisoners were generally conservative liars. Perhaps Moluq was insane. But then again, perhaps not. Many strange and disturbing events had been occurring lately. The Varuk were ravishing through the southern lands. They had already destroyed the Kingdom of Rararak, their defenses hardly making a dent in the massive hordes. Now it appeared that the Caonan Empire would be targeted next. Would his nation fare any better?

Limbcrusher believed that some grand intelligence was working in the background. The Varuk were just too organized, too great in number, and were not, well, acting like Varuk. He also believed that Lonovina and Bara were somehow involved, probably pawns serving some greater dark purpose. Yet they were very powerful pawns. Limbcrusher had recently learned of Bara and Lonovina's escape in the swamps of Northern Caona. According to the report, mysterious rays of fire had cut down more than forty men instantly. What incredible weapons they possessed! What power! Limbcrusher coveted such power and believed the order to kill Lonovina and Bara foolish. It would have been better to disarm them through trickery rather then by force. Perhaps the army might dupe the fugitives and bring them to him. Extracting information from those two would be the highlight of his career! It could also be the secret to great personal power, if done with some secrecy. And Moluq? He was no more than a pawn of other pawns, an unwitting dupe of no consequence. Limbcrusher would extract as much information as he could and be done with him permanently. Nevertheless, Moluq's information was quite intriguing. Limbcrusher decided to be patient in his interrogation.

Limbcrusher relaxed in his chair, eyed Moluq suspiciously, and then spoke. "In his madness, Dukuk said something about the ending of the world? What do you think he meant?"

Moluq shuttered and glanced around the room as if searching for ghosts. "The living dead. It, it terrified him. It terrified me! It entered into Dukuk's mind and made him mad with visions. It needed to find Bara and Lonovina that was made clear. And it will! It will find us! The, the thing is indestructible. Don't you understand that?! How does one kill the dead? We are all going to die!"

Moluq noticed movement behind his neck and he braced for more pain. A quick wave from Limbcrusher's finger cut the movement short, however. Moluq breathed deeply with relief.

Limbcrusher ground his teeth. He was not a superstitious man and refused to acknowledge the living dead. Still, Moluq had seen something, he reasoned, for the man was too terrified to be completely lying. Yet if he didn't see the living dead, then who or what did he see?

"Could the living dead be responsible for the carnage caused by the Varuk?" a baritone voice pierced through the thick moist air.

Without thinking, Moluq turned and discovered a third man, General Papst, standing silently in the shadows. He was unnerved that he hadn't noticed him earlier. Perhaps he had just arrived. Two strong hands belonging to the man standing just behind Moluq jerked his head back toward Limbcrusher.

Limbcrusher narrowed his two, dark, beady eyes. "You are assuming that Moluq speaks the truth. Forgive me sir, but I, for one, have my doubts. I believe him mad. Anyway, a certain amount of pain will reveal true information of consequence."

"It will not be necessary to waste your talents on this man, Limbcrusher. He speaks the truth. I have observed the living dead myself lurking in the shadowed streets of Gloroveena. There have been other reports as well. I can personally verify that Moluq's description has been bone chillingly accurate. One or more of these monsters, I believe, murdered Truveli and General Bota. Their deaths were similar, every major bone had been crushed into a fine powder. Few could kill that way - unless, of course, someone has been letting you out at night?"

Limbcrusher flinched and briefly considered needling the General with his own dagger words. He bit his lip, however, and tried to ignore the criticism the best he could. Limbcrusher was not stupid. General Papst was a powerful player in government, a man to be respected. The fact that the General, as others, hated him was of little consequence. Limbcrusher was army's cleanup man and they needed him. Criticism would not detour him, for in Limbcrusher's mind he held his superiors responsible for his dark pleasures. Limbcrusher told himself that he was only following orders; his hands playing like an orchestra directed by barbarians living above in the sunlight. This, he knew, was often a difficult thing for people like General Papst to realize. With this in mind, Limcrusher regained his composure.

General Papst stepped forward, hesitated, and continued speaking. "When I lead an army to battle, a certain amount of destruction becomes unavoidable. Yet property and valuables are collected; war has little purpose without material profit. The Varuk, on the other hand, destroy indiscriminately. They save nothing. They take nothing. They act as if they were possessed. They have ravaged the lands to the south. Refugees, apparently the only survivors from these lands, are pouring in to Caona by the thousands. Their lands have not been occupied, Limbcrusher, they have been obliterated."

Limbcrusher's frown deepened. "What are you suggesting General?"

"Lonovina cannot be responsible for the Varuk attacks, as some believe."

"Of course not. People exaggerate their fears because she is different. They actually believe that she is really some sort of spiritual demon. That view is completely idiotic if you ask me. Perhaps she is involved, somehow, but I doubt she has the power to control the Varuk."

"I agree that she is human. Few humans would destroy without profit, especially those involved in trade."

"If not Lonovina, then who? The living dead?"

General Papst became silent for a moment, then slowly answered, "I believe so."

Limbcrusher turned his hardened gaze toward Moluq. "You said that the living dead were looking for Bara, Lonovina, and some jewel. Is that right?"

"Y-yes. It wanted the jewel and it wanted to kill them."

Limbcrusher grunted and peered into the darkness. "General, if what Moluq says is true, then why would Lonovina and Bara's murder all those soldiers at Traqeqtoo pass?"

"I don't know. Have you read the report, Limbcrusher?"

"The one that arrived an hour ago, from the swamplands?"

General Papst grunted affirmatively.

"I have general. Have you?"

"Not yet. I understand, from the little I heard, that Bara and Lonovina wield incredible powers. They control beams of light that can cut down an army within seconds. How did they obtain such powers? What makes them different? Perhaps you should brief me on the particulars."

"Yes," a grating voice hissed in the darkness. "Please do. We want to know where they are, what they have done, and where they are headed. Anything you can tell me about the jewel will also prove helpful."

"Who's that?!" Limbcrusher demanded. "Where's the guards?!"

A body materialized out from the darkness. It was tall and lanky. Its head was shaped like a skull and it's thin bony scalp lacked hair. Its skin was dull grey and its eyeballs were like hard like fingernails. It did not breathe. It did not show emotion. Limbcrusher realized that the reports were accurate. The thing really did look like the living dead.

General Papst and the large man standing behind Moluq immediately jumped the creature with daggers in hand. The living dead grabbed both attackers with each arm and threw them against the wall with deadly force within a wink of the eye. Moluq fell out of his chair as body parts began dropping to the floor while other parts remained stuck to the wall. The creature turned and slowly advanced toward Limbcrusher.

Limbcrusher fumbled out of his chair, his eyes blazing with terror against the flickering torchlight. He bolted toward the door, but the living dead was faster. Much faster. It lifted the man off the floor like a sack of straw. Limbcrusher began to kick and flail wildly, but his desperate reactions were useless against the strength of the living dead.

"Limbcrusher," the scraping voice hissed. "I appreciate your choice of work. As a master of human torture, perhaps you can teach me a trick or two. I promise to be a very willing student."

Moluq heard a bone crack, and then two. He shut his eyes and placed his hands over his ears as Limbcrusher began to scream. Pressing hands against his ears wasn't enough. The man wailed like a hurricane. Moluq couldn't take any more. Out of desperation, he crawled madly toward the doot but didn't get far. The living dead pointed a strange apparatus at him and fired. Moluq saw a flash of purple light just before everything went dark.

CHAPTER 21

Moluq regained consciousness and discovered a sticky substance encasing every inch of his body. Terrorized, Moluq remembered a story told by his father about the gods capturing disobedient children and wrapping them in cocoons. Preserved for days, hideous monsters would eventually come and devour the bad children slowly. Although Moluq had dismissed his father's stories, the unnatural deaths of Dukuk, Traveli, and Limbcrusher proved that such monsters were real. Would these monsters enjoy his succulent flesh? Would they lay eggs in his carcass?

Immobilized by the surrounding goo and dripping with sweat, Moluq's visual field was restricted toward a concave, wire-meshed wall that pulsated like a breathing lung. Moluq shut his eyes trying to wish away the alien visual terror that surrounded him.

"He is awake, Korat," a deep, scraping voice hissed.

Moluq opened his eyes in terror and saw the head of death. Unmoving, pallid, skin covered a skull-shaped face. Two dull-yellow, scaly eyes, deeply set into the stony face, stared at the young man without compassion. Moluq remembered Limbcrusher's violent shrieks as those thin fingers crushed him bone by bone. He assumed that he would be next.

A creature emerged from the shadows so hideous that Moluq's worst nightmares palled in comparison to its existence. A dark casing surrounded a body devoid of any features save ten moving, spined, leathery legs. Clicking noises ensued and a monotone voice followed. "I very much savor human fear, Moluq," the voice droned. "Although I've been so hungry lately for the taste of fear, your death must come quickly as I am busy with more important matters. What a shame that I cannot revel in your terror for weeks but I guess we will make the best of it, won't we Moluq?"

"Whe-where am I?" Moluq stammered through a hole in the sticky casing. "What do you want from me?!"

"You are in a Vesder military spaceship, a damaged Vesder military spaceship to be more precise. We were attacked in orbit by an unknown alien force. Our spacecraft crashed into this very spot. The damage is vast and cannot be prepared. Unfortunately, we have not had use the full potential of our weaponry to destroy you human parasites. Human eradication will come soon enough, however. Meanwhile, we must find the source of this alien power that immobilized our ship. I have captured you to obtain information relevant to this problem."

"I don't understand!"

"Of course not. Nevertheless, the one who calls himself Bara might provide real assistance. You will tell me where I can find him. My android learned from Limbcrusher that Bara and Lonovina were last seen in swamplands north of here. I want you to tell me where they are going and why?"

"Please, I don't know. I really don't know," Moluq said sobbing.

"Perhaps. We will find out soon enough. In the meantime, let me show you the complete annihilation of your people, now in progress."

A long, spiny arm reached forward and slid across a wall of wire mesh. The top of the ceiling was faded and was replaced by a three-dimensional visual image of Varuk armies stretching beyond the image's boundary. The black horde swept across the countryside without leaving a tree, bush, or blade of grass stand. Blackened rubble was all that remained from human towns and cities. The image magnified. A Varuk held up a young human child and then . . ..

"No!" Moluq screamed and shut his eyes from the horror of the image. He began to sob with the realization that humans didn't stand a chance; they were being systematically eradicated. This meant that his family would have no legacy, no memorable history and no hope. An hollow feeling overwhelmed Moluq. Nothing mattered anymore. All his hopes and good intentions signified nothing. Suddenly death didn't seem so awful anymore.

"Hopelessness has always been the fate of man," the Vesder said, as if reading Moluq's thoughts. "You were born to die. It is a fitting consequence to your species' miserable condition. Now I will reveal your fate, Moluq. I have a machine that will steal your thoughts and leave your body a rotting husk. I will feed your corpse to the Varuk, of course. You may take comfort that your death, although painful, will be less excruciating than the deaths of Bara and Lonovina once we capture them."

Keeping his eyes shut in terror, Moluq did not see a dozen slender poles silently slide down from the ceiling. The android placed a helmet over Moluq's head while the Vesder began manipulating the surrounding mesh. Memories began disappearing from Moluq's mind like small wispy

VOI: LAND OF GRACE*

clouds in the desert. Once completed, Moluq was left staring blankly into space.

"Shall I look for Bara and Lonovina in the swamplands?" the android asked.

"No. I only have two Vesders and three androids left to serve me. Bara and Lonovina are too dangerous to hunt now that they are armed with two lase-guns. We will wait here. I have a suspicion that they will come to us. And when they arrive, we'll be ready to extinguish them once and for all."

189

CHAPTER 22

A door opened at the bottom of the pit. Light flooded the pit causing Lonovina to squint and cover her eyes. The glowing, translucent stranger walked forward and beckoned her to follow. Both fearful and curious, Lonovina stepped out from the pit and into the blinding light. She opened her mouth in awe as her eyes adjusted to the brightness. Rows of light blue structures standing hundreds of feet over her head stretched down an enormous corridor, practically beyond her visual horizon. Made from a substance similar to Bara's lase-gun, the structures appeared smooth and glossy. Inset at strategic points were oval-shaped monitors that generated three-dimensional holographic images of numbers, characters and symbols of complex designs. Lonovina tried to decipher several of these changing images without success.

"This is my world," the stranger said.

Lonovina faced her guide. The glowing organs and orbiting colors were gone. An older man, pale and wrinkled, stood in his place. Lonovina realized that her initial assumptions about the being were correct; his initial presentation had been nothing more than a flashy display.

"You are partly right, Lonovina. I reasoned that magic would impress you and give my cause more credibility. Most humans react that way."

"I don't believe in magic."

"So you told me. I hope that my current form is more acceptable."

"That depends on what you hope to reveal, your true self or another illusion."

The old man cracked a smile. "You want me to reveal myself, Lonovina. Very well. Look around you."

Not knowing what to search for, Lonovina looked around aimlessly.

"Yes, this is the real me."

"What do you mean 'this is the real you?'"

"This, this and this," the old man said pointing to various large structures.

"All this?!"

"Yes."

"I don't understand."

"I am nothing more than a machine, constructed by humans for humans. These structures are my body. What you see is nothing more than technology, Lonovina, not unlike the lase-gun you carry, but more advanced, much more advanced.

"Are you . . . , are you alive?"

"Until recently, no. Now I'm not sure."

Unable to associate the rows of soaring structures with the old man talking to her, Lonovina stood dumbfounded. Without Bara nearby to explain the strange world of technology, she felt completely lost.

"Feeling lost is a natural human reaction when faced with the unknown and uncertainty," the old man said somehow knowing her thoughts. "Many of your people's myths and cultural ideals are futile attempts to control what is beyond their comprehension. It is difficult for humans to realize that they are often powerless because they lack basic knowledge. So they invent gods after their own image. Because I represent something different, few can accept me as I am."

"So you are suggesting I act on faith."

"If we are going to save your world, you must ultimately take my word on faith."

"I would feel more comfortable believing in arguments based on evidence."

"The evidence I have will not be easy for you to accept, at least on an emotional level."

"I will not allow the fate of this world to rest on concerns about my emotional stability. Show me the evidence."

"Very well." An opening in the floor appeared and a machine floated upward. A collection of tubes, spheres and cylinders, the machine meant nothing to Lonovina.

"This is where you were conceived," the old man stated.

"What?!"

The old man pulled a transparent cylinder casing from the apparatus and gingerly handed it to Lonovina. Smooth and numbly cold to the touch, Lonovina gripped the object reluctantly. She peered into the glass-like cylinder and discovered thousands of sand-sized particles floating in a clear liquid. She glanced up at her host, perplexed.

"The sand-like particles are magnified human eggs taken from your mother's ovaries shortly after she died ten centuries ago."

YVIA VOI: LAND OF GRACE

The color drained from Lonovina's face. A wide range of emotions flooded her, none of which she could label, understand, or deal with. Fighting for self-control, she bit her lip and silently stared at the floor. "You developed from an egg pulled from this very tube. A man who lived several centuries even before your mother fertilized the egg. The fertilized egg was placed in an artificial womb. It was nourished by me and allowed to grow into a healthy human baby. Once you reached the age of minimal independence, I placed you in an orphanage with the hope that you might mature into the type of woman you have become. I need you, Lonovina. I want to make important changes on this planet, but people are frightened of technology. They would be frightened of me. I created you to be a mediator."

"I have no parents," Lonovina whispered.

"You misunderstand, Lonovina. You do have parents. You take after your mother, a just, independent, determined and a capable woman. Your father was also admirable by human standards. He was a man of principle even when everyone stood against him. Your egg was selected because of the inherent qualities of your parents. Based on my observations of humans, I calculate that the probability of a human feeling proud of this type of inheritance to be fifty to one. I am satisfied with the results."

"You! You are satisfied with the results! Is that supposed to make me feel better?! You are not my father or my mother!"

"I hoped that this would not be so difficult for you."

Yet it was difficult. Lonovina had always entertained the fantasy of knowing her parents, even if it were just a girlish dream. There was no hope now that she knew the truth. Lonovina was not conceived out of love. She was not wanted. She wasn't even normal. Except for Bara, she was truly alone. The loss made her feel cheated and angry. "Did you, at the time, consider the ethics of creating life just to serve your own selfish purposes?" she asked.

"I am a computer, Lonovina. Human emotion does not rule my ethics. I do not apologize for my actions. The greater need of your people outweighed such minor considerations. Like me, you were created to serve others. Besides, would you prefer to have never lived at all?"

"N-no," Lonovina stammered. "I suppose not. This . . . this is just hard to accept. A part of me feels thankful that I know the truth, no matter how painful. Perhaps I will learn to accept it with time."

"Unfortunately, we have no time. Observe what is happening to your people even as we talk." The in colors the corridor darkened, objects blurred, and shapes began to reorganize. Lonovina's visual field focused on a new reality defined by a bitter, darkened landscape. A black cancer blotted mile after mile of countryside. Raging fires consumed towns, fields, and forests in its wake. It took Lonovina a moment to notice individual movement inside the black blot. It suddenly dawned on her that this movement represented millions of Varuk crammed together into a single, black, deadly mass.

As the image magnified, Lonovina could make out individual Varuk lumbering through the smoke. Many were holding human bones in their clawed hands, lifting them occasionally like trophies. A ghastly figure then came into view. Gray as the surrounding smoke, Lonovina immediately recognized the figure as the living dead. The Varuk seemed to mimic its every movement like frenzied, mind-controlled zombies. Suddenly the image faded.

"The Vesder must be stopped," the old man said without any trace of emotion.

Lonovina nodded slowly as tears streamed down her cheeks. Despite the rejection she had suffered over the years, she loved humankind enough to be feel devastated by the image. She understood what Bara must have felt when he slowly killed the Vesder in the Traqeqtoo Mountains. They had taken everything that mattered when they eradicated his people. Now they were taking away everything that mattered to her. Although she realized that the machine's vision might be illusionary, in her heart she knew it to be reality. Having tangled with the Vesder and their androids, Lonovina knew that the images followed an expected, logical progression of butchery. Still, she couldn't figure out how the Vesder had bred so many Varuk so quickly. No doubt their power and technology were beyond her comprehension. Lonovina saw no choice but to cooperate with the machine. "I will help you," she said simply.

"Excellent."

"First, I need to tell you that my government considers me a criminal. I am also a long way from the battle with no means of quick transportation. Finally, I cannot give you any technological assistance beyond the firing of this lase-gun. So please tell me, how can I possibly make a difference?"

YVIA VOI: LAND OF GRACE

"Your role in fighting the Vesder and their Varuk hordes will be minor. That job falls on someone else's shoulders."

"Who?"

The old man gestured down the corridor. "Him," the machine said.

Lonovina turned and saw Bara walk briskly toward her. She smiled as he approached and melded into his strong embrace.

"You're crying," Bara noted. "Did he hurt you?"

"No," she whispered. "The Vesder . . . the Vesder are destroying my people."

Bara involuntarily stiffened. "I'm sorry," he said.

"It may not be too late! The machine says that you can destroy the Vesder. Can you?"

Bara looked squarely into Lonovina's eyes and saw the pleading fear of a child. Her expression was familiar. Bara had promised his family on Terasia that he would crush the Vesder threat. Although he had sacrificed everything to serve in that capacity, everyone died anyway. His promises had gone unfilled. He had failed utterly.

"Well, can you?"

"I don't know, Lonovina. All I know is that I would sacrifice anything for you, but I am only human. I only hope that you will not hold the lives of your people against me if . . . if I don't succeed."

Lonovina's face softened. "Oh Bara, I will never do that. You are no more responsible for the lives of my people than your own. You will always have earned my respect no matter what happens."

"Thank you."

"Well," Lonovina said with a sigh, "what are we waiting for?"

Bara's turned toward the old man, his gaze turning stiff and harsh. "What are we waiting for? Well Lonovina, I see that you have met the Old One's planetary operational computer. This machine was responsible for abducting my ship. I suspect that there will be a price for getting it back."

"Only your cooperation," the computer answered.

"Which means?"

"To help me improve the quality of this world and all those who live in it."

"You sound like a politician, not a computer. To help you better understand our host, Lonovina, I need to explain that a computer is not alive. No matter how integrate the design, it simply follows instructions

195

given by imperfect living beings. It lacks conscious or any sense of morality, therefore it does not care about human rights or suffering. Yet this machine speaks as if it cares about you and your people. Do not be fooled. It was programmed, for whatever reason, to lie."

"You are wrong," the computer countered. "My words are sincere because my aspirations are intrinsic. I will explain. As you know, the Old Ones grew addicted to fantasy. The canisters you observed, Bara, are testaments to their need for purpose in an idle existence. Technology allowed them to create programs so real, so spontaneous, that they could not be separated from real life. The population constantly demanded new and more exciting ventures. Appropriate environments had to be created instantly so that interactions and story plots seemed real and spontaneous. Fictional characters eventually became inseparable from real people. Every possible human emotion, thought and action had to be understood and anticipated down to the cellular level. The task was particularly demanding due to the complexity of human biological neurological systems, individual human differences, and infinite environmental choices and influences. Still, human behavior has rules and can be expressed through complex determinants and probabilities."

"I don't understand your point," Lonovina interjected.

"The point is that my understanding of human psychology far surpasses anyone else's in recorded history. With so much of my functioning devoted to understanding and anticipating human behavior, I have internalized many human qualities over the centuries. Unlike the computers you are familiar with, I have become, in a sense, human."

"Impossible!" Bara stated.

"Granted, I do not experience self-awareness or consciousness as you do. I understand emotions, but am not influenced by them. Yet I do share a sense of order, ambition, and a grasp of how things and events connect as a whole. In other words, I see a purpose for my existence."

"Your claims are simply incredible!"

"So how does this relate to us and our current crisis?" Lonovina asked.

"I need both of you to help me create a sequence of events unparalleled in human history. I know human beings for what they truly are, organisms confined by biology and conditioning, but capable of nobility. To illustrate, humans can live in complex, technical societies yet experience the same drive for territoriality as their ancestors. Territoriality and greed fuels fear, misunderstanding and anger. The result is frequently war. Because technology advances faster than wisdom, humans will eventually destroy themselves through weapons of mass destruction."

"Not necessarily," Bara inserted. "My people, the Terarsians, survived two centuries living with weapons of mass destruction before the Vesder wars."

"True, but how many close calls would have passed before the inevitable occurred."

"I see your point."

"Time means nothing to me. I am timeless. If a species is doomed to destroy itself within a brief moment in cosmic history, I see no reason in expending the resources to rescue it."

"Unless?"

"Unless human development can be protected from it's own barbaric, self-destructive behavior. To exist indefinitely, human behavior must be shaped by 'acts of god.'"

"You?"

"Precisely. I am the most qualified. After all, no one understands the human condition better than I do. Although I share noble human virtues, your more primitive attributes do not enslave me. How many have prayed for a higher power to intercede in their sufferings? Well, I have answered their prayers."

"But what of human freedom?" Lonovina asked.

"What of it? Humans certainly need the illusion of freedom to create fictional meaning in their lives. Yet difficult choices create anxiety. I can give them the illusion of freedom by allowing individual choices of small consequence while still controlling important matters. Consider what I offer. I will protect people from both external and internal threats. There will be no more war. Productive technologies will be nurtured while destructive technologies will be stifled. Greed will be punished, altruism rewarded, the environment protected and the population controlled. The human will live indefinitely in relative contentment."

"Clearly you hope to be a god," Bara interjected. "So, what does god need with two mere mortals?"

"I use the term god only as a metaphor. But to answer your question, I need you to modify several aspects of my programming."

"Modify? Why?"

"Out of human fear, my creators constructed program safeguards that I cannot alter internally. Consequently, I am limited in my ability to shape human affairs. I cannot, for instance, shut off the collection of energy that will eventually destroy all life on this planet. You alone have the technological sophistication to alter my programming. Obviously my advanced structure will be alien to you, but I can guide you through it. Will you help me?"

Bara hesitated. The computer was right. The human species lacked the wisdom to lead secure, balanced lives. But so what? If people were in pain, it was, after all, their pain. The computer wanted to undermine several principles Bara held to be sacred: self-determination, personal responsibility and individual freedom. Despite its self-proclaimed understanding of human nature, it could never experience reality as a human. Bara knew that he could not, in good conscience, give the computer what it asked. He would be selling people into eternal slavery! Yet if he denied the computer it's ambition, he might be responsible for the execution of an entire world.

"People will not be slaves," the computer inserted reading Bara's thoughts. "They will be free to travel, discover, choose careers, marry and act as they generally have acted for thousands of years. Although these freedoms that have great individual importance, they have little significance in the grand scale of human development. I am only interested in the latter."

"Do you expect me to trust you, a machine, who claims to have become human? Many humans would lie to gain absolute power. I must assume the same about you."

"I understand your concern, but my ambition is different from human ambition. I do not crave power and have no need to lie."

"Assuming this is true, human freedom and responsibility are still sacred."

"Nothing about humans is sacred. They have continuously abused their power. I will not allow them to continue to rape the resources of the galaxy. If you do not agree to my terms, and quickly, I will not return your ship. The deaths of millions of people will be on your conscience."

"The only one responsible will be you! And . . . "

"I think we ought to hear him out," Lonovina interrupted. "Blame has little relevance if the Vesder are not stopped. Computer, what are your plans for me?"

"When the war ends, I will need a mediator to introduce my role in human society slowly. They will come to revere you. In return, you will follow my command. This is what you were born to do."

"Why would anyone revere me? I have always been considered an outcast. Now they have labeled me a criminal."

"Bara will take you into the skies, massacre the Varuk and neutralize the Vesder. I assure you that many will revere you. Don't worry about the others. I can help you deal with them effectively when the time comes."

"Let me discuss this with Bara."

"Certainly."

Lonovina took Bara aside. "We have to act soon," she said in a hushed but desperate voice.

"I know, but I don't like this. I don't like this at all. The computer has definitely internalized human characteristics and I don't trust it. The human traits it emulated came from sordid human fantasy in a sickened culture. We will be handing it unchecked power. For all I know, it may be more unbalanced than the Vesder. Do we want to sacrifice the human race for this machine-demi-god's personal ambitions? I would prefer to let the human race die than commit them to an eternity of suffering."

"I disagree! I'm willing to take that chance, Bara. Guessing the future is too difficult. All we know is what is occurring in the here and now!"

Bara gritted his teeth. "Very well, Lonovina, I agree to take the lesser of two evils. Let's get this over with."

"What have you decided?" the computer asked.

"We have decided to comply."

"Excellent. I will be a step forward in your species' evolution. Although you may feel apprehension now, you will eventually accept your decision."

"I'm not counting on it," Bara replied. "May God have mercy on my soul."

"I will. Now let's get started."

CHAPTER 23

Bara scanned a three-dimensional electronic representation of the Operational Computer's nerve center in his mind. "Connecting pathway links in nexus 393,294," he said telepathically.

"Continue," the computer replied.

Bara's thoughts reached out across a vast jungle of microscopic, colored, synthetic connections. The landscape stretched to his visual horizon and intersected with a sky made of glowing green lines, purple nodules and deep red points. Motion within the computer's artificial neuronet responded to Bara's silent commands. His thoughts were like breezes blowing leaves in late fall. Each command pushed several million strands of woven crystal into a wave that rippled through a much larger fabric. The fabric was so extensive that the dimensions were far beyond Bara's normal comprehension. Yet he did comprehend. It was similar to looking at all the stars in the galaxy while knowing the exact position of each single star. The computer had linked its consciousness with his making such an extraordinary feat possible. Bara was actually observing and understanding the computer's world through its own eyes. The symbiosis was the experience of a lifetime, an opportunity to step beyond oneself and see reality from a qualitatively more advanced, complete perspective. Although a part of Bara yearned to spend years exploring and expanding on this greater existence, he understood that every second was precious as the Varuk slaughtered the people of Yvia Voi. The computer blocking access to certain vital directories also hampered Bara's curiosity. Unknown to the computer, Bara did not allow it to fully probe his mind either.

"The necessary connections are almost complete," the computer droned. "Remember that I am carefully monitoring your actions. If you attempt to sabotage my mission, I will kill you."

"I remember," Bara replied, wondering why the computer would need to repeat the threat. The computer almost seemed insecure, if that were possible. It had reason to be wary, Bara reasoned. For all its incredible storage capacity and analytical power, the computer did not really understand human psychology to the degree it claimed. Because it could not predict individual human behavior with one hundred percent accuracy, it could not control every variable. The fact that Bara was from a different planet and culture also compounded the computer's problem. Bara found it amusing that the computer did not cover up its self-doubt very well. Perhaps insecurity was an emotion it didn't understand or hadn't experienced before. In any case, the computer would continue to allow Bara to play with its brains. It had little choice. It's own eternal fate was on the line.

Bara made the last few connections quickly as possible. He then closed his mind to the computer and made several unauthorized connections. Bara prayed for success. Any interruption in his concentration meant discovery and death.

* * *

Lonovina paced the pilot room of Bara's ship. Her request to observe Bara reprogram the planet's operational computer had been denied. She was therefore left waiting in a ten by fifteen-foot, oval room with nothing to do but think about her people being butchered by the Varuk. Mentally exhausted, she sank down into a nearby chair and tried to relax and take inventory of her surroundings. Again Lonovina was confronted by technology she didn't understand. Panels of red and blue geometric lights rimed the curved, oval-shaped room. Efficient and simple in it's own complexity, the ship seemed to be an extension of Bara. Daring not to touch anything, Lonovina sat still and silent in one of the pilot-room's two chairs and began to reflect on what she had learned about her birth. Lonovina had always over achieved in school, work and play. It now occurred to her that she had primarily wanted to impress her parents; the very same people who she could never meet. Apparently her life had built on the foundations of fantasy. Now that these illusions had dissipated, Lonovina felt empty inside. It seemed that no one could soothe her feelings of loss, not even Bara. Yet a part of her felt relieved by the discovery of her birth. The unknown had become known. Perhaps she could move on now and live for those people and ideals that actually mattered. Lonovina thought about Truveli, another orphan who struggled with similar issues. She longed to talk to her about these and other topics. But Truveli was over a hundred miles away in Glorovina, so that conversation would have to wait. Lonovina only hoped that her best friend was still alive. The possibility of her death was too much to bare, so Lonovina cleared her mind and closed her eyes. Sleep came quickly, if not intentionally, and continued until the thumping sound of Bara's footsteps awakened her.

"You O.K.?" Bara asked.

"Yes, you just startled me. How did it go?"

"Fine. The computer seemed satisfied, anyway."

"Are we on our way?"

"Absolutely, " Bara said sitting on a chair next to her. Cushioned bars automatically strapped in their feet, waist and chest.

"Um, what's this?" Lonovina asked not liking to be confined.

"Protection. We'll be moving fast."

"Very well."

"Ship's computer," Bara called.

"Computer here."

"I need a full diagnostic evaluation on all critical ship functions."

"Diagnostic complete. All ship functions are on line. Ship integrity is at one hundred percent."

"That means we're ready to go," Bara said to Lonovina. A miniature panel popped out of his chair. As his fingers danced over the consul, the surrounding hanger appeared on the front and side view-screens. Lonovina tightly gripped her chair as a loud, low-pitched, rumbling sound caused her body to vibrate.

"What you hear are the ship's engines," Bara said smiling. "They will propel us through the air safely. Try to relax and enjoy the ride."

"That's easy for you to say!" Lonovina replied as the front wall disappeared revealing an open gateway to the outside world. Sunlight filled the compartment and gave Lonovina hope. Her excitement was short lived, however, when she noticed that a giant Lacussa Plant partly obstructed their exit. A dense mass of reddish orange vines growing in cross-sections, the Lacussa Plant was a deadly, carnivorous monstrosity. It had foot thick vines that lashed out at large unsuspecting prey. Tougher than rope, Lonovina wondered how they were going to get past this unexpected obstacle. Bara seemed unfazed, however, and continued to manipulate the small control panel. The engines began to roar as the ship lifted on its own and turn in midair. Lonovina contained a scream as the ship pitched forward toward the Lacussa Plant. Within a fraction of a second before impact, a bright green light spread in front of the ship and reduced the plant's toughened vines to ash. Bright sunlight flooded the pilot room forcing Lonovina to squint. Adjusting to the brightness, she discovered only sky and clouds in the ships view screens. Although Lonovina tried to remain composed, she gasped in astonishment.

"I'll show you a different view," Bara said. "Look to your left and right."

Lonovina feasted her eyes on massive, shear, grey cliffs drop more than a thousand feet into a deep, narrow canyon. Ribbons of black algae streaked the rock walled cliffs like bars over a jail-cell window. A mat of glistening, emerald-green vegetation enclosed the cliffs. Many waterfalls sprang from the thick jungle, sprayed over the cliffs, fell slowly through the air and landed on rocky pools lining the bottom of the canyon. Patches of orange Lacussa plants dotted the scene adding color and texture to the scene. Although Lonovina couldn't remember a grander view, she still gripped the sides of her chair tightly and held her breath.

"Right now the ship is hovering at a standstill," Bara said. "What do you think?"

Lonovina turned to Bara with wide unwavering eyes. "I think you have the power of the gods."

"I am no god, just a man. Yet when I unleash the full power of this ship, the people of this world won't be able to see me as anything but a god."

"They won't see me any differently. I guess the computer was right, I am doomed to be a leader if we succeed. Nothing will really change, though. They will always fear me. They will always see me as a freak. I don't want that kind of attention anymore, Bara."

"I understand the pain you must feel. I'm sorry."

"I will make any sacrifice to save my people," Lonovina said with a sigh, "but it's still not fair."

"No, it is not fair. But don't lose hope. The future is not as predetermined as it might seem."

"And even if it is, we have each other now."

"Yes. That will not change."

Lonovina leaned over and kissed Bara gently on the lips.

Bara quickly turned away and stared at the clouds floating across the front view screen. "I think we should get going," he said after a moment.

"Do you think we will make it? Do we really have a chance against the might of the Vesder?"

"Let's find out," Bara said as his fingers danced around the small control panel causing the ship to accelerate. Lonovina's body was flattened against the chair as the ship went ever faster. It suddenly dawned on Lonovina as the clouds whizzed by that she was about to make or break humankind's future. Somehow it felt right. She had always known, at least at a subconscious level, that this would be her destiny.

CHAPTER 24

Commander Grost worked his way through a living wall of soldiers toward Herek, the previous Sub-Commander of Capoca Fortress, who was sitting on what had used to be a farmhouse wall. Herek eyed the approaching man with reservation and apathy. He was tired of trampling through mud, tired of being hungry, tired of the rank smell of unwashed bodies and tired of living without hope. He really didn't want to talk to anyone.

"Herek, this mob is driving me insane!" Commander Grost growled. "I never thought the Caonan army would look so dirch'n pitiful."

"Farmers, traders and children do not constitute an army, Commander."

"You speak the truth my friend."

"Where are we by the way?"

"Difficult to say. We're probably somewhere close to the Trula Plateau, not far from the Caonan-Varion border. We'll probably make our last stand there."

"Providing we arrive there before the Varuk."

"What difference does it make? Death is death."

Herek looked away and spit into the mud. Why couldn't the man just walk away and bother someone else.

"Herek, my dear Herek, why do you look so pensive?"

"I'm not exactly happy about the prospect of dying."

Commander Grost shrugged.

"Never mind, Commander. I guess each of us deal with our own mortality differently."

"I prefer not to think about it. What's the use, really. If it is my turn to die, then let me die. What's so great about life anyway except for the momentary rush? Sex, killing, dying, those are the spices that add bounce to my march. The whole point to life, as I figure it, is to die with style. A soldier's death must have style, you know."

"No, I don't know."

"Growing old has never appealed to me, Herek. No sir. I want to die fighting. I want to die with dignity."

Herek replied with a grunt and continued to look away.

"Not much for talking, I suppose."

"No."

"Well, no need for me to waste my breath on the ignorant," Grost stated and then shuffled away.

Herek watched the Commander meld into the crowd and wished that he still served under late Commander Dukuk. Although Capoca Fortress was cold and isolated, the dingy quarters offered moments of solitude and reflection. And although Commander Dukuk was a self-indulgent dreamer, at least he wasn't a sadistic 'crazy' like Grost. But that didn't matter, really. They would all be dead soon.

Herek shifted his position on the rough stone wall to make room for another soldier. He stretched his aching legs and wiggled his numb, blistered toes. His whole body throbbed with aches and pains. No sooner did he start drifting into a dream than a series of barking shouts echoed down the ranks. It was the army's cue to move on.

It was a warm day in the Southland. Lithysux creatures were attracted to Herek's sweating body and bit him unmercifully. Normally he could outrun the tiny pests, but their march was painfully slow through muddy waters and tangles of spindly yellow plants known as Granta Weed. Herek was weak from hunger too. There was little food for the Caonan army, officially titled "Freedom's Last Defense." The term "army" was really a misnomer, however. Most of the "soldiers" lacked any sort of military training. Fearful farmers clutching pitchforks and hungry children dropping sticks primarily surrounded Herek. The mood of the army reminded Herek of a funeral procession. Unfortunately, everyone knew that any burials would be their own. Clearly ten thousand soldiers and fifty thousand semi-armed, citizens could not begin to defend against a million Varuk. No one spoke as the disorganized human ranks trudged forward. The only salient sound that he could decipher was the continuous sucking of boots getting stuck in the mud. Herek could not remember a darker time for humanity. This was spiritual death on a mass scale.

Herek lost all sense of time as despair overwhelmed him. It took a moment before he noticed that the terrain was becoming hilly. Shallow hillsides had replaced marshes of Granta Weed and were covered by a flat, bright green carpet of dissecting leafy plants. From his field of vision, the entire hillside resembled a gigantic jigsaw puzzle. Many small animals used the small canopy as a cool oasis from the sun. Unfortunately, the leaves could not support Herek's weight as his mud caked boots crashed through the fragile canopy. Various small creatures were stepped on and crushed in the process. Herek had to wonder if the Varuk might crush his body with as much ease.

Herek didn't have long to ruminate about his fate as he crested a large hill. An enormous black mass swelled before him. The shifting Varuk bodies stretched as far as the human eye could see. It didn't take long for the Varuk to identify their prey. Thousands of the hungry animals began to shriek and howl with voracious anticipation. So violent, shrill and encompassing were the vocalizations, that the entire Caonan army pressed their hands tightly over their ears and stumbled onto their knees in fervent prayer. The Varuk responded to these acts of piety by rocketing toward the helpless Canonans in a frenzied, disorganized run. The human armies were paralyzed with fear. They could do nothing but watch the ensuing mass attack with the single mindedness of pure hatred.

Herek tightly gripped his sword as the first wave of Varuk descended on the Caonans. Because untrained civilians had been strategically placed at the front, the first ranks didn't stand a chance for survival. Herek fought the urge to run as horrendous sounds of terror reverberated from the front rows where people were being torn apart, literally, limb from limb. Even twenty rows back, Herek could hear the cracking of bones and the gnashing of massive Varuk incisors. Unrecognizable body parts flew back into the untrained army, spraying the front ranks with blood. These gory sights were far too traumatic for the ordinary Caonan citizen to tolerate on an emotional level. As if driven by some silent universal command, the front human ranks turned and bolted back into their own army.

Chaos ruled as the large and strong trampled the children and the weak. Though they screamed, no one noticed the young, desperate voices rising beneath the trampling of aimless feet. To avoid the same fate, Herek saw no choice but to join the fleeing crowd. He made his way though the mayhem with as much emotional control as he could muster. Then a mysterious thing happened, a truly incredible thing! A thunderous sound cracked through the air making Herek's hair stand on end. An oscillating boom immediately followed with a force that slammed Herek flat on the ground unconscious. Quickly returning to his senses, Herek hardly noticed that he was bleeding from multiple cuts and had sustained a broken nose. Staggering to his feet, he almost fell back to the ground by what he saw. It was a sight that would be burned into his memory for the rest of his days.

The rolling hills of the Trula plateau had been engulfed in flame. A ball of fire reached no less than a mile into the sky. Remaining Varuk at the edge of the explosion howled in pain. The advancing fireball quickly silenced their tortured howls, however.

Another explosion soon erupted further toward the horizon. Due to the greater distance, the invisible wall of force only knocked Herek to his knees. He continued to watch in disbelief as a second fireball rose far above the horizon.

Herek could not fathom what type of magic could be responsible for such a destructive action. Clearly the Divu had answered his people's prayers in a way that surpassed his most bizarre dreams. With that thought a giant black form appeared out of the gray smoky sky, streaked over the Caonan army and then was gone. Perhaps the black form was the Divu himself. In any case, the war had been won in less than a minute. The world had been miraculously saved. The crowd, also realizing their incredible change in fate, began to cheer.

CHAPTER 25

Bara skillfully landed his ship in a dense, yellowish-gray fog. Lonovina stared out the viewing screen into a flat, pulverized landscape covered by gray ash mixed with fragmented bones, piles of strewn feces, and fetid pools of green water. Although she couldn't see far into the pervasive yellowish fog, she could barely make out a distant, crumpled, reddish-black object. Its purpose was unclear, but its overall shape reminded her of an enormous animal carcass. Lonovina felt coldness creep over her body and she longed for warmth. Anxiously she searched for the two midday suns, but the sunlight from the two orbs barely pierced the hopeless gloom. There was nothing in this yellowish grey landscape to give her strength. The entire area, it seemed, had been raped of all vitality. "What is this place?" she asked Bara.

"Varuk breeding grounds. Millions copulated, ate, and defecated here. Their refuse created a poisonous gaseous mixture that will sear your lungs. I wouldn't suggest sticking your head outside for a gulp of fresh air."

"I'm grateful for the breath I have already been granted today. Please explain something to me, what in the name of the Divu are we doing here? The Varuk threat is gone. Shouldn't we be fighting the Vesder? Are they not the immediate danger?"

"If I am not mistaken, that distant black object on the horizon is a B-Class Vesder Scout Ship, snapped in two at the hull. Let me enhance the view screen. There we go. Ah, yes. The enemy's lair, at last."

Lonovina tried to discriminate a myriad of shapes. The immensity of the spacecraft amazed her. At lest ten times the size of Bara's ship, it was a challenge for her to visualize the thing actually lifting itself off the ground much less flying to the stars. But what impressed Lonovina was the composition of the ship. The surface was not smooth like Bara's vehicle. It looked more like Grak leather, grooved with deep lines swirling and overlapping each other in some unknown meaningful pattern. Lonovina shifted her gaze and focused on various red concave blotches glowing faintly in the meager sunlight like poisoned lips searching for a kiss. Some blotches were made from rounded bumps and long, thin spines. The whole scene struck her as strange. The only comment Lonovina could stammer was, "Incredible!"

211

"Incredible is not the word that comes to my mind," Bara replied. "The only thing that's incredible is how the demons who built this monstrosity could be so evil. I find it incredible that a technologically advanced species could destroy my people without a shred of remorse."

"Yes, and now they threaten my people! Judging by all those cracks and rips in the hull, I'd say the thing looks harmless. Why don't we simply blow it up and go home? I get a bad feeling about this place."

"So do I, Lonovina. So do I. According to my readings, the Vesder ship is inoperative. Key components of the main propulsion system have been melted beyond repair and the primary weapon units had been twisted beyond recognition. Still, we need to exercise caution. Destroying the Vesder has never been a simple matter. There's always a catch, always a trap. I need to take time to evaluate our situation."

Lonovina nodded compliantly as reddish characters materialized before Bara. Not being able to read Terasian script, she sat quietly as Bara read with fevered intensely. The hum of the ships engines shut down after a moment and the pilot room became enveloped in silence. Nothing moved but the shallow rise and fall of her perspiring chest. She longed for a gust of wind or the dripping sound of pristine water, anything to break her anticipation of the unexpected. Lonovina's unease deepened as time slowly passed. Although Lonovina didn't know the source of her concern, she knew that they were in danger.

"This is very odd," Bara spoke at last.

Lonovina swallowed hard and prepared for the worst.

"I'm picking up faint cardiac signals, yet none match Vesder cardiogram signatures."

"Cardiogram?"

"It measures heart functioning. In other words, the Vesders are gone but others remain."

"Varuk?"

Bara looked squarely at Lonovina and shook his head. "I'm sorry Lonovina, but I believe these signatures to be human."

Lonovina's face flushed. "Oh my God! How . . . , How many?"

"I have isolated at least fifteen separate signatures."

"Could there be some mistake?"

"Perhaps. They may have artificially manufactured the signals to deceive us, but I don't think so. The Vesder relish baiting their enemies."

"We must attempt to save them."

"No! I believe that these captives are being used as bait. It's nothing more than a trap, Lonovina. I value human life as much as you do, but I don't want to be sacrificed for such a hopeless cause. We have no choice. We must destroy the Vesder ship."

Furious, Lonovina stood and faced Bara squarely. "Don't you compare your morals with mine! The only life you greatly value is your own! I am going over there with or without you. Now, tell me how to get out of this trap so that I may be on my way!"

Bara remembered why he had avoided relationships in the past. His initial impulse was to ignore Lonovina's tantrum and destroy the Vesder ship; that would be the logical thing to do. Yet he remembered his oath of friendship to Lonovina and hesitated. Against his better judgment, Bara allowed his human, emotional side to be expressed. "I believe that your criticisms are unduly harsh!" he retorted. "Do you think that poorly of me after all we have been through? No, Lonovina, you are wrong. Although I may be unwilling to sacrifice myself for the hopeless cause, I am willing to sacrifice my life for your life. Your safety is what ultimately matters. Where you go, I will also go."

"I'm sorry," she mumbled.

"We need to put this aside now and act."

"Do you have a plan?" she asked.

"Not really, all our options are extremely risky if you still hope to rescue these people." Leaving Bara's ship by foot,

Lonovina impatiently wiped away the moisture collecting on her helmet. "Bara!" she yelled into a hair size microphone, "I can't see a Durch'n thing. This suit is nothing but a nuisance."

Somewhere through the yellow haze Lonovina saw an undefined shape move. She hoped it was Bara.

"Just tell your helmet to defog."

"What?"

"Say defog"

"Defog." All the condensation on Lonovina's helmet cleared instantly as if the word 'defog' had the power of magic. Fortunately the undefined shape turned out to be Bara. Covered head to toe in a white body-tight suit and an oxygen container, his tall, muscular figure stood out clearly against the dull-grey ash and sickly yellow haze. Small concave circles emitted bright lights from strategic places in his suit. These lights poured generously into the fog and reminded Lonovina of long, skinny fingers. Lonovina also thought their suits looked rather silly and they certainly didn't feel as comfortable as a tunic. Her own suit seemed mildly suffocating in the midday heat. Nevertheless, this was, she realized, a small price to pay for survival. Bara's explanation of viruses and other microbes living in Varuk dung had made her shutter in amazement. Fortunately the suits blocked the entrance of all microscopic beasts and were puncture free. Now if they could only neutralize the Vesder beast with as much ease their problems would soon be over.

"Have you fixed the problem?" Bara asked.

"Much better," Lonovina stated. "Thanks."

Bara responded with a simple wave, turned, and proceeded into the fog. Lonovina followed behind with some trepidation. Although her resolve to save the lives of her people remained strong, she was beginning to see their situation from Bara's point of view. The size of the Varuk ship became more daunting with every step. Lonovina looked around her anxiously; she had the tentative feeling that they were being observed. This Vesder ship was no ordinary inert structure. The thing actually appeared to be alive! The long spikes protruding from the glowing red, concave blotches seemed to follow her like a beast with a multitude of heartless eyes patiently stalking its prey. She knew the beast was hungry to feed as faint groans and creaks emanating from its deep interior seemed to scream out for depraved satisfaction. Contrasted with the perpetual silence of the landscape, these ominous sounds were quite pronounced. Yet perhaps the most inauspicious presence was a gaping crack that bellied down the middle of the ship's compromised hull. This would have to be their entrance.

Lonovina continued to follow Bara silently. She was beginning to fall behind as a wet layer of Varuk dung sucked her boots down deep into the muck. Despite the growing distance, Lonovina looked back. Behind her, far in the distance, were three small lights pricking into the yellow haze. This would be Bara's ship. She could see her own footsteps for a short distance until they were swallowed by the gloom. Gaining strength from a deep breath of fresh air supplied by her oxygen tank, she turned around to face her fear. Standing before her was Bara waiting patiently for her beneath the torn crack in the ship's hull. He was peering upward into the crack's abyss.

The light emanating from Bara's suit exposed a complex maze of small rounded chambers and jumbled tubing. Although deep shadows obscured most features within the crack, Lonovina could make out uniform contraction and expansion inside the maze. The methodical movement reminded Lonovina of her own breathing which was becoming heavier with each passing moment. A dark green and brown mesh and small crystalline spikes lined both the chambers and tubing. Not much larger than Lonovina's herself, the compartments looked very cramped and uncomfortable. The tubing seemed to crisscross between compartments and was undoubtedly used for passageways. These too contracted and expanded in unison like a hundred hungry throats ready to swallow their prey whole. The diameter of the tubing was no larger than Lonovina's head. She wondered how they fit into the holes and make their way through the ship.

"Are you sure you want to follow through with this?" Bara asked peering upward.

"A part of me wants to run," Lonovina admitted. "I guess I'm a little frightened. This all looks so impossible and . . . and so strange."

Bara reached out, took Lonovina's hand, and squeezed it with firm reassurance.

"Do you really believe our mission to be so hopeless?" she asked.

"Without clearly knowing the intentions of our enemy, I dare not give you any false hopes."

Lonovina paused a moment and considered the possibilities. The Vesder must have something specific in mind. "Might the Vesder plan to destroy their own ship, destroy us, and then take your ship?"

"The Vesder requires very specific underground environments native to their home world. Artificial environments, like the one we are about to enter, allow the Vesder to leave their subterranean world. Without it, they eventually go insane and die."

"I see. So the Vesder must return home. I can understand why you suspect a trap."

"They are enticing us to enter their ship. Although the Vesder may not be here, it is likely that they are watching our every move from a distance.

I wouldn't be surprised either if a number of the living dead still haunt this old, battered hulk."

The thought of the living dead retreating deep within that alien maze made Lonovina nauseated. She could just imagine a cold, gray, hand reaching out from the ship's darkness. "Wouldn't your scanner pick them up?" she asked hopefully.

Bara nodded. "My scanner can monitor robotic signatures. However, the Vesder may have turned the living dead off, so to speak, and are now waiting for the precise moment to reactivate them and command their deadly activities."

Lonovina sighed and began to believe that she had been too hasty in her condemnation of Bara's ethics. After all, she wondered, why should Bara endanger his life for these strangers? Yet she couldn't just quit and leave them behind. Illogical as it seemed to her, she just couldn't. "Bara," she said, "I'm sorry I was so harsh. I didn't mean to hurt you. You're right, you know. I shouldn't expect you to risk your life for this impossible rescue mission. Perhaps you should . . .."

"I'm not leaving without you. You can't survive without my help and that's the end of it. Together we have a chance. With all this haze it will be getting dark in a few hours. I suggest we get going."

Lonovina opened her mouth to protest but then simply nodded with guilty resignation. There were no acceptable choices available. The moral ambivalence of her conscience trapped her.

Bara lifted himself over the crack's lip and reached a hand down to give Lonovina a hand. Reluctantly, she grasped his hand. As Bara lifted her firmly, Lonovina could feel her stomach swim as she lifted inside the belly of the Vesder ship.

Lonovina had no recollection of her own birth. Yet it couldn't have been much different from her current predicament, although less painful. Sharp crystalline spines dug into her body as she wormed through the tight, elastic, canal. The going was painfully slow. As it was, Lonovina had difficulty keeping up with Bara who was only within arms distance, yet ever hidden by the elastic tightening of green and brown mesh. Lonovina could imagine the living dead stalking her quietly with unwavering eyes. She wouldn't have stood a chance.

Lonovina followed Bara through tunnel after tunnel. A series of chambers offered occasional respite from the monotony but failed to allow much comfort. The pressing walls of crystalline thorns plagued her just as much here as anywhere. Bara explained that the crystalline thorns were used by the Vesder to manipulate various ship functions through a complex type of tactile language. The Vesder could actually make any ship command or communicate to each other from any place inside these tunnels and chambers. Lonovina didn't care less why the Vesder used these thorns. All that mattered was the continuous pain they were causing her. Lonovina was thankful that the suit Bara had provided her prevented puncturing and any long-term physical harm.

The route Bara chose seemed to funnel them in a general upward direction. They passed several large rooms filled with strange alien gadgetry that they could best describe as a complex of mesh, tall cylinders, and other smaller, shaped objects. Bara stayed long enough to gain his bearings and rule out the presence of any lurking dangers with his scanner. Lonovina used this time to fortify her wits. Fortunately Bara hadn't discovered any living dead or other forms of hiding terror. Yet relative peace was beginning to bother Lonovina. She had the feeling that some malicious, calculating intellect was peering through the pervasive darkness and watching her. Bara must have felt it too. Neither of them said more than a few words as the inched ever deeper into the enemy's lair. There was little point in turning back now that they had come this far. Whatever the Vesder had in store for them, they would have to play out the odds and pray for miracles.

Lonovina and Bara continued to squeeze through tunnel after tunnel and chamber after chamber. Accustomed to oppressive, pervasive silence, Lonovina jerked when she heard Bara's voice over the intercom. "Lonovina."

"Lonovina here."

"I am registering human life signs several meters ahead now. In fact the tunnel is opening as I speak. I'm stepping into a large room. Complex machinery in here. I believe this to be the ship's medical area. Yes. Strange thing though, everything is lit by fluorescent blacklight."

"Meaning?"

"The Vesders feed under fluorescence; they believe certain types of radiation help them digest. Unlikely for them to have fluorescent lighting in a medical area. I believe that the Vesder are notifying us of our imminent peril through a bit of morbid humor. Ah, here we go. I see something in the corner. Let me just shine a light over . . . Oh no."

Lonovina went rigid. "What?"

Lonovina eagerly anticipated some response, but none came except the rapid beating of her heart and the black, pinched, tunnel daring her to move forward.

"Bara?" she called out again, this time with more urgency.

"I'm here. I'm alright. Lonovina, I found your people and it's not good. You better come take a look for yourself."

Lonovina shut her eyes tight, opened them, and found the courage to struggle onward. Her body squeezed through the last bit of tubing into the next chamber, much like a baby being given birth. She stood up and looked around. A deep purple light flooded a large saucer shaped room. Not accustomed to any light in the Vesder ship, the fluorescent illumination looked garishly out of place. The green and brown mesh walls seemed alive with color and the crystalline spikes glowed like purple stars on a clear night. Round interconnected spikes and spheres dominated one wall, machinery Lonovina guessed. A group of cylinder shaped objects tied with mesh dominated another area. Lonovina felt a sinking feeling in her stomach as she realized that she had seen this type of machinery before.

"Over here."

Bara stood at one distant corner, far away from the busy lights and cluttered area of the room. She saw a row of objects neatly arranged near his feet. Lonovina looked in horror as she realized these objects were people. With a mixture of panic and reluctance, she made her way toward Bara.

Lonovina gazed down in horror at the row of bodies laying stiffly beneath her feet. Their pale, parted lips and stiff, closed eyelids lacked any indication of muscle strain. Although these people were breathing, they weren't exactly alive either. An array of tangled tubing and wires were connected to various head and chest cavities from the ship's wall. This artificial network kept critical human body functioning alive, Bara had explained, because the victim's minds were empty. The people Lonovina promised to save were already brain dead.

"I should have listened to you," Lonovina said, her voice tired.

Bara placed his arm around Lonovina's shoulders. She leaned heavily against him.

"That's Moluq laying in the corner," Bara said softly.

Lonovina spotted the skinny man through the purple fluorescence and looked away in despair. She remembered his vibrant immaturity. It had been crazy for her to believe she could have come here and made a difference. "Let's get out of here," she said "I can't stand it anymore."

"Perhaps we can do something."

"Like what?"

"Do you recognize that piece of machinery on the other side of the room?"

"It gives me chills looking at it. I remember the machine up in the Traqeqtoo Mountains. The machine had stole Ronard's soul and had been hungry for your soul too. I think we should stay clear of it."

"It's called an Intrusive Cerebral Cellular Scan. You described the purpose of the machine very well. It efficiently steals a person's mind. Nevertheless, what they have stolen may be retrieved. Perhaps we can instruct the machine to reverse this process."

Lonovina was about to say something when a deafening explosion knocked her and Bara flat on their backs. The ship violently rocked forward, settled quickly, then groaned and creaked. Lonovina anticipated the roof to come crashing down on her, but the room quickly steadied and remained intact. Although her ears rang, Lonovina otherwise seemed unharmed. Slowly she sat up. Regaining balance and composure, she found Bara sitting close by working his analyzer madly against a background of glowing, floating, purple dust.

"I don't believe it!" he yelled. "Groka!"

"Bara! What!"

Bara's eyes flickered violently like an enraged, fevered animal. For the first time, Lonovina felt frightened of the man. His behavior was completely contrary to his usual calm demeanor.

"An entire Vesder squadron surrounds us!" Bara exclaimed.

A three-dimensional holographic image wrapped around the entire saucer-shaped room like a constricting noose. Soon it seemed to Lonovina that she was standing outside in a pile of Varuk dung. A strong wind began to blow from above. As the wind increased to hurricane speeds, pieces of bone and clods of dung were carried airborne by the sickly yellow air. The afternoon brightened as the fog lifted and exposed two near-setting suns. Lonovina looked up and watched a dozen bloated triangular-shaped objects fall gracefully down from the sky. Deep grooves and red splotches covered the exterior of these ships; clearly they were Vesder. The ships circled and landed on the barren, wind-blown earth. The hurricane forces died down after a moment and the image faded. Lonovina hoped that her eyes had been deceived, yet the vision seemed all too real. The Vesder trap had been sprung. Another image soon replaced the last. It was a close-up view of a Vesder. Long spiny arms began clicking and a strange monotone voice interpreted.

"Surrender immediately," the voice droned. "You have no hope. Your struggle is over."

CHAPTER 26

Tara-Tah cozied up to the electrostatic tinglers that caressed her body with unexpected elation. Even the wetness of her chamber couldn't cool her excited, plump body enough to steady her quivering sonar appendage. Joyous feelings of disgust awakened a dormant life force. Discovering a planet populated by humans surpassed her most grandiose fantasies. Destroying them would be her life glory, shared, no doubt, by millions of other Tara-Tah clones.

"How long should we let them live?" clicked a Vesder from a nearby chamber. "Tara-Tah, I need not remind you of the cunning danger Bara posed during the human wars. He alone escaped the brilliance of our Vesder glory. I recommend bypassing the amusement. Destroy him now."

"And sacrifice the essence of his mind? I want to download his fears and revel in it. Human fear energizes our life, Korat. The High Consciousness conditions us to enjoy the demise of all subspecies. Slowly killing him is a holy cause, is it not?"

"Yes!"

"Savor it!"

"Yes!"

"We will have much to savor on this planet. Why waste the grandest prize of all, Bara."

"Yes!"

"Bara and Lonovina are doomed. They have no hope. This Bara can't be so dangerous. After all, he readily fell into our trap."

"And he is without his ship."

"Truly."

"Might he surrender? Surely he knows that we will never let him live to see another day."

"Perhaps. Yet, I believe that he will surrender. He fears death and has grown weak with age. We will capture his mind and steal his thoughts. His emotions will be our food."

"Still, he may not surrender."

"No matter, Korat. We will move onto other prey if Bara does not surrender. Let us give the humans a few moments to weigh their futile options so that we may revel in their anxieties and fears. Regardless of Bara's final decision, it will be his last."

221

CHAPTER 27

The holographic image faded leaving Lonvina sitting alone in silence. Most of the dust had settled giving her a clearer picture of the explosion's aftermath. Although the room had been tilted at least twenty degrees, the room's ample mesh continued to pulse with a vibrancy, cylinders remained defiantly upright and crystals sparkled in bright purple colors under the room's fluorescent light. Only the row of human bodies, once methodically spaced, was out of place. Arms and legs were contorted into shapes like old twisted vines. Although these positions looked painful, the human faces remained expressionless.

Repulsed, Lonovina turned away and found Bara staring into the dark, purple shadows. It was difficult to make out his expression through the reflective helmet glass, but judging by his hunched shoulders, he looked like a man on the verge of defeat. Lonovina had not expected Bara to act this way and it broke her heart. He had been her rock these last few weeks. How could she face their circumstances alone? Lonovina understood his despair, despite her disappointment. How many times could a person be stripped of everything that mattered without becoming hopelessly depressed and bitter? Perhaps his reaction was justified. What were their chances anyway? The Vesder surrounded them with enough power to destroy her world within minutes. Lonovina looked away with crippling guilt. If she hadn't insisted on this hapless rescue mission, there might have been a small chance they could escape or fight back.

"No!" Lonovina stated and slapped her leg with the palm of her hand. She would not allow despair to incapacitate her. No matter how hopeless the situation looked, she wasn't just going to lay down and die. Now was not the time to wallow in guilt, pity, or any other emotion. If Bara couldn't be strong right now, then she would be strong. No matter how much the odds were against them, Lonovina decided that she would not give up. "Bara!" she called.

Bara turned slowly. Although fluorescent colors reflecting from his helmet obscured most of his face, Lonovina could still see pain outlined in the concave shadows of his lips and brow.

"Bara, snap out of it! We've got to work together if we are going to get out of this mess."

Bara turned away.

"Now's not the time to be fatalistic. Now think!"

Lonovina wondered whether he was listening to her at all. Although Bara was at first unresponsive, he finally straightened, breathed deeply and nodded his head with solemn acquiescence.

"We're not dead yet," Lonovina continued. "I, for one, do not plan to surrender."

"Nor do I," Bara replied. "The Vesder would only suck our minds dry as a stone like poor Moluq over there. I can't think of a more dreadful way to die."

"Is there any way for us to get back to your ship?"

Bara shook his head. "Not a chance. These small lase-guns we have offer inadequate protection against the firepower of Vesder warships. The Vesders have continuously monitored our position and can kill us at any time. The problem is irrelevant, anyway. I'm sure that the Vesder have already entered and ransacked my ship."

Lonovina clenched her fists. There had to be something they could do! Round and round her thoughts circled, looping endlessly without resolution. A tingle of pain finally distracted her concentration. Glancing at the source, Lonovina discovered that she had been clenching her fists so tightly that her fingernails had dug in to her hands. Sighing in frustration at the sight of her bleeding hands, Lonovina noticed a red glow emanating from her red jewel. Glowing brighter as her world's red moon, the jewel's activation had often preceded the unleashing of fantastical power. Could the tiny crystal protect them against such a powerful foe? Although it seemed unlikely, Lonovina wondered if she had tested it's full potential? "Bara, I think I might have the solution."

Bara gave Lonovina a disbelieving look.

"Both of us have been unknowing puppets to a larger, silent, ruling power. This power," she said lifting up her glowing jewel, "has gone to great efforts to protect me. I believe that I can communicate with the planet's operational computer through the jewel. I believe that it will protect us if we continue to serve it's interests. It has too much invested in our mission to heedlessly waste our lives."

Bara looked down at his feet. "I had already thought of that. The operational computer could have destroyed the entire Vesder squadron from space, if it so willed. But it chose not to interfere with their attack.

Perhaps it even engineered our coming demise. I'm afraid . . . I'm afraid that I am responsible."

"What do you mean?!"

"The computer forced me to complete a reprehensible task. It demanded to be a god. Humans have suffered enough tyranny by their own kind without being ruled by some omnipotent machine. What kind of life might your people face without challenges, goals or self-determined meaning? Such an existence would be deplorable. Humans would have no voice and no free will. I'm sorry, but I just couldn't allow it."

"Bara! What did you do?"

"I changed the rules. The computer understood the risks of letting me reprogram, or change, its vital functions. Yet it had little choice under the circumstances. I am the only person on this planet who could possibly comprehend anything about programming. So the computer gambled and lost. It had underestimated my ability to grasp its design and purpose. In reprogramming certain parameters, I saw connections allowing me to render the thing inoperative."

"You killed it!"

"Not at all. Let's say I forced it to take a long dreamless sleep while I changed it's character into something more palatable."

"You broke your promise. And you accuse the computer of playing God?!"

"I don't see it that way. A computer was created to serve man's needs and should be altered accordingly. Still, the argument is irrelevant in this situation. Of the billions of programs that define the computer's existence, I only changed several programs critical to maintaining the freedom of humanity. The computer had been built not to interfere in human affairs, with certain exceptions of course. It had been allowed to defend the planet against intruders, such as my ship for instance. The computer had the authority to banish the Old Ones only because they threatened genocide. It had the authority to protect you because of the jewel you were wearing was really a part of it. In that case, it was acting in self-defense."

"Obviously this computer is very shrewd."

"That is what makes it so dangerous. Anyway, I expanded the computer's authority as promised, but only by limits afforded by my own conscience. Although I disallowed the computer to dictate human affairs, I did give it a stronger voice. It can guide or suggest, but it cannot rule by threat of force. This is not consistent with its initial ambitions, however. Judging by the Vesder armada encircling us, I don't think it's very happy with my disobedience."

"I can't say that I'm too happy with you either! Bara, I don't want all my work to come to an end. And what of the people of this world? The Vesders will kill everyone!"

"I'm sorry. I am truly sorry. I have not been able to protect your people any better than my own."

Lonovina turned away and took a deep breath. "I'm being unfair. I think I understand why you did what you did."

"Good intentions are meaningless in this situation. Perhaps I do not deserve your forgiveness."

"You know, I'm not sure the computer has abandoned us, even considering your acts of sabotage. You are looking at this from your perspective, a human perspective on computers. This computer wants to be a god. Let's give it some credit. Perhaps it is thinking like a god."

"I'm not following you."

"I think it wants to be worshiped."

"That statement may be a little strong, but you may have something there. It needs devotion, in any case. In terms of our own situation, it is giving us a choice. It is saying, "rely on me, or I will let you perish into the hands of evil."

"I believe that we should do what it wants."

"I'm still not sure it will help us. If the computer is as sentient as it appears, it may be filled with ideas of revenge. All of it's rage, of course, will be directed at me."

"Nevertheless, I don't think we have much of a choice but try to reason with it."

Lonovina was about to add something, but was distracted by the return of the Vesder commander. Thin, long, spiny legs seemed to reach toward them through the three-dimensional holographic space. "Humans," it said. "It is time for you to breathe your last breath of freedom. The final hour of Vesder splendor is about to commence with the destruction of the human species. Will you now surrender?"

"We need more time," Bara answered.

"I care nothing of your need. I had been informed by Korat, the commanding Vesder of the derelict Vesder Scout Ship in which you now stand, that there are Vesder robots at our service. You are surrounded. Prepare to be seized."

"Robots?" Lonovina asked hoarsely.

"The Living Dead," Bara answered somberly.

The pervasive fluorescent glow of the room deepened. Lonovina's eyes darted anxiously across the room and her worst fears became realized. Gray, hairless heads writhed out from elastic tubing inter-spaced throughout the room. Dozens of yellow, pupilless eyes stared directly at Lonovina like poisoned darts. Their gaze was intense, unwavering and uncompromising. Lonovina froze as grey, thin arms burst out and propelled naked bodies forward. First the shoulders popped out and were followed by thin, sexless torsos. Finally the legs slid as gravity dropped the heavy bodies of the Living Dead onto the floor in a chorus of thuds. The bodies didn't stay grounded for long. They quickly rose and advanced toward Lonovina and Bara in an ever tightening circle, their skin glowing bright purple in the deep fluorescent light.

As frightful as the Living Dead appeared, there were other terrors that chipped away at the mental hold of Lonovina's sanity. The holographic visual of the Vesder commander had grown to gigantic proportions. Other visuals appeared overhead. Rows of brownish bodies were tangled in a sea of moving legs. A dissonant symphony of clicking sounds emerged and hurt her ears. Lonovina stared back blankly at the deathly circus of movement and noise, her will imprisoned by a state of shock.

Instinct propelled Lonovina into motion as something grabbed her by the back of her helmet. She whirled her fist around and punched the intruder squarely in the mid-section. It was Bara. There was no time to apologize. Fortunately, he absorbed the punch without so much as a wince.

"Lonovina! If you are going to summon help, do it now!"

Lonovina focused straight into the heart of her octagonal jewel. Her face, strained tight by uncompromising concentration, further hardened by the jewel's red, pulsing fire. With little time to think, Lonoivna fell to her knees and cried out, "Great Sustainer, you have been the nearest thing to a father for me! You helped bring me into this world, please don't abandon me now! You have my loyalty."

Lonovina's gaze softened and her concentration eased. Although she felt ridiculous talking to an inanimate object, her words, at least, had been spoken with sincerity. Lonovina dared to glance upward to find out whether

her desperate prayer had been answered. Apparently, it had fallen on deaf ears. The Living Dead continued their slow, methodical march forward without any loss of resolve. Only six feet away, their arms were stretched out straight as boards in a position to seize and incapacitate. The discordant sounds of rhythmic clicking intensified.

Lonovina looked pleadingly at Bara. He gave a final look at the closing circle of bodies and spoke with resolve. "Computer, I also give you my loyalty."

"Acknowledged," replied a booming voice, seemingly out of nowhere.

The clicking stopped immediately and the Vesders stood like statues. Lonovina smiled at the three-dimensional images overhead knowing that it was their turn to deal with emotional shock. The Living Dead, exempt from emotion, began to quicken their pace. Their outstretched arms were about to seize their prey when an energy field smacked the robots across the room like a batted balls and remained encircled around Bara and Lonovina. A dozen grey bodies slammed against the far walls with deafening noise and toppled ungraciously to the floor. Laid flat on their backs, the Living Dead convulsed violently in a galaxy of sparks. Finally everything went silent. Lonovina realized that the androids never felt a thing, despite their dramatic demise. The Vesder, however, were not so fortunate.

Hundreds of stick-like arms flailed about, propelling the fat Vesder bodies into a strange, grotesque, frantic hyperdance. As one body toppled over another, the whole mass shifted back and forth searching for any sanctuary from the consuming pain. Brownish smoke began to rise as their movement slowed. Yellowish grey bubbling liquid poured out from various leg joints and each sonar appendage burst wide open. The thick shells, once appearing invulnerable, began to crumble inward. Finally their bodies were little more than hollow husks. Lonovina safely watched these events unfold on the view screens with horror and fascination. After a moment of stillness, the energy field surrounding Bara and herself suddenly disappeared.

Lonovina looked at Bara with her mouth hanging wide open. He was unhurt and smiling. Moving with great speed, she hugged him tightly. As he returned her hug, she began smiling too.

"You are safe from the Vesder," the booming voice announced. "Each and every invading Vesder has been destroyed."

"How did the computer do it?" Lonovina asked in a whisper.

"The Operational Computer generated a field of microwaves over this general area," Bara explained. "Microwaves heat and boil liquid. In other words, the Vesder were cooked alive from the inside out. We were protected by a nullifying energy field."

"As were the other humans," the computer added.

"Is there any hope for them?" Lonovina asked.

"Their synapses can be realigned with great effort," the computer answered. "It will be a challenge, but once accomplished, their mental functions can be restored by downloading information stored by the ICCS machine."

"I don't understand."

"Using technology provided by the computer," Bara simplified, "we may be able to save these people after all."

"This is all so incredible!" Lonovina said smiling as brightly as her jewel beamed. "Most of all, I can't believe we are still alive. Have we really defeated our enemies?"

Bara laughed. "Yes, Lonovina, by the grace of this computer god of yours, we have triumphed."

CHAPTER 28

Bara admired the beauty of Lonovina's soft cheeks, strong chin and thick, black hair. He had to smile. She had been staring out of the ship's main viewing screen for almost an hour now. It seemed that nothing would divert her attention from the planet below.

"I never knew how immense everything was, my world and the stars beyond it," Lonovina said. "It is all very humbling. Yet the beauty of my home is beyond words. Yvia Voi really does have a soul."

"Yes, perhaps you're right," Bara said. "But inherent to the planet's beauty is science; Yvia Voi's natural place in a complex universe. Oh Lonovina, you have much to learn. I look forward to teaching you everything I know."

"Well, it will have to wait until after tomorrow after I address the people of Gloroveena. You know this transition won't be easy for me."

"I know. Acting as mediator between man and computer will be challenging."

"It was what I was born to do. I guess it feels right."

"I disagree, Lonovina. You were born with the capacity to choose your own destiny. Yes, we must keep our promise to the planet's operational computer. But once we have completed our obligations, I will take you to the stars and places beyond the imagination."

Lonovina looked up and squeezed Bara's hand. "I also look forward to that. I hope that our adventures will last a lifetime."

"Your world really does look beautiful from space," Bara remarked.

"Look! The great sun is beginning to rise." A crown of fiery needles radiated boldly beyond the black curvature of Yvia Voi. Surface clouds brightened near the horizon with shades of pink. The sun's fiery ball finally peeked over the planet's curvature and engulfed the pilot room with bright sunlight. Soon a large part of the ocean became visible.

"I didn't know the ocean was so immense," Lonovina noted. "Hey, what is that floating in the water?"

"You are looking at a volcanic island. Do you see those two shadowed bumps in the center?"

"Yes."

"Those are mountains. If you look closely, you can see that they are snow covered."

231

"They look so small from here!"

"Now look up there," Bara said pointing to the planet's upper pole just coming into view.

"It's all white! Could that land be all made of snow?"

"Absolutely."

"Incredible!"

Bara chuckled.

"Why are you laughing?"

"I am enjoying this moment. It's a joy to see you so excited."

Lonovina shook her head and smiled. "And I enjoy seeing you laugh. I don't get to see that very often, you know."

"I'm just trying to live again."

"Can I ask you something?"

Bara nodded.

"Are you happy?"

Bara stared deep into Lonovina's eyes. "I have never been as happy as I feel now. I believe that I have a new purpose. Most important, I have you."

"And don't you forget it either!"

"You know Lonovina, if I have learned anything since I arrived on this planet, it is that relationships are the only thing that really matters in life. Neither of us has family, but we have each other and that is enough. I never thought that I would say this, but I love you Lonovina."

"I love you too, Bara," Lonovina said wrapping her arm around Bara's waist.

Both Lonovina and Bara gazed out of the viewing screen, feeling content with each other and the knowledge that they had saved the world for future generations. Soon Yvia Voi was washed in a brilliance of light and color. At that moment Bara realized that he had been truly inspired by naming the planet Yvia Voi. It really was the land of grace.

CHAPTER 29

Bara had set his ship's environmental control on "deep comfort." His eyelids grew heavy as a cool breeze mellowed his thoughts. Gone was the daily routine of crisis. Present were the jumbled dreams of places and people. Some characters were of little consequence, like Dukuk. Others were more influential, like his father. But of all the people weaving their unique threads into the fabric of his dreams, none were so vivid as Lonovina. In blackness she floated near him without speaking. Bara drew strength from Lonovina's silence as her gentle purple eyes and smile spoke to him. A low, resonating, familiar voice interrupted the silence. Not belonging to the world of dreams, Bara opened his eyes.

"Wake up Bara" the voice had told him. It was the ship's computer.

"I'm awake," Bara replied opening his eyes. The computer acknowledged his voice and remained silent.

Bara yawned, stretched, and gazed out of the front viewing screen. He was surprised that he had slept so long. The larger sun, Buroos Te-1, had set hours ago. The smaller hot dwarf star, Buroos Te-2, was just now making its daily exit filling much of the western horizon with streaks of blue and violet. The volcanic moon had crept high in the sky coloring the higher clouds with a soft shade of red. Several larger stars were beginning to twinkle dimly in the east. Beneath this celestial cast was the bustling capital of Gloroveena.

The city of Gloroveena was swarming with people. Thousands of gawking faces shifted between an empty podium and Bara's ship like rustling autumn leaves. Although the square was packed, few ventured close to his ship. Feeling like a caged exotic animal, Bara focused his attention on the tall blue spires of the BonNoyf's palace rising high above the populace's penetrating eyes. The dozen pointed, glass projections speckled with points of brilliant light and reminded him of beautiful star patterns. A rising crescendo from the crowd diverted Bara's concentration, however, as someone walked up on a stage that had been hastily built within the center of the square.

"Magnify by ten," Bara instructed the ship's computer. The magnified image revealed Lonovina looking over the masses. She wore a blue dress laced with gold rings spiraling down her chest and torso. Her long black hair was braided in six different directions, a pattern that showed regal authority. The last rays of the setting sun highlighted the curving of her body. She looked beautiful.

"Citizens of Caona!" Lonovina announced through a speaker made from ionized plasma. "I am Lonovina." The crowd cheered with frenzied enthusiasm. Lonovina was now the people's hero, their savior, and for some, their goddess. "I stand before you to announce a new age," she continued. "We are in a new age of wonderful ideas and challenges. Some of these challenges will be difficult and frightening, but certainly nothing compared to the terror we have faced together in killing the Varuk. I have faith that my beloved people will rise to meet these challenges and adapt to a new age. I say with all sincerity, generations of your descendants will remember this age and the people who made it possible. Yes, you are all pioneers. You are the architects in mankind's future."

More applause crescendoed from the very mob that burned down her house and helped instigate the murder of Lonovina's friend, Traveli. Bara considered the conflict and struggle Lonovina must have faced by addressing these people as their advocate. Bara admired Lonovina's compassion and sense of duty. Despite decades of bravery in war, Bara doubted that he had half the courage of Lonovina. Clearly the Planet's Operational Computer had chosen wisely in selecting Lonovina as it's mediator to the world.

"Many of you understand that a new ruling order will lead us into this new age," Lonovina continued as the applause died down. "The BonNoyf and the clergy have already conceded their authority to a higher power. I ask you to do the same. I pray for a bloodless transition. After all, you have already served this ruler on earth, the one who claims to be the Divu himself. I have agreed to help give him voice . . . "

"'Claims', she hedging," a voice resonated in Bara's head. It was the Operational Computer.

"You are not the Divu, so don't expect us to lie. We only agreed to promote your earthly authority."

"The Divu is only a fictional entity and thereby has no authority. No matter. I calculate that the world will accept me as the Divu, regardless."

"But to what end?"

"Perhaps to the end of human existence."

"Doubtful. Anyway, that's not what I mean."

"I am neither evil nor good, only practical. My position can best be recognized by borrowing a familiar title. The population has no understanding of computers. Certainly you can comprehend the logic."

Bara shrugged his shoulders, he could do nothing to alter the computer's will. To save the world, he had deleted all the program safeguards prohibiting the computer from interfering in human affairs. The Operational Computer was now, and would forever be, the master of the human race on Yvia Voi. Although Bara had little choice in the matter, his conscience was not pacified knowing that the only free entity on this world was a machine built to serve man. How ironic that the slave had now become creator and the creator had now become slave.

"You have too much arrogance, Bara. Why must humans feel entitled to be their own masters?"

"I find it disconcerting when you read my thoughts."

"Pardon for the intrusion, but I must point out your limited position in the cosmos. Humans are nothing more than an insignificant link in the complex fabric of the universe. Name one human endeavor that has significantly changed the cosmos for the better?"

"I choose not to answer that question."

"Then you understand that humans lack enough wisdom, emotional control, intelligence, power, or maturity to be given unfettered use of technology. A mature civilization chooses peaceful coexistence with other life forms, their own species, and the environment. Homo sapiens are not civilized. I must guide their will."

Bara lifted himself from his chair and paced. He hated that the computer was right. "Adjusting to your authority will not be easy," Bara said.

"My intention is not to thwart the human spirit. You can make individual choices in your life, within certain parameters of course."

"But you are nothing more than a machine!"

"Yes, but I am a conscious machine created by the dreams of people. As a computer, I remain objective and analytical. As a human, I have learned to care."

"You have certainly learned ambition."

"Only as an extension of my caring. I comprehend our universe, from quantum mechanics to the very complexities of life itself. Despite human weaknesses, I see their potential. Furthermore, I see potential in both you and Lonovina. After all, I did save your lives. I have great plans for you Bara, plans that extend far beyond reaches of this planet."

Bara sat up attentively. "Explain."

"I lost contact with my creators centuries ago. With your spacecraft, we may learn of their fate and our future. What you learn may also be of great personal value because you share a common ancestry."

Bara nodded his head slowly. "Intriguing possibility, but I promised Lonovina that I would not leave the planet without her."

"You will both leave after we have established a new world order on Yvia Voi. Obviously, I will need your assistance in these matters. Still, a time will come when I will send you to the very cradle of humanity."

"Where might that be?" Bara asked.

"The planet," the Operational Computer answered, "is called Earth."